FALLOUT GIRL

A Hollywood Lights Novel

The Hollywood Lights Series
Book 4

KATIE ROSE PRYAL

Blue Osprey Books

Copyright © 2025 by Katie Rose Guest Pryal

All rights reserved.

Pryal, Katie Rose Guest 1976-.

Fallout Girl : A Hollywood Lights Novel / Katie Rose Guest Pryal.

ISBN Paper: 978-1-947834-84-2

ISBN Ebook: 978-1-947834-85-9

1. California—Fiction. 2. Los Angeles—Fiction. 3. Love—Fiction. I. Title

813'.6

Updated Blue Osprey Books Edition, 2025
First Blue Crow Books Edition, 2018

Blue Osprey Books

Published by Blue Osprey Books,
a division of Pryal Consulting, Inc.
Chapel Hill, NC
blueospreybooks.com

In *Chasing Chaos*, Pryal pierces L.A.'s film industry veneer to find complex and relatable characters and then winches the ties between them, pulling the reader right into the fray. The result is as psychologically astute as it is engaging.

Kathryn Craft, award-winning author of *The Far End of Happy*

As glamorous and mercurial as Hollywood itself, *Chasing Chaos* is a novel that glitters.

New York Times bestselling author Eileen Goudge for *Booktrib* Magazine

In *How to Stay*, engaging characters lead the reader through a poignant and layered narrative about the universal desire for something so elusive—a safe place to fall.

Amy Impellizzeri, award-winning author of *Why We Lie*

How To Stay is an intelligent romance. The central tension isn't whether the girl will get the guy, it's whether she will let herself–something all readers can relate to and enjoy.

Brandi Megan Granett, author of *Triple Love Score*

Modern, fresh, and entirely credible, *Fallout Girl* is a love story wrapped inside a heart-rending struggle for personal freedom.

Washington Post bestselling author Sonja Yoerg for *Booktrib* Magazine

Fallout Girl is a dangerous, sexy, motorcycle ride of a story, which pulls off the feat of being both humorous and heartbreaking at the same time.

Sandra Block, author of *What Happened That Night*

Fallout Girl is compelling story of friendship, family, and love with a honest look at mental illness that doesn't shy away from the painful realities so often hidden beneath the surface.

Susan Bishop Crispell, author of Dreaming in Chocolate

A gut-wrenching journey through darkness to redemption, one that proves that love, and family, can conquer anything. *Take Your Charming Somewhere Else* is her best yet. Do not miss this emotional tour-de-force—or anything Pryal writes.

Washington Post bestselling author Kelly Harms

For M, who never doubts me
For E, who inspires me with his fearlessness
For A, who inspires me with his joy

Author Note

Some people, like me, need content warnings to allow us to fully engage with and appreciate our world, including books.

This book contains flashback scenes of child abuse and neglect by parents, of attempted killing by poisoning, and of self-defense killing by gun.

The main character of *Fallout Girl* has bipolar disorder, and I'm a bipolar-autistic author. Like all of the books in the Hollywood Lights series, *Fallout Girl* centers neurodiversity and carefully handles trauma.

Chapter One

Cameron University, January 1997

No one meant more to Miranda George than her little brother Charlie.

November of his senior year of high school, when he'd said that he'd wanted to come and check out Cameron University to kick off his college tour, she'd told him no. No way. Cameron was not where she wanted her little brother to go to school.

Miranda had only chosen Cameron so she could be close to her parents—close to her mom, Sorcha. Her mom needed her, after all. Her mom did not need Charlie. Charlie could go anywhere he wanted. He could go to Yale, or Stanford. Cameron, an hour and a half from their family home in Winston-Salem, was an overrated shithole, an ivy-league imitation full of self-important douchebags— of both the student and the professor variety.

But Charlie had argued that a "college tour" was a good excuse to come visit his big sister for the weekend at college, and she'd relented. She'd never been able to say no to him, not even when they were kids. So now he was visiting, and Miranda's roommate Tonya was spending the weekend in her boyfriend's room so Charlie could sleep in Tonya's bed. Although once Charlie had arrived on Friday afternoon, Tonya had taken one look at Charlie and seriously considered dumping her boyfriend. Girls always did that—Charlie was six-foot, four-inches of J. Crew-model perfection mixed with an overdose of charisma. But Tonya had regained her senses and left, and Charlie had insisted Miranda take him out for the night.

That's how she'd ended up at this fraternity party—Miranda George, at a fraternity party—with her friend Daphne Saito and Daphne's jackass boyfriend Sutton. Sutton called Miranda *The Fat One* behind her back, but he was too stupid to realize that Miranda overheard him. Miranda couldn't really argue with Sutton's assessment of her body since his girlfriend Daphne was a size two, if that, and Miranda was five-ten and with thighs that could only be described as Rubenesque.

Daphne lived in an off-campus apartment with Sutton because Sutton had already graduated and couldn't live in the dorms. But because Sutton was immature and had no life, he still came to his fraternity's parties. The only reason that Miranda was at this party was Charlie. He'd begged and cajoled her into taking him to a frat party, insisting a frat party was part of the essential college experience.

He wasn't wrong. It's just that Miranda hated the college experience. Most of it, anyway.

So here they all stood, in the common room of Sutton's fraternity house—Sutton, Daphne, Miranda, and Charlie.

A couple of years ago, Cameron University had suffered from a high-profile news story that revealed its debauched lifestyle to pearl-clutching middle Americans. After the story broke, Cameron's administration cracked down on the free-flowing beer and booze at fraternity parties. Now, the beer was dispensed by professional bartenders that the frats had hired through the school, and only beer —not liquor—could be served officially. Unofficially? You could go upstairs and take a shot, or snort, of whatever you wanted.

But Miranda didn't drink. Miranda didn't drink because she liked having her bearings. She also didn't drink because she'd seen what drinking had done to her mother. Sure, her mother had other problems, but the drinking made them a lot worse. The technical term, Miranda had learned in her psychology class, was *self-medication*. When Miranda had been a kid, she hadn't cared what the technical term was. She'd only known that her mother could be either loving or violent and unpredictable. Miranda had also known that her father would never protect her or her brother.

Charlie, though, had no qualms about drinking. She'd been bailing him out of tight spots with alcohol since he'd turned fourteen, when he'd called her from middle-of-nowhere Forsyth County after his friends had all gotten arrested and he'd been the only one who'd managed to evade the cops. Despite her annoyance that he'd been drinking at so young an age, she'd been proud that he'd applied the wisdom they'd picked up as the children of the go-to defense lawyers in the state of North Carolina. While all the other party kids had taken off running from the cops, Charlie had dived under one of the parked cars and kept quiet, only emerging after everyone else had gone.

She looked at Charlie's blond head now, making its way toward the bar with a fake ID so perfect that no one would ever yank it. After all, Miranda herself had gotten it for him. She leaned against the wall and waited, arms crossed over her chest.

Charlie returned with two red plastic cups of beer. He sipped from the one in his right.

"What's that?" she said, nodding at the cup in his left hand.

"Seconds." He took another chug from the cup in his right, then gave her a winning grin.

Sutton came over with a guy in tow. Sutton had the good sense to be charmed by Charlie. If he'd been rude to her brother, Miranda would have had to murder him.

"Hey Chuck," Sutton said.

Miranda groaned. What a dick.

Sutton continued. "This is Morris. He's a freshman, just pledged. I thought you might want a partner in crime for tonight."

Charlie, who could get along with anyone, gave Morris a smile. "Sure, man. What's up?" Charlie downed the rest of his first beer, stacked the empty cup under the one in his left hand, then held out his right hand in greeting.

Morris shook it. "I see you got starter drinks. Wanna head upstairs for the real deal?"

Charlie grinned. "Absolutely, man."

Miranda rolled her eyes.

———

IT WAS GETTING CLOSE TO TWO O'CLOCK IN THE MORNING, AND MIRANDA had resorted to going from room to room looking for her brother. She'd asked Sutton where he thought Charlie would have gone, and Sutton had said something about maybe Charlie scoring some ass and that Miranda shouldn't be a cock-block.

Fucking Sutton.

She wasn't truly worried about Charlie. He was savvy and knew how to take care of himself. But she was tired and wanted to go back to her dorm room and sleep. She wasn't going to leave him at an off-campus party by himself. They'd hitched a ride to the party with Sutton and Daphne. The frat house was a good twenty minutes' walk from her dorm. That was a long way to go in the dark of winter at two in the morning when you were drunk and didn't know your way.

No. She needed to find him and get a ride home with Sutton and Daphne.

She knocked on the next door in the hallway. Her fifth. The door, which had been cracked, swung open. A group of four guys and two girls sat in a circle on the floor taking shots from a bottle of tequila.

Gross.

One of the guys eyed her up and down.

She fought back an eye-roll and spoke to the guy who was checking her out. "I'm looking for Morris. He's a pledge. You know him?"

"Wanna drink?" the guy said.

"No. Morris?"

"I'm not Morris."

Jesus. "Yeah, I know that. Have any of y'all seen Morris?"

"I think so," one of the girls said. "I feel like I saw him in the bathroom."

The girl *felt* like it? Did she feel like she could give a straight answer?

Miranda left the door open and headed to the bathroom. Sutton and Daphne were waiting for her in the common room downstairs.

She just needed to find Charlie, and then she could finally go to sleep and pretend she'd never come to this party at all.

She pushed open the bathroom door, and the smell hit her like a board—urine, naturally, but also vomit. Liquor-tainted vomit. She knew that smell.

It meant someone was in trouble.

"Come on, man." She knew that voice. It was Charlie's, and he sounded panicked. Miranda took a deep breath, her heart settling into a slow rhythm, a familiar rhythm, one that meant she had a problem to solve and that she would solve it, no matter what.

She headed into the bathroom and found Charlie kneeling over Morris's still form. A dribble of vomit hung from Morris's mouth.

"What happened?" she said, squatting at Morris's side.

"I was waiting for him to come out of the stall after he booted, but then he collapsed. I had to crawl under the door to unlock it. I think he hit his head on the toilet."

"Stay here," Miranda said. "I'm going to get help."

She ran from the bathroom and entered a room directly across the hall. A guy was lying in his bed, on top of his blankets, ass bare to the world.

She flipped on the lights. "Where's your phone?" She scanned his room. There, on his desk.

"What the hell?" the guy said, sitting up. She ignored him.

She grabbed the cordless phone, dialed 9-1-1, and gave the address of the fraternity house as she headed back into the bathroom.

"I'm giving the phone to my brother now," she said to the operator. She tossed the phone to Charlie. "It's 9-1-1. Stay on the line. I'm getting Daphne."

Morris didn't look good. He looked pale and way too still. Miranda knew he didn't have much time.

Miranda ran from the bathroom and down the stairs to the common room.

She needed Daphne. She couldn't do this by herself. She couldn't protect Charlie and save Morris at the same time.

The common room was empty except for a few party stragglers. She called out Daphne's name, dashing from the room and into the foyer. She ran out into the parking lot.

Sutton's car was gone.

She was alone with her drunk, underage brother and a kid who was dying of alcohol poisoning.

Sutton. Sutton had a car phone.

She ran back inside and up the stairs. She flung open another door. This room was blessedly empty. She grabbed the cordless phone and dialed Sutton's phone from memory.

"Yep," he said.

"Sutton. It's Miranda. Where the hell are you?"

"We're almost back to our place. We thought you'd left."

"Put Daphne on the phone."

There was a pause, and then Daphne's voice. "Hey Miranda. We honestly thought you'd left, you were gone so long."

"I need you to turn the car around, right now."

"What's happened?"

Miranda explained. "I need you to come back and get Charlie." Miranda heard sirens. An ambulance. She glanced out the window in the bedroom. She gritted her teeth. Police cruisers pulled up behind the ambulance.

"Hurry, Daphne. The police are here."

Daphne spoke with Sutton, her voice muffled. Then she came back on the line. "I can't."

"You what?" Miranda's voice raised at the end.

"I can't. Sutton says I'll be arrested for underage drinking. I'm only twenty. You're safe because you didn't drink anything."

"Charlie is wasted, and he's saving that guy's life."

"I'm sorry, Miranda. Charlie will be okay. Tell him to go hide someplace." She paused. "Maybe you shouldn't have called 9-1-1."

Miranda hung up the phone, cursing Daphne to hell.

———

AFTER ASSESSING THE SITUATION, THE POLICE ARRESTED CHARLIE ON THE spot. While the paramedics loaded Morris into the ambulance, the police put Charlie into the back of a cruiser. He caught Miranda's eye and nodded. The message was clear. He would say nothing.

Of course he would say nothing. They both knew what to do in a situation like this. Their parents were Sorcha and Charles George.

Miranda, though, was stuck. She was twenty minutes from her

dorm—and from her car—and Daphne and Sutton weren't coming to help her. She was worried about Morris, and she was worried about Charlie. She was torn.

Fucking Daphne.

She ran up to the ambulance and looked into the back. The paramedics were frantic in a way they hadn't been frantic before.

Miranda stepped closer. One paramedic was administering chest compressions. Another was injecting something into Morris's IV. Morris's eyes were half open, unblinking.

Morris was dying.

She stepped back from the ambulance.

She knew how long it would take to book her brother at the jail. She had time to make it back to her dorm, get her car, get down there to meet him. Once in her car, she could call her father from her car phone.

With one last glance at the police cruiser pulling away with her brother, she turned and ran all the way back to her dorm.

After she got in her car, she dialed her father's mobile phone.

"Charlie's been arrested."

Silence.

Truly, her father was the worst.

"We were at a fraternity party. A kid got alcohol poisoning, and we called 9-1-1. The cops arrested Charlie because he was on the scene and had been drinking."

"Charlie was helping the sick kid?"

"Yeah."

"That's good. It'll work in his favor as a mitigating circumstance. How's the kid?"

"I think he's going to die."

A pause. "That's not as good for us strategically. If Charlie had saved the kid's life, we could paint him as a hero."

Wasn't Charlie still kind of a hero? Miranda wondered. "When are you coming down to help?"

"I'll send Amanda. She's perfectly capable of handling this."

Amanda was her parents' newest associate. She wasn't much older than Miranda. She was kind of a shark though.

Still. "Don't you want to come and help out your own son?"

"It's unnecessary. This is run of the mill. Amanda will be there in two hours. She'll meet you at the station."

"Dad, I really think you should come. It would mean a lot to Charlie."

Silence. "I can't come running every time you two get in a scrape."

Miranda hung up. No one was coming. No one was ever coming. Not her father, not Daphne. No one.

Chapter Two

Los Angeles, April 2005

On a Thursday night in the Laurel Canyon mansion of a reclusive movie star, Miranda George shuffled a deck of cards. Next to her on the gray leather couch sat Sandy, the owner of the mansion. Across from her sat Marlon, Sandy's handyman and de facto adopted son. Next to Marlon sat Timmy, her college friend Greta's husband—as of yesterday. Glancing around, it was hard to believe this house had just hosted a wedding.

Miranda didn't really know any of these guys. She was here because she was friends with Daphne Saito and Greta Donovan. Sort of friends. The three had gone to college together back in North Carolina years ago. At the moment, Greta was outside in the driveway trying to talk Daphne off of an emotional ledge. Miranda's job was to keep things together inside.

Miranda dealt another hand of spades. She'd just taught the three guys how to play—incredibly, none of them knew how. She would have preferred to have Sandy as her partner, not Marlon. Sandy had by far the best poker face of these dingbats. Plus, Marlon was distracted by the goings-on outside. He kept glancing at the door, hoping it would open and reveal Daphne, whom he'd finally figured out was the love of his life.

Timmy, as opposed to Marlon, was feeling good. He knew his wife was coming back to him.

Yesterday, Wednesday, while Timmy had married Greta in this very house, Marlon had seriously screwed things up with Daphne. Miranda might be only sort-of friends with Daphne, but when Marlon had torn into her yesterday, hurling unfair accusations and causing her so much pain, Miranda had wanted to kill him. Now he was beating himself up for it, and she was letting him do it. They all were. He needed to suffer some.

She eyed the pile of cash in the middle of the table. Of the four of them, she needed that money the most. Sandy didn't need it—he was a bazillionaire. Marlon didn't need it; he was the bazillionaire's heir. Timmy didn't need it; he owned both a successful restaurant and his own production company on the West Side.

Miranda was the only one of them who was homeless and unemployed. Daphne was letting her stay in the guest room at her condo, but Miranda had no significant source of income. She eyed the pile of cash again. Marlon needed to get his act together and help her win this damn card game.

She'd suggested they all play cards after Greta had stepped outside to wait for Daphne to arrive. The guys were acting crazy with worry. Miranda hadn't been too worried. She'd known that Daphne was in trouble, but she'd also known that Daphne was a survivor. After all, the reason they were only sort-of friends was because Daphne had sold her out in college to save her own ass. Miranda could respect that kind of survival instinct, even though she'd hated Daphne for it at the time.

Tonight, Daphne might have chosen to disappear and leave all of these fools behind, but that would have been her choice. And Daphne would have been all right. She would have made it.

Miranda looked at her cards, then tried to catch Marlon's eye to help them make a good play.

He was staring at the door, a look of yearning of his face.

She sighed. This game was hopeless.

Next to her, Sandy chuckled.

"Something funny, old man?" she said.

"Your partner is out to lunch."

She narrowed her eyes at him. "At least there's one person on my team who knows how to play spades."

"You're talking about yourself."

She nodded. "You and Timmy are getting trounced despite my partner being lunchy."

Sandy chuckled again.

Miranda scowled. Scowling was better than being starstruck. She was trading jabs with Alexander Martin. His last name might as well be *Oscar*. And he'd insisted she call him Sandy.

She was definitely starstruck.

The front door opened, and Greta and Daphne stepped inside. Marlon dropped his cards on the floor, staring at Daphne with reverence, the card game forgotten.

Miranda stared at the ceiling, begging a god she didn't believe in to give her patience. Sandy laughed, low enough that only she could hear, and placed his cards face-down on the table.

Greta and Daphne stopped in the foyer, surveying the group around the coffee table.

Greta Donovan stood six-foot-one in her bare feet. She had broad shoulders, narrow hips, long legs, and perfect muscle tone. She'd been a swimmer her whole life, and it showed. She also had brilliant red curls that she currently wore pulled back in a ponytail. She wasn't conventionally pretty—in fact, she'd been a goofball in college. But she'd grown into her own in the years since. And she was honest, loyal, and smart as hell.

Miranda liked Greta a lot.

Daphne Saito, Miranda's current roommate because Miranda had run away from home and other things, looked like a supermodel. Full stop. Her parents were Japanese immigrants who'd settled in North Carolina. She'd grown out her black hair from the short bob she'd worn in college, and now it hung in long layers around her face and shoulders. She also wore a killer pair of leather pants.

Daphne observed the cards and the pile of cash on the table. "Miranda?" Daphne asked. She sounded like she'd just discovered her priest getting nasty in the confessional.

What was the problem? It was just a little gambling. Miranda had been gambling—unlawfully—since she was fourteen.

"We're playing spades," Miranda said. "They don't know how."

She gestured at the guys gathered around the table. "Can you believe it?"

"Seriously?" Daphne said.

Greta, who stood a step behind Daphne, was turning red with suppressed laughter.

"What?" Miranda said. "They were all making me crazy with their manly pacing. God. Back and forth. Back and forth."

"I do not pace," said Sandy, elbowing her.

"Correction," Miranda said. "Timmy and Marlon were doing manly pacing. Sandy was lurking." She turned to Sandy and muttered, "Vast improvement, dude."

Sandy smiled at her. Miranda leaned back, allowing herself to be charmed by Sandy despite her efforts to remain unmoved. Sandy, who must have been in his fifties, was still a total fox. She couldn't believe that she was sitting next to him on his couch, though she kept her disbelief well hidden. He was as big a movie star as you could be, and he was elbowing her in the gut.

She wished, hard, for less of a gut, for the six-pack abs of Greta or the tiny waist of Daphne. Back home in North Carolina, plenty of guys thought she was pretty—and she could even pull off beautiful with her attitude problem and the right lipstick. But here, in Los Angeles, she barely registered as cute.

She shook her head. She didn't care. She couldn't care. After all, there was nothing she could do about immutable facts.

Suddenly, Marlon stood, putting his chair between himself and Daphne, as though he were afraid of her. The whole reason the group of them were here at Sandy's house was to see if Daphne would show up—show up for him. Marlon was so in love with Daphne it hurt to look at.

So Miranda looked away.

Miranda wondered what it would be like to have someone adore her that much. She knew that sort of love wasn't coming for her. She just wasn't made that way. She was okay with it, most of the time. There had been one person, but in the end, they'd decided they'd be better as friends.

Or rather, she'd decided. He would have kept trying to make things work. God, why did people keep trying with her?

That was the way it always went for Miranda. She knew she

hurt people—so she was selective. She picked people who were emotionally bulletproof—like the wealthy sons of her family's friends back home—or people who didn't care about her very much.

She didn't have the strength for anything more than that. At twenty-seven, she felt like she'd lived three lifetimes.

Sandy stood. "I'm exhausted."

Me too, Miranda thought.

"Lock up when you all leave, OK?" Sandy headed into his palatial kitchen toward the master suite. According to Daphne and Greta, no one had ever been into his master suite except Marlon, who lived in the apartment over the garage and worked as Sandy's assistant and handyman. Greta and Daphne were allowed to come and go from the house as they pleased, but that part of the house was Sandy's sanctuary.

"We have an annoying brunch to get ready for, Greta," Timmy said. "We should get home."

Tomorrow, Timmy and Greta were having a meal with Greta's dad. Yesterday, he'd flown in from North Carolina and crashed the wedding. Greta really didn't like her dad. In fact, Greta's dad was worse than Miranda's own. Miranda's dad was mostly neglectful. Greta's dad had thrown Greta out of his house when her mom was dying of cancer and he'd wanted to shack up with his graduate student.

"See you in the morning?" Greta asked Daphne.

At Greta's words, Miranda assumed that Daphne had decided to stick around after all, instead of disappearing from their lives. When Miranda had woken up from her nap earlier that day, Daphne had packed her things and taken off, apparently for good. Before she'd taken off, she'd left Miranda a key to her condo, which Miranda had thought was really nice of her considering everything Miranda had done to piss her off the past few days—and considering the fact that Miranda hadn't seen her since college.

"I'll be there," Daphne said.

"You should all come," Greta said to Miranda and Marlon. "It'll make my dad extra uncomfortable."

Miranda avoided a reply. She would not be going to the family brunch. "I'm heading home, too," Miranda said. "Well, to your home,

Daph." She picked up the cash from the table, stuffing it in her back pocket.

————

WHEN THE FRONT DOOR TO SANDY'S HOUSE CLOSED BEHIND HER, Miranda vigorously ignored the feeling of wrongness that rubbed over her skin. Sandy's house, a mid-century steel-and-glass affair that hung off the edge of a cliff, was far more spectacular than the stately southern mansions of her parents and their friends. And her parents —well, her father—was rich as hell. But Miranda refused to be cowed by the house, by its owner, by the neighborhood, by any of the L.A. fabulousness that she suddenly found herself in the middle of. She refused to give in.

She stepped forward, her foot touching concrete, leaving behind the warm stone of the porch.

She refused to think about her mother, dead. She refused to think about how she'd died.

Miranda refused to think about why she'd run away from her parent's home without word, what she'd recently learned about herself, and what she'd packed in her bag—the pills, still sitting in their bottles, tiny, gray unexploded bombs.

She walked to the edge of the driveway, where a dense forested area blocked all view of the road leading to other Laurel Canyon mansions. She stared at the darkness, and the darkness stared back.

"Miranda." A voice called to her from behind. She turned to face him. John. She supposed she would call him a friend, even though she'd only known him a few days.

After all, she'd only been in Los Angeles a few days.

"Wait for me," John said. He'd been hanging out in his car while she'd been handling things in the house.

She snorted. "I can hardly leave without you, can I." She didn't have a car. Back when everyone had been so worried about Daphne, and they'd decided to converge on Sandy's house, John had driven her to Hollywood from Daphne's condo in Brentwood.

She smiled to herself. She liked Sandy, even if he was as rich as hell. And Miranda had an innate mistrust of rich people.

But the gathering was dispersing, and it was time for her to head back to reality—to Daphne's condo where she was going to rent a room until she found her own place.

Or until she decided to do something else entirely.

If you'd told Miranda three months ago that she'd be living in the Los Angeles home of Daphne Saito, she'd have told you to go to hell. After all, Daphne was an undependable jerk whom Miranda hadn't spoken with in years. But a lot had changed in three months. And here she was, living in Los Angeles in the home of Daphne Saito, who'd let her asshole college boyfriend Sutton call Miranda fat on a regular basis and had been such a coward she'd let Miranda's brother get arrested for trying to save a kid's life.

"You probably could leave without me, actually." John said. "It wouldn't surprise me if you could jump-start one of these cars around here." John glanced behind him at the six-car garage that jutted off the house and the collection of cars all around them in the circular drive, including Sandy's hot-as-hell Aston Martin.

Miranda frowned. "I don't steal from people I like."

"Noted."

"And I don't want a car," she said.

"This is L.A." he chided. "You have to have a car."

"I want a motorcycle."

John's mouth fell open for a moment until he seemed to realize he was catching flies, and then he shut it. "You know how to ride a motorcycle?"

She nodded. "I know all the ways to make a fast getaway."

He looked thoughtful. "It's not that late yet. A dealership might still be open, especially in the valley."

Ah. He was still trying to make her happy. Good. "You know where to go?" she asked.

"There's a strip of car dealerships in Burbank. I bought my car there."

She knew that John hadn't lived in L.A. proper for very long. He'd moved here from Orange County, about an hour away. And he drove a Camry. She and Daphne agreed it was the most boring car in the world.

Miranda climbed into the passenger seat of his boring car. He headed out of Sandy's driveway, up Sandy's street to Laurel Canyon, then up some more, and then down into the San Fernando Valley.

———

Around eleven o'clock that night, Miranda pulled into the parking lot of Daphne's condominium building on her new, black Suzuki SV650. Tomorrow she'd take it someplace to get the factory tailpipes replaced with an after-market set that looked and sounded less goofy. The pipes were the only modification she'd make. At five-foot-ten, she was tall enough to stand over the bike at its factory height, so she didn't need to have it lowered, and she didn't care enough about bike styling to do anything else to it.

Plus, it was pretty sweet as it was.

She'd also bought a helmet and an armored jacket, both in white—opposite of her customary black clothing. She'd bought black Kevlar-padded gloves. She already wore calf-high leather boots over her tight jeans, part of her regular uniform—she had many pairs of tight jeans, and many pairs of black boots, but most of them were back at her parents' home in North Carolina.

Correction. At her father's home in North Carolina.

She'd already spent plenty of her father's money in the few days since she'd arrived at Daphne's apartment with nothing more than what would fit in her college backpack. She'd filched her mother's no-limit credit card before leaving home, and she was on a spending spree until her father Charles cut her off.

She only hoped that her father wasn't vindictive enough to turn her in to the cops.

She also knew that using her mom's card risked giving away her location. But she figured that Charles George, Sr., had better things to do than dash across a continent to track down his daughter. Plus, he'd have a hell of a time tracking her down here. It wasn't like L.A. was a small town.

She was aware, however, that Charles had more than a few private investigators at his disposal. He was an attorney, and rich-man's defense work paid well—in both cash and connections.

She removed her helmet and pulled her phone from the black, ballistic-nylon messenger bag she had strapped across her chest. The bag was the last item she'd purchased tonight. She knew she'd need something to haul her stuff around in. The bag had cost five hundred dollars, and it was completely waterproof.

At the dealership, when she'd been tossing accessories onto the counter to purchase, John had watched in silence, his lips pressed together as though he'd been wanting to say something, to perhaps encourage her to think twice before spending so much money.

He didn't know the first thing about spending money. Miranda's mother used to spend that much money on dresses that Miranda would wear only one time.

What was ten thousand dollars? Her mother made ten thousand dollars in a day. In an hour.

Had made.

Miranda dialed her phone, her feet resting on either side of her bike, a closed garage door in front of her.

"Hello?" Daphne sounded like Miranda had woken her from sleep.

"You're not here, are you."

"What?"

The lights were off in Daphne's foyer. It didn't look like Daphne had made it back home from the gathering at Sandy's house. That meant that Daphne and Marlon had finally sealed the deal. Good for her.

Despite Marlon's bad behavior yesterday, Miranda believed that he was good for Daphne, and she for him. He was protective of his family, sure, but Daphne was his family now, and Daphne needed family. Marlon took care of people—it was his superpower. And Miranda couldn't begrudge Daphne a little caretaking.

Marlon had made a mistake. Marlon could be forgiven.

But now Miranda was stuck outside Daphne's house, alone. "Do you have an extra garage-door clicker?" Miranda asked. "I am now in possession of wheels."

"Um, yeah. In the console by the front door. Top-left drawer."

"Say hi to Marlon for me." Miranda could hear a grumbling voice in the background.

"What? Okay."

Miranda hung up, then kicked down the bike's stand. She dashed up the steps to Daphne's front door, unlocked it, and fished around in the console for a garage door opener. When she found it, she ran back down the stairs, opening the garage as she went. She pushed her bike into the garage, into the space next to where Daphne usually parked her car, then set the kickstand again. Then she shut the garage door behind her. She hung her shiny white helmet from the black handlebars, stuffed her gloves inside her helmet, then climbed the stairs that connected the garage to the front porch.

Once she was locked up safe inside Daphne's condo, she considered calling John. She'd heard Marlon's gruff post-sex voice in the background when she'd called Daphne, and the sound had made her both jealous and sad. Not jealous of Daphne's having Marlon in particular—lord, he was not her type—but jealous of her having someone at all.

The look in Marlon's eyes tonight when Daphne had stepped through the door had caused Miranda to feel as though her own gut were getting ripped out. She'd never have that, she knew. But she could feel something, an echo of that, perhaps. For a little while.

Miranda knew that she needed to keep John at arm's length. Not because she was worried about hurting John, not at all. She never worried about hurting guys. On the contrary—she always, one-hundred-percent-of-the-time hurt them. Hurting was a given. It was only a matter of when.

But she wasn't quite ready to hurt John, not yet. He was useful. After all, she had a vehicle now because of John's knowledge of L.A. She needed his knowledge. She hated not knowing her way around. She hated feeling helpless.

So she couldn't sleep with John tonight.

Her phone rang. Of course it did. John was, after all, a nice guy.

"I'm home safe," she said before he could ask.

"Just checking," John said.

"Odds were low that I would crash on my first ride."

"That's not how odds work."

Miranda knew that, actually. She loved Las Vegas.

"You don't need to worry about me," she said.

John was silent on the line. "I'm not sure that's true."

"Do you have any more pot?"

"Come on, Miranda. Let's have an actual conversation."

She didn't want to have an actual conversation. She wanted to forget why she'd run away from home. She'd told John about her mother's funeral on Monday, but she hadn't told him why her mother's funeral had been on Monday, or the fact that her mother had died months before. She'd let John, along with Daphne and everyone else, make incorrect presumptions about her mother's death.

She knew that as soon as she mentioned the truth aloud to anyone, including herself, she'd have to deal with it.

John wanted to have an actual conversation. Jesus. Here she'd been starting to like him.

She supposed she was going to have to sleep with him after all. It was the only way to get a guy to shut up.

"Fine," she said. "But I don't want to talk on the phone. You'll have to come over. I'll leave the garage open for you. Don't hit my bike when you park."

————

BEFORE JOHN ARRIVED, MIRANDA MOVED HER BIKE TO THE VERY TOP OF her parking space, giving him room to park his car in her spot as well. She left the garage door open for him, then headed back inside.

The time before his arrival she spent in Daphne's guest room, which was now her room. She grabbed her old backpack from the corner and dropped it on the bed. It held everything she owned, except for the fancy dress she'd bought for Greta's wedding, which hung in the closet, and the shoes that went with it, which she'd tossed on the closet floor. She wouldn't be needing those again any time soon.

She reached into the very bottom of the backpack and pulled out three prescription pill bottles. She held them, contemplated them. She thought about how much time she had before John arrived. She thought about a diagnosis that might as well be a death sentence.

Not tonight, she thought.

She placed the bottles into an interior zip pocket of her new messenger bag. Then she stuffed in her laptop and charger and her black pullover sweater into the bag as well. The rest of her clothes she left in a near-empty drawer in the bedroom dresser.

A little while later, she heard the garage door closing. She opened the front door to greet John. She wore a slim, scoop-necked black t-shirt, black panties, and nothing else. Her long, dark blond hair hung loose around her shoulders, and she gave them twenty minutes, tops, before they were going at it in her room.

John stood on the threshold, gazing at her bare thighs. He swallowed hard once, twice, then three times. She waited for him to gather himself.

"You coming in?" She turned, knowing the back view was even better than the front. She might not be skinny, but her legs were toned and shaped well—she had some lucky genetics working in her favor.

At the thought of her having lucky genetics, she almost snorted.

She heard John step into the narrow foyer and shut the door. She heard him slip off his shoes. She heard him pace behind her into the living room.

She sank onto the vinyl couch, the one Daphne called The Lifeboat. An accurate descriptor, actually, given how large, orange, and squared-off it was. John sat at the other end.

She leaned back against one of the couch's arms and plopped her feet in John's lap. She'd painted her toenails the night before while she and Daphne had sat around drinking and smoking weed together. She'd used a navy blue color. She liked it.

John, without thinking, rested a hand on her foot and began to squeeze her arch.

It felt amazing. She shut her eyes.

When she opened them again a few minutes later, he was watching her.

"Do you think the bike will finally get your dad to cut you off?" he asked.

"Maybe. I haven't thought about it."

It was the truth. She was actively not thinking about her dad. She was annoyed that John was making her think about her dad.

While giving her a foot massage.

What was wrong with him?

She'd met John two days ago at a restaurant here in Brentwood, around the corner from Daphne's condo. Miranda had only arrived in town the night before, and she and Daphne had eaten breakfast together before Daphne had headed to a work meeting. After Daphne had left, John had come up to Miranda asking who her friend was.

Turns out Miranda wasn't the only person who slept with guys for terrible reasons. But Daphne was with Marlon now. Thinking about Daphne and Marlon together tonight, Miranda fought hard not to make a pinched face. They were just that sweet.

John had sworn he wasn't interested in Daphne, although Miranda couldn't see how that was possible, given that Daphne looked like a goddess put on Earth for men to fall over themselves for.

After Miranda had met John earlier that week, she'd spent most of her time with him. The past few days, he'd driven her around town while she'd restocked her supplies. He'd been a good sport. Correction: He'd been a good friend. She'd even dragged him to Greta and Timmy's wedding yesterday as her date.

That had been a terrible thing for her to do, throwing Daphne's one-night-stand in her face like that. John hadn't been happy about it either. And yet John had come through tonight when Daphne had needed help. Miranda, without a car, had called John. And he'd helped her without question.

John really was a good guy.

Miranda pulled her feet from John's lap and crossed her legs. She studied him. He kept his brown hair short, clipped close on the sides, but with sideburns that accentuated his jawline. His brown eyes were warm, honest. Under her appraisal, he gave her a funny half-smile, like a brave soldier facing a firing squad.

She sat forward on her knees and kissed him.

He kissed her back, and she felt heat. The heat felt glorious.

She straddled him and they kissed again. He wrapped his hands around her waist, running them up her back. She pressed her body into his, and he groaned. She nibbled at his ear, smiling.

And then, suddenly, he stopped, pulling away from her.

"Let's not do this, Miranda." He kept one hand on her cheek, cupping her ear.

"Are you serious?" she asked, incredulous. "You're turning me down?"

"I'm as surprised as you are, but I'm going to leave now. Unless you want to actually talk to me."

"Sure we can talk." She smiled, putting all sorts of promises in her eyes. "After."

"We won't talk after, and you know it. You'll throw me out."

She'd known he was smart when they'd first met. It was the only reason she'd been able to tolerate him. So she didn't bother denying his accusation.

"Can I ask why you're turning me down?" she said, flopping onto the couch next to him.

"I actually like you," he said. "So I would rather not give you a reason to throw me out."

"I don't need a reason to do that."

He laughed, hard, at her words. "I don't want to fill some preconceived L.A.-guy stereotype that you've concocted in your head so that you can feel justified when you throw me out."

"Sleeping with me would turn you into a stereotype?"

"Of course it would. You're vulnerable. Your mother just died."

She frowned. "You're not even from L.A. You're from the Midwest."

"Doesn't matter. You'll argue that because I choose to live here, I've bought into some personality type."

She narrowed her eyes. "Why do you think you know me so well?"

"I don't think I know you well at all."

He did, though. He was calling all her plays. "So you won't come to bed with me tonight?"

He shook his head.

She lay back onto the couch, covering her face with her hands. "Even if I beg?"

"Please. Don't beg." His voice sounded strained.

She moved her hands from her face, grinning. "Don't worry. I never beg."

"Thank god. I was reaching the end of my strength."

"Go. I'll see you tomorrow or something."

"Or something? Do you want to make a plan for tomorrow?"

Did she? Maybe a little. But she wasn't going to make any more plans, ever again. That was the only thing she knew for certain. "No. I'll text you if I feel like it."

John stood. "One last chance. Conversation, not booty call."

All she wanted from him was enough sex to ruin their friendship so she wouldn't have to have a conversation. Couldn't he see that? The very last thing she wanted was conversation.

Maybe she'd feel differently tomorrow. Tonight, she wanted to smoke the last of the pot she had stashed in her bedroom drawer and then pass out.

"I'll lock up after you leave," she said.

He stood a moment, staring down at her, as though he wanted to say something more.

She raised her eyebrows at him and gave him a half-smile. "Having a hard time walking out?"

"Yeah." He stuffed his hands in his pockets. "I am."

"That's because your instincts know you're making a bad decision."

"I know I'm making the right decision." He leaned forward, putting his face closer to hers. "You're worth waiting around for." As he strode toward the door, he called over his shoulder. "See you tomorrow."

She lay back on the lifeboat and frowned.

Chapter Three

Miranda woke early the next morning, Friday. The sun barely broke through the barred window of her bedroom. She was still jet-lagged.

She staggered to the shower, using the fancy shampoo and conditioner Daphne kept in her guest bathroom. As she dried off, her phone started ringing. She'd left it charging on her bedside table. She sat down on the edge of the unmade bed and picked it up.

Her father.

She silenced the phone.

She finished drying off, dressed, and dried her hair. Then she pulled her hair into a tight twist at the nape of her neck, wrapping the bundle with two hair ties to make sure it was secure.

As she left, she grabbed her white motorcycle jacket from the foyer. She dashed down the steps to the garage, noticing the empty space where Daphne's car should be. She was sleeping in, then. Good for her.

Miranda hopped on her bike and headed out.

She arrived at her family's bank in downtown L.A. just as it was opening. She knew that what she was about to do was a little dodgy. So she figured she might have better luck at a central branch of the bank.

And if she didn't have good luck, at least she'd be closer to the jail.

She pulled off her helmet and undid her hair ties, shaking her hair loose. Then she strolled through the double plate-glass doors. She had to pass through a metal detector, and she nodded to the guard as he looked inside her bag and helmet.

The bank took up the entire first floor of the tall office building. Private banker offices lined the exterior walls, except the farthest wall, where the tellers stood behind a bullet-proof glass barrier. The central floor was covered with workstations where lower-level bankers sat behind formal wood desks, meeting with loan applicants and folks opening accounts too small to rate a private office. Men and women strode around in dark suits trying to look busy. She knew that look—lawyers at her parents' firm pulled it off better than these bankers did.

She searched for a target.

There.

A youngish banker sat at a desk in the middle of the open space, typing on his computer. His blond hair was shaggy, his face tan. He might be a banker, but he fancied himself something else. Miranda would figure out what that was and use it against him. And hopefully she would get out of here with what she needed.

She headed over to his desk, stopping in front of him, waiting for him to look up. After a moment, he glanced up at her. And then looked again, taking in her tight jeans, her fitted black blouse that she'd bought at a boutique on Montana Avenue that accentuated her strengths. She smiled at him, her reddest lipstick drawing attention to her full lips.

He stared for a full five seconds. Yes. She'd picked a good target.

"I'm hoping you can help me," she said. "I seem to be in a bind."

"Okay." He cleared his throat. "Like, sure."

"Wonderful." She sat in one of the two chairs that faced his desk, and placed her coat and helmet in the other. She checked out his name placard. "So, Mark." She spoke his name like she was eating chocolate—slowly, and with a lot of tongue.

He flushed. This really was too easy.

"I'm visiting L.A. from out of town. I have my credit card. Can you advance me some cash?" She pulled the card from her wallet. "It's this card."

When he saw the card, precisely what kind of card, his eyes widened.

"I'm sure that won't be a problem, Ms.?" He paused.

"George. Sorcha George."

"Thank you, Ms. George." He took the card from her hand, then handed her a pen and a pad of paper. "Just write down the amount you would like advanced."

Miranda wrote $10,000, then handed the pad and pen back to him.

"If I could just have your ID, I'll get this taken care of."

This was the tricky part. Miranda's ID had gotten her this far—it had even worked at the motorcycle dealership. Granted, the dealer hadn't been eager to kill the sale. She handed over her North Carolina driver's license. The name read *Miranda Sorcha George*.

Blondie Mark didn't even glance at it. "Please, wait here," he said.

She nodded.

He entered one of the offices, one with a large glass window. Through the window, Miranda saw a woman with her hair pulled back in a severe bun and wearing a maroon suit.

They talked with their heads tilted close together. Then a short while later, Blondie Mark reemerged and returned to his desk.

"Um, I'm like, so sorry, but my manager needs to talk with you for a sec. Can you come with me?"

"Of course." Miranda gathered her things.

Maybe it would be jail after all.

Miranda entered the glass-windowed office. She took a seat before the banker could offer her one. She knew how to act put-out.

"Is there a problem?" Miranda put every bit of George family scorn into her voice.

The woman banker spoke. "I'm sure you understand, Ms. George, that with such a large withdrawal, we need to be careful with security."

"It's not that large of a withdrawal," Miranda snapped.

The woman blinked. "Right. The name on your ID doesn't match the name on your card, not exactly, so—"

"It doesn't match exactly because your system keeps substituting my preferred name for my legal name. I'm not sure why your system can't get it right, but surely that's not my problem. As you can see from my ID, I am, indeed, Sorcha George." Miranda leaned back in the leather chair as though it were her throne.

"Regardless—"

"Regardless, I don't have time for this. What do you need for the transaction?"

"We could call the designated phone number on the account."

"You could, but since I'm sitting here and not in my house, that won't work, will it." Miranda paused. "Would you like me to verify my signature?"

Miranda had learned to forge her mother's signature when she was twelve.

The woman bit her lip. She was starting to feel uncertain. "Protocol requires the phone call."

Miranda could only hope that her father wasn't at home. "Have at it." She waved her hand.

The woman picked up the phone and dialed. And someone answered. Miranda kept her face still, but her heart started racing.

"Is this Mr. George? Your wife is here. She would like to withdraw a sum of cash—" The woman stopped speaking, cut off by Miranda's dad.

Miranda tried not to smile. She wondered if this woman had ever been interrupted so much in her entire life. Georges were an impatient lot.

She also wondered how her father had taken the news that his dead wife was at a bank withdrawing money.

"We just need you to verify that Miranda Sorcha George is indeed your co-account-holder's full name. The card seems to have an inaccuracy."

And here was the moment of truth.

"Thank you for that verification. I just need to ask you some security questions to verify your identity."

As she did so, Miranda wondered why her father had given her a pass. He hadn't even asked about the amount of money. She should probably double it. It wasn't like the card had a credit limit. And now that Sorcha was dead, no one would be buying couture.

No one would miss twenty thousand.

Twenty thousand it was.

Plus, she had a feeling this transaction would be her last dance with Sorcha's card. She needed to make it a good one.

The woman banker hung up the phone, looking unsettled. Charles Senior had that effect on most people.

"Could you please confirm how much you would like advanced, Ms. George?" the woman banker said.

Blondie Mark stepped forward from the corner where he'd been waiting, passing her the slip of paper on which Miranda had written the initial amount.

"Make that twenty," Miranda said. "Which is still not that large of a withdrawal."

"Right away." The woman banker stood, turning to Mark. "Go back to your station."

Mark hustled out, the poor thing, in woefully over his head.

Fifteen minutes later, Miranda slid a narrow envelope into her bag and left the bank.

Outside in the bright April sun, she was pulling on her jacket when her cell phone rang. It was her father. She couldn't ignore him this time.

"Hey Dad," she said, squinting into the sun's reflection off of a tall glass building.

"You're alive, then."

"Why wouldn't I be?" But she knew why he was asking the question. And she knew the question was legitimate.

"A psychiatrist might call riding around Los Angeles on a motorcycle parasuicidal."

"Lots of people ride motorcycles here. The parking sucks."

"Lots of people aren't you."

"Are you concerned about me, Dad?" She filled her voice with faux surprise.

"Do you have enough cash for whatever little adventure you're on?"

"Never," she said.

"I hope that's not true. I've cancelled the card."

She hung up. That was all the information she needed.

She slung her bag over her head and across her chest, then pulled on her helmet, fastening it under her chin. She tucked her hair under the collar of her jacket. Long hair really wasn't a good pairing with a motorcycle.

She tossed the black credit card into a public trashcan before hopping on her bike and pulling into traffic.

———

DAPHNE SAITO ARRIVED HOME FROM THE BRUNCH SHE'D HAD WITH GRETA and Greta's dad around two o'clock. She'd spent the night in Sandy's guest room with Marlon, her—well, her boyfriend. After everything that had happened that week, her best friend Greta's wedding, the tragic car wreck, and her own near catastrophe, she could barely believe that she'd escaped with a happy ending.

And she owed that happy ending, in large part, to Miranda George, her surprise houseguest, who still had a haunted look about her when she thought no one was watching her closely.

"Miranda?" Daphne called out as she slipped off her shoes. "You here?"

Miranda wasn't in the kitchen. She wasn't in her bedroom or bathroom. Daphne was just grabbing her phone to call her when she heard the garage door opening. She slipped her shoes back on and stepped onto her front porch, opening the gate that separated the porch from the garage. In shock, she watched as a muscular, sporty, metal-framed motorcycle rolled in, ridden by a guy in white.

Wait, no. By a woman in white.

Miranda pulled the helmet from her head and hung it from the handlebar.

"Seriously?" Daphne asked.

Miranda climbed off the bike. "Can you cut hair? You seem like someone who would know how to cut hair."

In fact, Daphne was excellent at cutting hair. She'd grown up poor, and she'd had three little sisters.

"A motorcycle?" Daphne asked, following Miranda inside. "Are you crazy?"

"Why is everyone freaking out about the motorcycle?"

"Who is everyone?"

"You, John, my dad—"

"You spoke to your dad?"

Miranda huffed. "Can you cut hair or not?"

Daphne knew she wasn't going to get anywhere with Miranda by taking a direct approach. She would try a flank attack instead. "Sure, I can cut hair. I have shears in my bathroom."

Miranda followed her into her bathroom and sat on the closed toilet lid, unbuttoning her blouse and tossing it on the counter. Daphne draped a towel around Miranda's neck and held it shut with a hair clip. Using a spray bottle, she spritzed water on Miranda's hair, and then she began to comb it.

"What were you thinking for a haircut?" Daphne asked.

"It needs to be short enough to fit under my helmet. It's getting tangled when I ride fast on the freeway."

Of course Miranda would want a serviceable haircut for her motorcycle helmet. Miranda was a curious mix of practical and completely and totally not.

"And make sure it's long enough in the front for me to pull back if it gets annoying," Miranda added.

"How about a blunt bob, angled a little longer in the front."

"Fine. Whatever."

Daphne smiled. She slipped a comb through Miranda's long hair to part it, and clipped it up on her head. Daphne chewed her lip, thoughtful. Miranda's hair had always been one of her vanities. That she was so willing to part with it today, and with so little concern, worried Daphne. What else was Miranda willing to let go of? She'd already abandoned what was left of her family. Her entire life would fit in the messenger bag that was currently leaning against the shower enclosure.

Having recently considered disappearing herself, Daphne knew the signs of someone shedding the attachments of the world around her.

"You sure about this?" Daphne asked, holding up the scissors.

"You're like a worried grandmother."

Daphne snipped, holding up a ten-inch length of hair. She handed it to Miranda. "Here you go. No more tangles."

Miranda held the top of the lock with one hand and rubbed the length of it with her fingers, then she laid it carefully on the counter next to her cell phone.

"I invited Marlon over for dinner tonight," Daphne said. "I thought the three of us could eat together. He and I owe you a lot."

She and Marlon owed Miranda everything, really. The last two days, Miranda had come through in surprising ways. But now that the crisis was over, Miranda had turned dark, dark like she'd been when she'd first arrived on Monday night. And Daphne could tell that she was upset about more than the old pain of a college betrayal. No. She was upset about something else, something to do with her mother dying. Miranda was still keeping secrets. Daphne wanted to know what they were.

Daphne looked in the mirror at her work on Miranda's hair. One side hung in a sculpted bob. The other was a ragged mess. Daphne smiled.

"What?" Miranda demanded.

"Tell me what happened with your mother."

"I did tell you."

Daphne sat on the edge of the tub. Miranda rotated on the toilet bowl until she was facing her.

"I know there's more to the story, Miranda." Daphne twirled the comb in her hand. "I'm not cutting any more until you spill."

"How do you know there's more?"

"I spent half my life handing out keys in a no-tell motel. I can read people."

"So you're holding my haircut hostage?" Miranda sounded incredulous.

Daphne nodded.

Miranda narrowed her eyes. "Why do you care, Daphne? My mom died. What else matters?"

Daphne refused to be cowed by Miranda's anger. "You matter to me, Miranda. You're not all right. I can't help you unless you tell me what's going on."

Miranda pressed her lips together. Daphne wondered if Miranda was stubborn enough to walk out of the room with half a haircut.

"Since when do I matter to you, Daphne?" Miranda's voice was a near-whisper.

Was this the problem? The one time Miranda had asked her for help, Daphne had been too scared—too easily influenced by her silly college boyfriend—to do the right thing. But surely Miranda could see that Daphne cared about her now. Daphne had taken Miranda into her home. What else could Daphne do to prove to her that she could be trusted?

"I let you down, it's true," Daphne said.

"Charlie got arrested. A kid died. I needed your help and you didn't come."

Those were all true things. Daphne had done some things in her life that she was ashamed of, and abandoning Miranda that night in college ranked high.

"I'm sorry about all of those things. I'll keep apologizing. It'll never be enough to make up for what I did."

"God, Daphne." Miranda rolled her eyes. "You don't have to be so decent."

"What happened with your mom, Miranda?"

Miranda sighed. "She didn't die from alcohol. She killed herself. Like, in a more intentional fashion."

"What happened?"

"The usual." Miranda shrugged.

"Miranda." Daphne wasn't letting it go.

"She shot herself."

Daphne raised her eyebrows in surprise. She'd worked the counter at her parents' shitty motel from the time she could see over it, so she'd learned a lot about people. She'd bolstered that knowledge with psychology courses in college, and as a screenwriter, she made a point to know all she could about human behavior. And one thing she knew for certain was that it was very, very unusual for a woman to kill herself with a gun.

"Who found her?"

A long pause. "Charlie."

Charlie, Miranda's precious little brother. But there was a lot more information in that pause than Miranda was letting on. Daphne considered pressing for more, but she'd asked enough of Miranda for today.

Daphne stood, slipping her fingers back through the grips of the shears. Miranda turned to face the mirror again. As Daphne shaped Miranda's hair, she spoke. "I know you feel like you don't have a family any more. That's why you came here. But the thing is, we all felt that way—me, Greta, even Sandy and Marlon. So we made our own family. We started over. You could be a part of our family, too."

Miranda said nothing.

———

While Daphne finished cutting her hair, Miranda considered Daphne's words about making a new family, about starting over.

At the very least, she'd be starting over with new hair.

But she refused to lie to herself. Daphne's words sounded so good that Miranda wanted to cry—if she were the kind of person who cried about things like that.

If she were the kind of person who could let herself have a family. But she'd had a family, and that family had destroyed itself.

Instead, once Daphne pronounced her haircut finished, she entered her room in Daphne's gorgeous Brentwood condo and dialed John. She didn't need a family, she needed an easy lay and drugs.

"Can I come to your house? The love birds are cooking dinner at my place tonight." Miranda couldn't bear the thought of sitting through dinner with Daphne and Marlon, not with the rotten way she was feeling.

"I guess so." John sounded unenthusiastic about the prospect of her company.

What the hell?

"I guess so, and therefore I can come over?" she asked.

"I definitely want to see you, Miranda. I'm just not in love with the idea of you coming over to my place."

"Yeah, Daphne did mention that your place needed a lot of decorating." After Daphne had spent her one night at John's apartment not that long ago, she'd left John with a fake name and fake phone number.

"Give me a break, Miranda."

Daphne had picked John up at a swanky Santa Monica nightclub and left him at dawn. Miranda would feel bad for him, except she didn't feel bad about things like guys getting to sleep with gorgeous girls with no strings attached.

Please.

"I can't help it that you slept with my roommate before you met me. That was your decision, not mine."

"And you're never going to let me forget it, are you."

"Probably not. I'm getting way too much mileage out of it."

John sighed. "Come on over." John gave her his address. "Do you want me to pick up food?"

"Yes. Preferably those pot caramels. They were delicious."

"You can't spend every day high, you know."

"I can try."

"You won't be able to ride home if you get too messed up."

"Oh goodness me," she said with mock concern and a thicker southern accent than usual. "I'll have to stay with you then."

He laughed. "I was asking for that one."

Miranda fished her keys out of her pocket. "I'll be there in five minutes."

"It should take you fifteen."

"I know."

She didn't say good-bye to Daphne when she left. What Daphne had offered was so tempting, she needed to walk away from it, and soon.

Chapter Four

J ohn Wesley hadn't lived in L.A. long. He wasn't expecting to like the place. But it was good for his work, and he loved his work. And liking L.A. had kind of crept up on him.

He built websites for companies, all kinds of companies, from law firms and medical practices to restaurants and nightclubs. His business was steady, booming even. He'd just hired a kid fresh out of college to work for him because he needed an extra coder.

He didn't have an office, just computers rigged up in his studio apartment and a couple of laptops for when he went to meetings. His assistant, Deon, had his own gear, too. Deon was psyched to have the job because it paid for his tech habit. Deon still lived with his parents, and now he could write off nearly all of his expenses. But the kid was a genius, and when he wasn't playing Warcraft, he worked at a supersonic pace. Which was good because they were getting more and more clients.

At the moment, on a Friday afternoon, John knew he should be working to meet a deadline for a new restaurant in Santa Monica that wanted their site mock-up ready for viewing by Monday. Sitting at his desk—a piece of countertop he'd picked up from an office supply store, set across two metal file cabinets manufactured circa 1960—he leaned back and laced his fingers behind his head.

He should be working, but he was unable to say no to Miranda George.

Nothing in his life had prepared him for anything like Miranda. He was from a small suburb of Columbus, Ohio, perhaps the most boring place on Earth. He was grateful that his parents had raised him in such a quiet place. It was so safe that the kids were allowed to walk alone up to the ice cream shop, and it was so quaint that it had an ice cream shop in the first place. His dad worked for Honda, and his mom taught piano out of their house. His parents had let him take over the basement with his computer gear and basically live like a troll all through high school.

He'd gone to Ohio State for college, like half the kids at his high school, where he'd majored in computer science. At graduation he'd said he wanted to move to California with his best friend. His parents hadn't batted an eye. They'd offered him a thousand dollars to get started, helped him pack his car, and told him not to do drugs.

The best friend, whom they'd all called Turbo since they were in the second grade, had wanted to be an actor. But Turbo had ended up a server at a fancy restaurant in Newport Beach. And Turbo did an awful lot of drugs. He knew how to get the best weed. After living in Orange County with Turbo for a couple of years, John knew he needed his own place, and he knew he needed to move to L.A. He wanted to be in the city. Plus, the late—and raucous—nights of the restaurant industry didn't work for him.

God, he was so square. He'd never cared before now. Before Miranda.

Miranda would be here any minute, given her new vehicle and how she'd likely be operating it. It drove him nuts that she was racing over on that motorcycle, and he would have offered to pick her up except he knew she would have laughed in his ear.

He stood. The head of his bed was pushed against the back wall of the studio. His desk ran along the entire wall to the left of the bed. The door to the bathroom was to the right, next to his dresser. His kitchen, near the exterior door, had a bar that kicked out a bit so he didn't need a table, thank god, because there wasn't room for much else, just a leather loveseat he tucked in the corner facing the bed so he had a place to sit that wasn't his desk. The apartment was small, but it was his—meaning he wouldn't accidentally find Turbo's cocaine in his sock drawer.

He quickly made his bed and tossed a pair of dirty socks into the laundry basket in his bathroom. He put all the dirty dishes in his sink —no time to wash them—and wiped down the counter with a paper towel.

He grabbed a hammer from the drawer in his kitchen. Daphne had been teasing about the unfinished state of his apartment, so he supposed he should hang some of his artwork. He'd gotten three framed prints hung before there was a knocking at his door.

He tossed the hammer back into its drawer. His heart rate kicked up. Damn.

He opened the door and pretended that he wasn't immediately turned on by what he saw.

Miranda stood there in painted-on jeans tucked into black leather boots, her white leather jacket still zipped tight over her hips and breasts. She held her helmet in one hand and her bag in the other.

And her hair. She'd cut it.

Before he could stop himself, he reached out and ran his fingertips along the bottom edge where it tracked her jawline.

"Daphne cut it for me," she said. "What do you think?"

She already knew the answer. He could tell by the glint in her eye. So he did what he wanted to do every time he saw her, what he resisted doing because he knew it was the easy play, because he knew she expected it. He grabbed her wrist and pulled her to him and kissed her like tomorrow wasn't coming.

When he finished, he stepped back. "Come on in."

She looked stunned.

Well. He should have kissed her like that sooner.

She shook off her surprise as though she'd never felt it.

Didn't matter. He'd seen it.

He gestured behind him. "You can put your things on the floor by the couch." Someday he might have a side table. But today he did not.

She set her bag and helmet down, then unzipped her jacket. She wore a fitted black t-shirt that said Suzuki on it. He recognized it from the night before. The dealership had given it to her when she'd bought her bike. She'd walked in the door, picked a bike off the floor, and paid in full, all in about forty-five minutes. A shirt had been the least they could do for her, really.

"Thanks for taking me in for the evening." She laid her jacket on top of her bag and helmet. "I'm really glad that Marlon and Daphne worked through their problems and found love and all. But I would have stabbed myself with something if I'd had to hang out with them."

"Not a fan of happy endings?" he asked.

"Well," she said, grinning at him, "not that kind."

"I can't decide if you're a grown woman or a thirteen-year-old boy."

Miranda laughed. "I know I'm interrupting your work. Don't lie. I can work too."

"What are you working on?"

He knew that Miranda did freelance writing of a variety of kinds —for lawyers, for magazines if she could get it, and for websites. It was the last kind that had caught his attention when she'd described her work, but they'd been kind of busy the past couple of days, so he hadn't pressed her on the details.

He was a coder, and a pretty good designer too, but he wasn't a writer. He relied on his clients to provide the copy for their websites. But more and more he was realizing that it'd be better to offer copywriting services as well.

Working with Miranda George seemed like a terrible idea.

"I'm writing a resume and cover letter for a client. Their desperation breeds work for me. After I'm done with that, I have to turn a 400-word blog post into a 1000-word blog post for a mortgage company." She flopped onto his couch and unzipped one tall, black leather boot. He couldn't keep his eyes off that zipper.

Working with her would be a terrible, terrible idea.

"Anyways, I can sit here with my laptop, and you can go back to the control center of the Death Star over there." She unzipped the other boot. "Then we'll get high and eat. Sound good?"

He shook his head. He'd never seen someone so keen on keeping her mind off of the things that were hurting her.

"Sounds good," he said.

Her phone rang. She stood to fish it out of her jeans pocket, and he couldn't keep his eyes off of her perfect ass. How was he supposed to get work done? She was a walking distraction.

She frowned when she saw the number, and silenced the phone.

"Your dad again?" he asked. Her dad had called a few times the past couple of days, and she'd never answered.

"Not this time. In fact, I finally spoke to him this morning. He cut off the credit card, the asshole."

John nodded. "Sorry." He knew that she was disappointed. She might act flip about it, but it was a big deal for her to lose that credit card. "Who was that?"

"My brother."

She hadn't talked about her brother much, only to say that she didn't feel bad about ditching her father because her brother was still back east with him. That meant she'd left her brother behind, too, as though leaving him behind didn't mean anything. Yet here her brother was, calling her.

People cared about Miranda George. But for some reason, she wasn't letting them reach her.

John knew guys in college and after, guys who'd had crazy girlfriends. Girlfriends with issues, baggage, or whatever you wanted to call it. He'd always figured he'd find some girl from an ordinary family like his own to spend his time with. A girl who returned her parents' phone calls. Who had parents. Who didn't steal things or take unnecessary risks or dash across the country to hide from something so obviously painful that he could read the pain in the way she held her laptop in her clenched hand and in the severe cut of her hair. Maybe he wouldn't have been able to read it a few days ago, but he could read it now.

Miranda was dying inside.

John didn't want a normal girl. He wanted Miranda, and he wanted to know what was hurting her.

God, he was done for.

He sat on the edge of his bed, facing her. "Can I ask you a question you won't like?"

She raised her eyebrows. "Living on the edge?"

"Why did you bring me to Greta's wedding, when you knew I'd hooked up with Daphne?"

Miranda lay against the back of the sofa, crossing her sock-clad feet under her legs. How she could bend that much in those tight jeans was a mystery.

"First of all, I wasn't certain you'd slept with Daphne. It was merely a deduction."

John had a feeling that Miranda could make a living on accurate deductions. He should take her to the underground poker games Turbo liked to frequent. He wouldn't be surprised if she could count cards.

"And sure, Daphne's my friend now, but she screwed me over in college pretty bad once. I was still angry about it. I felt like I owed her one."

"That's a long time to hold a grudge. Five years? Six?"

"We were sophomores. So, more like eight."

"What did she do to you?"

"She didn't do it to me. She did it to my brother."

John worked to keep his expression even. This was the most interesting piece of information he'd ever gotten out of her. She did, indeed, care about her brother. Deeply. She cared enough about her brother to risk her friendship with the girl who'd given her a place to live.

"Will you tell me what happened?"

"I guess so. Like you said, it was a long time ago."

"I'd still like to hear the story." In fact, he was dying to hear the story. Miranda talked about all sorts of things, but not about her family.

Miranda told him about a college party, and a boy who died, and a brother who was arrested, and a friend who hadn't come to her aid because she was too busy looking out for herself. When she described the phone call to Daphne, and Daphne's words rejecting her call for help, he could hear her throat tighten, as though the event had happened yesterday.

"You don't do that," Miranda said. "You don't do that to someone who's your friend. You might be afraid, but you suck it up and you get smart and you figure out how to help anyway." She snorted. "I mean, who couldn't outsmart the dipshit Feltham cops? She was so selfish."

"Is she still?"

Miranda was silent for a moment. "No. She's changed a lot."

John really wanted to ask another question—*Have you?* But he didn't. He knew that would be too much. She'd clam up. But he also knew the answer already. She hadn't changed. She was still loyal as hell, and competent, and good in emergencies—he'd seen that first-hand—and scary when angry. And she still believed that she couldn't truly count on anyone. Daphne may be giving her a place to stay, but Miranda was ready to pack everything she owned into a single bag, the one he'd watched her buy at the dealership. She was ready to be homeless again, ready to be betrayed again. Even if she didn't realize it.

John had his work cut out for him convincing her otherwise.

Miranda's phone rang once more. She glanced at the number and frowned, silencing it.

"Your brother again?"

"Yeah."

"Why don't you want to talk to him?"

Miranda narrowed her eyes. "No."

"What?" he said, confused.

"No, I'm not answering that question. Don't you have work to do?"

John smiled. "Sure. Let's work for a couple of hours, and then we can order pizza."

Miranda relaxed, pulling her laptop onto her knees. "Sounds perfect."

———

DAPHNE HAD SAID JOHN'S STUDIO WAS KIND OF A SHITHOLE, BUT UPON seeing it, Miranda disagreed. He just hadn't lived there long. He was still hanging his artwork, but at least he had artwork. And his couch was really comfortable. His desk, which ran nearly the length of one wall, had about fourteen different computers on it, but since his apartment seemed to double as his office, she could understand why he'd need all that stuff. And he'd even made his bed.

It had been two hours, and she was still thinking about that kiss he'd hit her with when she'd shown up at his door.

She'd finished most of the work she needed to do that day to meet deadlines. She wasn't really worried about money at the moment—not with the envelope currently zipped in her coat's interior pocket—but she wanted to stay in good standing with the freelance agency she worked for. Blowing deadlines would mean no more jobs.

She wasn't sure if she would need more jobs when her money ran out, but she wanted to keep her options open.

That kiss, though. Where had that come from? John had spent the entire week dodging her attempts to get past his defenses. She wanted more.

She wanted more. The thought zipped through her like a bolt of energy. The kiss, sure, but also his directness, his refusal to give in to her. His brown eyes which managed to be kind and sexy at the same time.

She wanted more. Damn it. She didn't think she'd find anyone she cared about as much as she'd cared about her ex, Matthias. She'd loved him. But Matthias had moved away, and then her mother had died, and now he seemed to belong to a different lifetime.

She didn't expect to find someone good again. She didn't want to. It wasn't part of her plan. She considered leaving John's apartment right then, making up some excuse, but then she remembered Daphne at the house with Marlon. She had nowhere to go.

That left her with only a few options.

"I'm done with my work," she said.

After a moment during which he typed furiously, the screen a white field with a bunch of letters and numbers and other characters on it, John glanced over at her. "I could be done."

"Can I please have a caramel?"

John seemed to have an endless supply of delicious pot caramels. He said his old roommate, who lived about an hour south, brought them as gifts whenever the guy had to crash at John's place after a wild night in L.A. *I would have preferred something more useful,* he'd told her. She thought the caramels were perfectly useful. They made everything blur.

He opened a mason jar tucked behind one of the giant computer monitors on his desk and pulled out a piece of candy wrapped in clear cellophane. Then he joined her on the couch. She held out her hand, and he dropped the candy in it.

Finally. The piece was about three inches long. She knew that normally a person would eat half now and half later, maintaining a chill buzz over time. But she didn't want a chill buzz. She wanted to deep-six these thoughts of family and love.

She unwrapped the piece and chewed the whole thing, swallowing it slowly, tasting the flavor of sweet and bitter. She leaned her head back against the couch and glanced at John, whose eyes had been following the progress of the caramel into her mouth.

She blew him a kiss.

He shut his eyes and shook his head.

"Why won't you sleep with me?" she asked, stoned enough to let down her guard somewhat. "I know I'm not hot, objectively, but surely I'm hot enough to sleep with."

"You can't possibly believe that I don't think you're hot."

"I'm not fishing for compliments, you dodo."

"Of course not."

She shook her head, and the room twisted around her. "No."

He chuckled. "You would never."

"Objectively speaking, Daphne is beautiful. I'm slightly above average. Especially in Los Angeles, which attracts women who are preternaturally gorgeous."

John shook his head. "Allow me to clarify. What I want to do is remove your clothes and toss you on my bed."

"Oh, let's do that, please." She grinned.

"But that want conflicts with what I want even more."

Desperation filled her. She had to make him stop talking. He was about to say something she didn't want to hear. Couldn't hear. What he wanted could never happen. And the fact that she was maybe wanting the same thing too? That made it even worse.

She and John—the way he wanted? A cute apartment? Two boring cars? Normal jobs? Normal anything?

It wasn't, as they say, in the cards.

She thought of Marlon and Daphne, getting ready to cook dinner together, how happy they were, and she wanted to scratch her arms until they bled. Until she could feel something that would focus the pain inside her, the pain that was scraping the inside of her body over and over until she was a thin shell.

She needed another caramel.

Before John could tell her what he wanted more than a fuck, she stood. But she stood too quickly, losing her balance, and she stumbled into the countertop. She took hold of the edge to stabilize herself until the room stopped twirling around. Then she walked to his desk and grabbed another caramel from the mason jar.

"Really?" he said, standing behind her. "Those are strong. Even Turbo says those are strong." He sounded worried.

She popped the caramel in her mouth. "Can I pass out on your bed? You can go back to work."

He pulled her to him, kissing her temple. "What happened to you?" He brushed her hair back from her face, and his features started to blur.

"Can't you see?" The room tilted. She liked it. "I'm in pieces."

Dizzy, she closed her eyes. He guided her to the bed, and she slept.

Chapter Five

Around six-thirty on Saturday night, Miranda pulled her bike up to the valet stand at Rivet, one of the hottest restaurants in Los Angeles, and stopped. Dinner wasn't until seven, but she wanted some time to case the place before her friends arrived. She flipped up her helmet's visor when the valet approached.

"I'm here with Greta Donovan's party," she told the woman. "Is there a place I can park?"

The valet, dressed in a sharp red suit perfectly tailored to her form, nodded. "Of course." She gestured to a narrow spot just to the left of the main entrance.

"Thanks, Lady," Miranda said, flipping down her visor. She motored into the spot and killed the engine.

As she was climbing off her bike, a familiar car pulled into the restaurant drive. It was a dark gray Aston Martin, the sweetest thing she'd seen on four wheels since she'd arrived in L.A., and everyone in L.A. had a nice car.

That was Sandy Martin's car.

Sandy emerged, spoke to the valet in fluent Spanish, and handed her his keys. Miranda would have sworn that the valet was blushing as she climbed behind the wheel.

Miranda strolled over to where Sandy waited for her by the steps leading up to the entrance. His gray hair was cropped short, his blue eyes piercing even from a distance. He was a handsome dude. He wore well-fitted jeans and a slim, button-down shirt, and his fit form was apparent even underneath his clothes. Weren't dudes supposed to start melting in their fifties? This guy looked as muscly as he had twenty years ago. When he smiled at her, she gritted her teeth, refusing to reveal that her heart sped up. She would not let on that he had that kind of effect on her.

"Nice wheels," he said, nodding at her bike.

"Finally." She heaved a sigh.

"What do you mean?"

"Everyone else has been freaking out like a granny that I'm riding a motorcycle."

Sandy laughed. "After what I've done in my life, I'd be the last to judge." He gestured at the entrance. "Shall we?"

Miranda turned her eyes on Rivet. The building, she knew, was an old city storage facility for road equipment. From the outside, the restaurant looked like a windowless box. There was no sign with Rivet's name, only the numerals indicating the street address in spot-lit chrome above the entryway.

Through a combination of disaster and luck, Timmy, Greta, and Sandy were the owners of Rivet, and Rivet was one of the most exclusive restaurants in Los Angeles. And here she was, walking into that exclusive restaurant with Sandy Martin of all people, getting ready to meet up with Timmy, Greta, Daphne, and Marlon.

As though she belonged with all of them.

She shook her head. She'd come to L.A. to get away from belonging.

She followed Sandy through the tall double doors and into the restaurant, and again she worked hard to hide her reaction. The interior of Rivet couldn't have been more different from the exterior. A dark wood bar ran the entire length of the left wall. The rest of the room was paneled in dark wood, with wide-plank wood floors and dark leather upholstery on the seats and booths. The place was like a rich man's wet dream, complete with spectacular, sparkling starlets every few feet.

She felt her face flush, remembering her intoxicated conversation with John the evening before. What was happening to her? She didn't care if she were a beautiful starlet. She was herself. She knew her strengths.

She shook her head, removing thoughts of starlets, and of John, from her mind.

Rivet's host approached them, a young man, certainly younger than Miranda. He was in his early twenties, although he looked like a teenager. His dark suit was well tailored, though, and well made. Spiffy clothes seemed to be the Rivet uniform.

"Jonas." Sandy greeted the host, then he nodded at Miranda. "This is Miranda George, an old friend of Greta Donovan and Daphne Saito. She just moved to L.A. Been here about a week."

Miranda thought it was a stretch to call her an "old friend" of either Daphne or Greta, but she wasn't going to correct Sandy.

"It's great to meet you, Miss George." Jonas smiled, revealing either the luckiest dental genetics ever, or at least ten grand in orthodontia.

She figured it was the latter. "Please call me Miranda."

"That's what Mr. Sandy always says." Jonas flushed a deep scarlet. "I mean, Sandy."

"It's all right, Jonas." Sandy smiled kindly. "Our table ready?"

Miranda was certain that Sandy's table was always ready, considering he owned not only the restaurant but also two Academy Awards for Best Actor.

Jonas grabbed six thick leather menus from a stand by the door. "Follow me, sir."

"After you." Sandy held out his hand for Miranda to take the lead. When she didn't step forward immediately, he chuckled. "Don't like having people at your back?"

"It's fun to follow you. I get to watch idiots trip over themselves when they see who you are."

Sandy paused, looking at her thoughtfully. "You don't think highly of people."

"I'm selective." As a rule, Miranda indeed didn't think highly of other people. But she wasn't going to tell Sandy that. Her misanthropy was not her most charming quality.

"Where do I fall?" Sandy surprised her by sounding genuinely curious, even concerned.

She smiled, trying to lighten a conversation that had grown darker than she'd planned it to. "I'll let you know after I've bought you a drink."

"You're buying?" He sounded surprised. Good.

"Doesn't happen to you often, does it."

"Nope."

"Everyone deserves to be treated now and then, Sandy."

Sandy smiled, thoughtful. "After me, then."

————

ALEJANDRO MARTINEZ, KNOWN AS ALEXANDER MARTIN TO MOST OF planet Earth and Sandy to his friends, felt all of his fifty-seven years standing next to Miranda George. He hadn't felt old in a while, but he had thirty years on this girl, and he didn't like it.

When she'd breezed into his house for Greta's wedding in a killer black dress, he'd found her distracting, but that was all. Lots of women in L.A. were distracting. When she'd saved Daphne and torn Marlon to pieces in the process, she'd caught his eye. She was irreverent, profane, and funny. Her ass was to die for. She rode a V-twin sport bike like it was no big deal.

He wanted to see her ass on that V-twin sport bike.

She also, apparently, already had a guy, some dude she'd brought to the wedding and had been torturing every day since she'd arrived, according to Daphne.

John Something.

He led her to their table, a round six-top at the corner of the patio closest to the bar and farthest from the band, the best table, naturally, because the manager of Rivet wouldn't give them anything less than the best. Jonas set the menus down.

"Have a good dinner, Sandy. Miranda." Saying their first names seemed to cause the kid physical pain.

"Thanks, man," Sandy said. He turned to Miranda. "Seems we're both a little early. Want to head to the bar? I believe you owe me a drink."

"Absolutely." She unzipped her white leather motorcycle jacket and draped it on the back of a chair. Sandy gritted his teeth—either that or he was going to drop his jaw. Underneath her jacket, she wore what looked like no more than a black silk handkerchief. It draped across the front and covered up the important parts and left her back almost completely bare, but for two ties, one at the neck and one at the waist. When she turned her back to him, he swallowed hard.

That's when he noticed her haircut—sometime since he'd seen her last, she'd lopped off her long mane of hair. Her sharp bob revealed an uninterrupted line from the back of her neck all the way down her spine to that one skinny bow tied at her lower back.

Jesus. What a view.

She turned, eyes narrowed, pinning him with a look. "What?"

"Nice shirt."

She shrugged. "I was in a hurry when I left home. Had to pack light."

She headed to the bar, and he followed, eyes never leaving her tight behind.

Sandy knew he should not be having thoughts like this about Greta and Daphne's friend. Greta and Daphne were like his daughters. Marlon was like his son. That would make Miranda a niece or something. Except she was exuding all sorts of vibes—she was sexy, she knew it, and she wanted him to know it. When she reached the bar, she looked over her shoulder at him and smiled, her lipstick as red as at least five of the seven deadly sins.

Yep. She wanted him to know it.

She was probably screwing with him. The problem was, it was working. This shit never worked on him. He'd thought he was immune. But her energy—it was intoxicating. Talking to her was like being swept along in a storm, and she made you like it. Her unpredictability was refreshing, especially for him, when nothing surprising seemed to have happened to him in decades.

Quentin, Rivet's bar manager, was working the outside bar tonight. Sandy caught him eyeing Miranda as he made his way over to her. Apparently Quentin wasn't immune to her, either. Sandy looked at her mouth, at her full lips.

She wasn't a beauty, but she was stunning.

"Hello, Sir," Quentin said to Sandy. "What can I get you tonight?"

Sandy watched as Miranda looked Quentin over. Quentin was a good-looking dude in his thirties, with black hair and dark eyes and a sexiness that kept the ladies buying drinks and the men talking, hoping Quentin would be their friend. When Miranda flashed

Quentin a red-lipped smile, Sandy felt himself grow unreasonably jealous.

"I'm buying," Miranda said. "And I'm picking."

Quentin raised his eyebrows at Sandy in question. Sandy nodded.

"Four Herraduras, please." She placed a one-hundred-dollar bill on the bar. "No need for the accessories."

Quentin lined up four glasses and poured four shots. He slid the glasses forward. Miranda picked up one and nodded to Sandy to do the same.

"One goes fast," she said. "One goes slow." She threw back the first shot, placed the glass down, and then picked up the second.

Sandy followed suit.

If Miranda thought she would be able to work him over with tequila, she had another thing coming. He'd been drinking people under the table for decades. He could barely remember the 1980s. His yoga instructor kept trying to get him to do a detox, whatever the hell that meant, but he wasn't going for it. He liked his whiskey, and his heart and other important parts were working perfectly. His doctor came and checked him out every three months. He might be in his late fifties, but he looked no older than forty.

Why was he thinking about his age? He never thought about his age. He didn't give a damn about his age.

He glanced at Miranda, who leaned her back against the bar next to him, scanning the enclosed patio.

As though she'd felt his eyes on her, she cut her gaze to his. "Why do you hang out with Greta and Daph?"

"You don't think your friends are cool enough to hang out with?"

"Don't play coy. My parents are the best lawyers in the South." She paused. "My dad is."

"Am I about to be interrogated?" He raised his brows.

She pinned him with brown eyes lined in black. "Answer the question."

Ordinarily, Sandy would not put up with a kid snapping questions at him the way Miranda was doing, but he was drawn to Miranda's directness. She wasn't asking questions to be nosy or greedy with information about his personal life. She was driven by a mix of fiery curiosity and protectiveness. He liked both qualities.

"How much do you already know?" he asked.

"Some. You met Greta and Daphne through Daphne's old boss. Y'all own this restaurant." She examined him, her eyes tracking all over his face. He wondered what she saw. "But it's obvious that you care more about them than you would about regular business partners. That wedding alone—you didn't have to do that for Greta and Timmy. So, why? Why throw the wedding of the century at your house for a couple of kids?"

"They snuck into my life, didn't they."

Miranda nodded. "I'm wondering how they did it."

It was a fair question. "This is a town where everyone lies. Where everyone wants something from someone else. Where you can't count on anyone for anything." He sipped his drink. "But every person coming here tonight is honest, gives more than she takes, and is always there when you need her." He paused, considering his own explanation. "Those are rare qualities."

Miranda nodded, seeming to accept his words.

"My turn," he said.

"Seems fair."

"Where's your guy from the other night?"

She looked at him out of the corner of her eye and gave him a close-lipped smile. "I have no idea."

"What's his name?"

"John."

Sandy had been hoping he would get his last name out of her so he could run a background check on him. No luck, though—Miranda seemed to know what he was about. So he tried to keep it cool. "You could have brought him along."

"I know." She was still smiling. She was definitely on to him. He wondered if that was good or bad.

"You going to tell me why you didn't?"

"He wouldn't fit on the back of my bike."

Sandy laughed. "Is he out of the picture already, then?"

She narrowed her eyes at him. "No."

Ah. A nerve, there. "You like him?"

Miranda's face softened. "He's a good person."

"You say that like it's an unusual thing for you to find."

A strange look came over her face, like she'd been wearing a mask of a girl, but then she'd dropped it, and an old woman had taken her place, a woman even older than Sandy himself. "You seem like a good person, too," she said.

"I don't know about that. My ex-wife might have a different opinion."

She threw back the rest of her tequila. "You should stay away from me. They should all stay away from me." Miranda gestured at the empty table where her friends would soon be joining them.

"Why's that?"

"You know the fable about the scorpion and the frog?"

"Does this have to do with your mom killing herself?"

Her face went stony. "Daphne's a motormouth."

Sandy gave her a look. He wasn't going to reveal his sources. Both Daphne and Greta had told him on separate occasions that Miranda had come because her mother had died. That she'd arrived the very night of her mother's funeral. Just yesterday, Daphne had told him about Miranda's mom shooting herself.

"Fine," Miranda said. "So you know something. But none of you know what happened."

"So tell me what happened."

Miranda smiled darkly. "Not a chance."

Sandy gestured to Quentin. "I'll have another."

Miranda set her glass down, too. "I'll have a double. Pour it on top, please."

Sandy's eyebrows shot up. "Don't you have to drive home?"

"Back off, Dad."

Having her call him Dad bothered him a hell of a lot more than he liked.

"Besides," she said, "I'll just hitch a ride with someone if I get wasted. Maybe with you. I've been dying to see the inside of your car."

The thought of Miranda inside his car didn't bother him at all.

Quentin set their drinks on the bar. "I'll get this round," Sandy told Quentin. Quentin would put it on Sandy's tab.

Across the patio, a couple he knew waved at him, and he waved back.

"You don't have to hang out with me," Miranda said. "I'm sure you have far more interesting people to talk to."

Sandy chuckled. "I don't know about that."

"You're just nosy," she said grumpily.

"And you have chutzpah."

"I've got nothing else, do I." She sounded incredibly sad. She leaned forward, resting on her elbows on the bar, her short hair falling forward and obscuring her face. But her hair accentuated her slender neck and her bare shoulders. She'd put on some sort of skin cream that was glittering in the light from the festoons draped across the ceiling. Her bare skin glowed.

When she looked at him again, her black-lined eyes were red, but there wasn't a trace of tears.

"Tell me what happened," he asked again.

"I can't," she whispered. "If I talk about it, I'll fall apart."

At those words, he stopped resisting. He put his arm around her shoulders and pulled her to him, brushing his lips across her temple.

She leaned into him, her bones going soft, and Sandy knew in that moment that he'd make terrible decisions where this girl was concerned, given the chance.

———

During dinner, Miranda watched Marlon with Daphne and Timmy with Greta. She said little. After sparring with Sandy at the bar—and sucking down four shots of tequila—she was feeling wiped out. The food tasted great, which was good, because she needed something to absorb all that liquor if she was going to make it home in one piece. Sandy hadn't been wrong to express concern about her riding after drinking. She knew it was stupid. She was going to do it anyways, but she knew it was stupid.

Her phone buzzed. She pulled it from her coat pocket. Her brother Charlie, again. She silenced her phone. She wished he would stop calling. She had nothing to say to him, and he knew it. She'd told him as much before she'd left. But Charlie was a stubborn asshole. Almost as stubborn as she was.

"Who was that?" Sandy asked, leaning close to her.

Despite herself, Miranda felt warm under Sandy's attention. She knew what she was feeling was probably starstruck bullshit for a movie star. Except, she wasn't starstruck. She'd been with Sandy through a crisis. She'd only known him a few days, but they'd already created a tentative friendship. So why couldn't she stop thinking about his eyes? Those blue eyes had been on every movie poster she could remember since she was a kid. The important part of that sentence was *kid*. He was too old for her. More importantly, to her friends, he was like family.

Her phone rang again, and again she silenced it.

Sandy was part of this makeshift family. She looked around at the five people at the table. Marlon, Daphne, Timmy, Greta, and Sandy. She looked at the restaurant that they owned, at the two best friends —sisters, really—at the center of it all. She looked at Daphne.

Realization hit her like a hammer.

Shit.

Miranda had to get out of here, away from Daphne and this family she'd made.

Miranda had made a terrible mistake. Based on the Daphne she'd known from college, Miranda had thought she was coming to stay with an undependable airhead. But she'd been wrong. It turned out she was staying with a girl who wanted to adopt her. Miranda didn't want to be adopted. She *couldn't* be.

She was feral. She was the scorpion. She didn't belong here.

"Whoever it is that keeps calling, he's really trying to get your attention." Sandy was leaning close, his eyes mesmerizing her despite her best attempts to ignore them.

And then a plan formed in her head, and she knew what she had to do. She knew how to escape Daphne's well-meaning grip.

Miranda allowed herself to feel the heat of Sandy's attention. She drew that heat into herself, spun it, grew it, and gave it right back with a half-smile and half-closed eyes.

She knew the moment the heat hit Sandy. His eyes widened a fraction. His lips parted.

"I might need a ride home after all," she said. "I'm still feeling the tequila."

"I'm happy to oblige." He rested his arm across the back of her chair.

"My bike will be safe here overnight?"

"Your bike won't stay here overnight. I'll have it brought to you."

"So many talents," she said. "And so little time."

He stared at her intently, as though considering a serious proposition.

"It was my brother on the phone," she said. "Since you asked."

"What's his name?"

"Let's get out of here."

He hesitated for a moment, then stood. She did the same.

Before he could speak, she stepped in. Lies were required, and lies were one of her areas of expertise. "It will surprise none of you to learn that I'm too drunk to ride my motorcycle home."

"I, for one, am unsurprised," said Daphne.

Miranda nodded at her. "Sandy here is going to drop me off at home, which means none of you have to cut your double-date short. Sandy, take a bow."

Sandy didn't bow.

"Spoilsport," she said to him.

Marlon stood, stepping around Daphne to speak to her. He reached out with his hand, and she couldn't avoid taking it in her own. She met his earnest gaze. "Thank you again, Miranda, for sticking by Daphne when I didn't. I owe you." He paused, as though considering whether he wanted to give her his first- or second-born child in return for her help that week. "I owe you everything."

Well, it appeared she could have her pick of the Marlon Barringer offspring.

She'd pass.

"You don't owe me anything. Y'all would have done it for me." It was probably true. That was why she was leaving.

Marlon nodded. "Safe trip home."

After a round of goodnights from everyone, she grabbed her jacket and helmet and strode from the restaurant, Sandy trailing behind her.

She took care to remember every detail of Rivet as she passed. By the end of tonight, she wouldn't be welcome here anymore.

Chapter Six

Standing on the walk outside Rivet, Miranda waited while Sandy spoke at length with the valet manager. Another valet driver had been dispatched to bring his car around. She examined the men and women arriving at Rivet for the night, some dressed in suits and dresses, some in jeans, all making some sort of statement. One couple, a man and woman in their forties by the look of them, both arrived in black—she wore a simple black dress, he black pants and shirt. Together, they reminded Miranda of her parents: a powerful team. As they left the valet stand, they tried to avoid looking at Sandy, and they failed. He was one of those people you couldn't help but look at. Honestly, she couldn't believe how good he filled out his jeans. She looked at his thighs and simply couldn't help licking her lips.

As the couple passed, the woman's eyes caught on Miranda. The woman's gaze narrowed in judgment. Miranda knew she was supposed to look away from that sort of glare, to shrivel and shrink.

Miranda did not shrink for anyone.

"Hi," Miranda said, giving the glaring woman a small wave and a taunting smile.

The woman froze in place.

Sandy turned to Miranda then. "Hand me the key to your bike. After Rivet closes, Manuel here will bring it to Daphne's house."

The woman glanced from Sandy to Miranda.

"I know, right?" Miranda said to the woman. "I can't believe he talks to me, either."

Sandy glanced past Miranda, taking in the annoyed face of the woman, and the man standing just past her.

"Making friends, Miranda?" he asked.

Miranda shrugged. "Unlikely." She spoke to the woman's perfectly groomed eyebrows. "I'm Miranda. This is Sandy."

"I know who he is," she said to Miranda, her words clipped. She turned to Sandy. "Sandy, we've met. Melinda Jarvis." Melinda Jarvis held out her manicured hand.

Sandy shook it. "Ah, yes. Good to see you again." He waved at the man holding the door. "Enjoy your evening." He hooked his hand through Miranda's elbow and led her down to the drive. He spoke in her ear. "You don't have to try to get under every person's skin, you know."

"To be fair, I didn't have to try very hard." Miranda glanced over her shoulder. The door was closing on the Jarvis couple. "Who were they?"

"Agents. Very powerful agents."

"So, they're like lawyers, except less educated and more blood-thirsty?"

Sandy shook his head, laughing. "Give me the keys to your bike."

"Your guy is going to bring it to Daphne's house? You sure about that?" Miranda raised her eyebrows. Were they still pretending that he was leaving her at home, alone? "What good will it do me down in Brentwood when I'm up in Laurel Canyon?"

Sandy tilted his head slightly, taking in her face. She wondered what he was looking for. For a small moment, she feared he found her lacking. She shook off that fear—she was who she was. There was nothing she could do about it now.

All she had was herself. She only ever had herself. She reached deep inside and found the strength, and the arrogance, that had sustained her throughout her childhood and teenaged years, throughout four years at cut-throat Cameron University, and she gave him a toothy smile.

"Chicken?" she said.

He chuckled, a deep sound, and it made her shiver. "Never." A look of wry acceptance passed over his handsome face. "To my house, then." He held out his hand for the key.

She dropped it into his hand. He took it to the valet.

When she heard the sound of twelve silky cylinders pulling into the valet drive, she turned her head to watch. No car sounded like Sandy's. No car looked like it, either—like a bullet just exploding from a gun.

Miranda shoved all thoughts of bullets and guns from her mind.

A valet opened the passenger door for her, and she climbed into the car, setting her jacket and helmet at her feet. Against her bare back, the leather of the seat felt smooth and firm, like a hug. She nestled in, resting her head back.

Sandy pulled out of Rivet's drive, and Miranda was across the Rubicon. There was no turning back from this night. After tonight, she'd be alone, again.

She felt deeply relieved.

She figured she might as well make small talk on the path to ruination. She turned her head so she faced Sandy, studying his famous profile. She reached over with a finger and brushed his shoulder. He smiled slightly. She traced his jaw. The lines of him. They were so perfect.

"See something you like there?" he asked.

"I don't have to tell you you're stunning. You already know." It was true. She could tell he was confident and aware of how he affected those around him.

He glanced at her. "There are things I know about how the world works. And all those things seem to alter when I'm around you."

"I'm electing to take that as a compliment."

"I meant it as one."

He pulled to a stop at a light, reached over and took her face in his hands. She froze in surprise at his touch. His eyes traced over every inch of her face.

Then he kissed her, his mouth pressing against hers, sucking all sound and light and energy from the car. She shut her eyes, leaning toward him, feeling the heat travel from her belly down her legs, up her spine, everywhere, until she was hot all over.

A horn honked behind them.

He sucked her bottom lip.

"Jesus, girl." His voice was a deep grumble.

He sped from the light, tossing her body back into the seat's embrace.

"How much farther to your house from here?"

"Too far."

She laughed loudly. "I'm going to ask you personal questions."

"In for a penny." His voice still grumbled.

"You speak Spanish, and your real name is Alejandro. So what's your real last name?" Miranda covered up her body with her jacket like it was a blanket. The night was getting cool, and she was still shivering from the kiss.

"I changed my last name legally a long time ago. Martin is my last name."

"And you probably got all the legal records wiped. Yes, I know you're very scary." She waved her hand in the air dismissively. "Tell me your real last name."

Sandy laughed. "I've never met anyone who talks to me the way you do."

"Not since your first Oscar nomination, anyway."

"My father's last name was Martinez."

Miranda hadn't known for sure that Sandy had changed his last name—she'd deduced it based on his first name, and based on his perfect Spanish. And now, based on the way that he said the word *father* with such venom in his voice, she had an idea about why he'd changed it.

"You didn't like your father much. Is he dead or disappeared?"

"Both. After my mom finally got the guts to throw him out, he disappeared completely. I kept tabs on him, though, once I was able to do so."

"Because you're very scary." She gave a false shiver of fear.

He gave her a look out of the corner of his eye. "I got word that he died when he was seventy-six. About eight years ago. He died suddenly of a heart attack."

"Did you pick Sandy as your nickname? Or did your mom?"

"My mom did." He gave her another look. "You know you're very intuitive."

"Not at all, actually. Daphne is intuitive. I'm logical."

"Is there a difference?"

"Of course. Daphne relies on feelings when she makes observations." Miranda stuck out her tongue. Who had time for feelings. "Whereas I can articulate the evidence that I use to draw my conclusions. For example, you would never use a nickname your father gave you because you despise him. Thus, your nickname must have come from either you or your mother. That's hardly a complicated deduction."

"You said your parents are lawyers."

"My father is a lawyer." Her mother was dead.

He paused. "My mistake."

"Don't feel bad. I keep making that mistake, too."

They drove in silence for a while, and he turned on Sunset Boulevard.

"I see we're taking the slow way home," she said.

"It's fun to bring newcomers up here at night."

Miranda could only agree. The billboards on Sunset stood as tall as buildings. The lights from homes cascaded down the brush-covered hills to her left. The wide, wide road was covered in L.A.'s automotive glory. All of it was a delicious sight to take in, especially from the passenger seat of Sandy's Aston Martin.

She chuckled. "You have the same last name as your car."

"That's not why I buy them."

"Of course not. You're way too stuffy to do something like that."

He looked at her, eyebrows raised. "You don't actually think I'm stuffy."

"No." She smiled. "Where was your dad from?"

"Right here," Sandy said. "He was an original Californian. My mom was a transplant from Minnesota.

"He taught you Spanish."

Sandy nodded. "Honor the ancestors."

Miranda snorted.

"How about this," Sandy said. "I'll tell you about my dad if you tell me about yours."

"You first, since you've already started," she said. And hopefully he'd forget about her end of the deal.

He nodded in agreement. "I really looked up to my dad. He built family homes. That's what he sold to people—the idea of family. He had a wife and a kid at home, and he was this family man. But he was cheating on my mom all the time. I found out when I was fourteen. I walked in on my parents fighting about it. My mom decided to stay with my dad, but I could never look at him the same again."

"He burst your pretty bubble?"

Sandy nodded. "After that, I was always looking for things to go wrong. I was always suspicious. And then, one night when I was in high school, I was out at a bar with some friends, and I saw him there with another woman. I confronted him right there at the table. My dad claimed she was a colleague from work, but I knew he was lying. I'd watched them for a while, see. The way their hands kept brushing, the way he'd kept his arm around her chair. He'd lied all those years, to me and my mom. Everything he'd ever said was a lie."

Sandy didn't sound angry. He sounded resigned, as though this were a battle he'd fought, and lost, a long time ago.

"I'm sorry, man," Miranda said. "Dads are the worst."

Sandy laughed. "You are a funny girl, Miranda."

Miranda smiled. She supposed being called funny was better than being called harsh or caustic—two words thrown her direction far more often. "You didn't cheat on your wife. So why'd you break up?"

"Not intuitive?"

"That's logic. We reject the behaviors we hate the most. Thus, you didn't cheat on her. I say that with, oh, ninety percent certainty."

Sandy nodded. "She cheated on me."

"We are in Los Angeles. Cheating is a prerequisite for marriages here, right?"

"I think it was my fault, though. I think I believed that all marriages were doomed to fail, so I didn't fight very hard for my marriage when things got bumpy. I just withdrew. She went her own way after that."

"I can buy that reasoning to a point. But if she were worth her salt, she would have fought hard, too. I think you didn't fight, and she also didn't fight. You can't have two people throw in the towel."

"No, you can't."

Miranda thought of how much her mother hadn't been able to do, and about how much her father hadn't been willing to do.

Sandy turned left off of Sunset and headed up into the hills above. Up and up his car drove, taking on the curvy roads with grace. Miranda caught glimpses of the houses tucked away to her left and right, shrouded in trees and darkness. She'd been up here before, for Greta's wedding, and again a couple of nights ago. But tonight she was arriving for an entirely different reason.

There was no turning back from this. What she was about to do would destroy any chance she might have had of a life out here with her friends. That was why she was doing it, after all.

She reached into her coat pocket and pulled out one of Turbo's caramels. She bit it in half and chewed. She held up the other half to Sandy.

"Want to get high?"

He took the caramel from her and looked at it, and then gave her a grin. "Sure." He popped it in his mouth as he pulled into his driveway.

———

As he parked his car, Sandy chewed the pot candy Miranda had given him. It was good stuff. He should know. He'd survived the seventies on a prescription of weed and tequila.

He glanced at Miranda. At that moment, talking about his family, he realized he didn't even know her last name. He didn't know anything about her history. He knew she'd buried her mother on Monday, and that was all.

"Come on," he said. "Let's go inside."

She opened her car door before he could get it for her. Then she fished out her jacket and glossy white motorcycle helmet—so little protection for her body as she'd traveled to Rivet tonight. The thought of her on a motorcycle made him want to wrap his arms around her body to keep her safe. The feeling was strange. She wasn't a small thing, quite the opposite. She was tall—although with Greta around, tall took on a new meaning. Miranda wasn't as tall as he was, but she was close, and he was just over six feet. She wasn't frail—she had curves, strong legs, and that killer behind. And she wasn't a shy thing—she'd tear you to pieces if you showed weakness.

So why did she make every part of him feel protective? Something inside her was fragile, begging for care.

He was a bastard. He knew she was fragile, and he was taking her into his house anyway.

She smiled at him over a bare shoulder, the tips of her sharply cut hair caressing the bare skin. "Just so you know, I'm not having second thoughts."

"No?" Look at that. She'd read his mind.

"I don't do second thoughts, and I don't do regrets. Both are a waste of time." She stopped by his front door, waiting for him to open it.

"It's unlocked."

"Fascinating." She pushed the door open. Two large, brown dogs came tearing around the corner from the kitchen, toenails sliding on the wood floor. Miranda glanced at him again. "You going to handle this?"

"Hey girls," he said, stepping past Miranda into the house. His dogs, Jodie and Foster, immediately lost their aggression and turned into cheerful, drooling idiots. He scratched their ears. "Go lie down." They turned and ran back to their beds.

Miranda walked through the sitting area and straight to the sliding glass doors on the far side of the large room. She pushed them open. She stepped onto the deck and kept going, all the way out to the railing, leaning over it, gazing out into the brightly lit valley below.

He loved this view. He'd built this deck many years ago so he could stand right here and know where he was in the world.

"So many people," she said once he'd joined her.

"True."

"All doing awful things to one another. No wonder you want to live up here alone."

He'd never thought about it that way. He realized then what drew him to Miranda, aside from her obvious physical attributes. She had a dark streak a mile wide, and he wanted to step inside it.

"I've got Marlon up here with me." Marlon, his handyman, his stand-in son, his friend, lived in the apartment over the garage.

"For now. He'll be leaving you soon."

"You think he'll leave? It's a pretty sweet apartment. He and Daphne could live there."

She looked at him, her brown eyes sparking with the lights of the valley. "Yes. I'm certain he'll leave."

Sandy thought about his own dad, how he'd left even when he'd technically stayed around, how it would have been better for him to have just gone than to have continually humiliated his mom. It had been over thirty years since that confrontation in the restaurant, and talking about it with Miranda made it feel like last week.

"I realized something in the car," he said. "I don't know your whole name."

"Surely you've slept with nameless girls before, Mr. Martinez."

"Name, please."

"My full name is Miranda Sorcha George. Sorcha is my mother's name." Then she muttered, "Was."

"We had a deal, I believe." He leaned back against the railing. "Dad stories."

She frowned. "I'd hoped you'd forget."

"I bet you did." He glanced at the bottle of scotch on the sideboard just through the glass doors. "Do we need drinks for this?"

She nodded.

She leaned forward on her elbows and waited while he filled two glasses. When he returned, he paused for a moment in the doorway, taking in the sparkling skin of her back, her narrow waist, her tall black boots, her long, long legs in tight, tight jeans. He wanted to kiss her again. But he knew that once that all started, there'd be no stopping.

"Here," he said. "I hope you like scotch."

"My parents are lawyers. Of course I like scotch." She took a sip. "My dad is a lawyer. My mom was a lawyer. She was the better lawyer, in fact."

"What kind of law?"

"They're criminal defense lawyers. The well-paid kind. They were prosecutors when they were younger—that's where they met—and then they left to start a defense firm. Federal and state. All over North Carolina. Other litigation too, high-profile stuff. They were always on the news. Anyways, my mom had her problems."

Miranda's cool façade broke, just for a moment. Sandy got a

glimpse of real pain around her eyes, carving her cheekbones, pulling against her mouth. His curiosity immediately went to that small word, *problems*. He knew there was a lot more hidden there than she was sharing. That word held, perhaps, the secret to everything. He would come back to Miranda's mother's problems.

"And your dad?" he asked.

"My dad was never there for us."

"Us?"

"Me and Charlie. My little brother."

Sandy waited. She was struggling to get something out.

"I've never told anyone this before. I don't know why I'm telling you."

"Marlon says that it's easy to talk to strangers."

She gave him a half-smile. "I loved my mom. Really. She was there for us when she could be. The problem was, there were lots of times when she couldn't be. She was sick. And when she was sick, she could be scary to us, to me and Charlie. We looked to our dad to keep us safe, but he never did. I never really understood it. My mom had untreated bipolar disorder. I know that now, but I didn't know it as a kid, and I wouldn't have understood it even if I had known."

Sandy took in that information. So Miranda's mother had problems—a disease that could be treated, but wasn't. One that was a disaster when left untreated. Sandy knew a lot of people. And he knew people with mental illness.

"Why didn't she get treated?"

"At first, I thought that my father refused to believe the illness was real. And honestly, when she was healthy or just a little manic, my mom was a superstar. I believed my asshole of a father encouraged her to not get treated so he could have his Ferrari of a wife and law partner. You know, super high-performance, but breaks down a lot."

He did know. He used to own a Ferrari. The thing had never run.

"But I was wrong. She tried to take medicine, but then she would go off of it when she was feeling better. That's part of the illness itself —the resistance to taking your medicine. It was so hard to watch."

Miranda quickly looked away from him. She took a big sip of her drink, downing the scotch like it was water.

"So instead of treating her illness, she drank. And when things got really bad, we had this private psychiatrist on call who would come

over and handle things at our house before they got too out of hand."
She shook her head. "I've been managing her episodes ever since I
graduated from college. That's why I never left home." She turned to
face him, suddenly urgent. "But she was a wonderful person, Sandy. I
loved her. You have to understand that, okay?"

Sandy wasn't sure where the urgency was coming from, but he
understood the need to be believed. "I understand."

"So my mom was sick, but my dad was worse. He was just cold.
When Charlie was arrested in high school, he didn't come to help.
When we were little kids and hid from our mom during her episodes,
he didn't help us then, either."

"You're supposed to be able to count on your dad to stand up for
you."

"Right. But not my dad. He never stood up for me or Charlie. Not
once. We could never count on him."

Sandy heard a hardness in her words. She could never count on
her father, sure, but there was more. Miranda believed she couldn't
count on anyone. He could see it plain as day.

"So there you go. The whole story. I loved my mom, but she was
sick. And at the end—well." A dark look passed over her face, and
then it was gone. "And my dad, he was so cold that I wonder if he
ever cared about us at all."

"So you grew up self-sufficient."

"I had to."

"What about Charlie?"

Her face closed down, its lovely lines turning hard. "What about
him?"

"Why are you ignoring his calls?"

"Who says I'm ignoring him?"

Sandy chuckled. "Come on Miranda. I watched you silence your
phone during dinner."

"I need a break from my family, that's all." She looked back out at
the valley.

"I do not believe that's all. But I won't push."

She scowled at him. "Thank you for your generosity, your
majesty."

He couldn't keep his eyes from her full, red lips. "Keep up the
sass, Miss George."

"Don't worry. I'm southern. It comes naturally." She looked at the half-full glass of scotch in her hand, then tossed the rest of it back.

Her throat moved as she swallowed slowly, and she shut her eyes. Then her tongue darted out to catch a drop that lingered on her bottom lip.

He leaned forward and caught that lip in his own. She startled, then relaxed. He took the tumbler from her hand and tossed it, along with the one in his own hand, onto the floor of the deck.

"Sandy," she burst out, half-laughing.

"They didn't break."

"You couldn't have known that they wouldn't."

He rubbed his now-free hands up her bare back as she leaned against the railing. Her skin felt even better than it looked. How was that possible? "I made a deduction." He kissed her neck. She let her head fall back, giving him more room to work.

Her entire body came to life beneath his hands, and he felt grateful.

The way this girl walked around in her body, so matter-of-fact— he knew she thought she wasn't beautiful, and he knew where she was coming from. She wasn't dainty and delicate like the starlets flitting about at Rivet. If she were going to compare herself to them, she was going to come up short. But she was bold, and curvy, and unabashed about any of it. Marlon had called her a tornado on two legs. That was about right.

And tonight, she was his tornado. He couldn't wait for the storm to hit.

"Come on." He tugged at her hand.

She slowly opened her eyes, fixing her gaze on him, so dark and full of heat. For a moment, he thought they could just start right there on the deck.

"Do I get to see what's inside Sandy's mystery rooms?"

"They're not a mystery." His rooms were his sanctuary, sure, but not mysterious. Marlon went in there to fix things.

"Please. Daphne and Greta have known you for years and years and have never crossed the threshold."

Could that be true? She must be exaggerating.

By the mocking gleam in her eye, he could tell she was not exaggerating.

"If they haven't, it was merely an oversight."

"Whatever you say, Sandy." She followed him through the kitchen and then through the doorway into his suite of rooms. His bedroom was to the right, with sliding doors leading onto the deck. His bathroom was to the left. Straight ahead was another room that he used as an office, one that Marlon called *the divorce room* because he said that husbands in the doghouse would sleep in there.

Marlon wasn't wrong. Sandy had slept in there during the final months of his own marriage.

She stepped ahead of him into the bedroom, taking in the low-slung king bed, the chrome floor lamps arcing from two corners, the seven-foot-wide painting hanging on the wall over the bed. There was hardly any furniture in here, Sandy realized, seeing the room through Miranda's eyes. At least the place was clean.

"Did Marlon paint that?"

"Yeah."

"Where's all your stuff?"

"I guess I don't have very much stuff."

She turned to face him. "Me neither."

He lifted up her handkerchief-shirt with two fingers. "You had to pack light."

She nodded, biting her lower lip.

He reached behind her back and untied the lower bow. The shirt fell loose against her torso. Then he reached up and untied the bow at her neck, and the shirt dropped to the floor. He exhaled. "Ah, Miranda." She was stunning, staring at him boldly in her jeans and nothing else. Her eyes—they were so old. Those brown eyes had seen decades of pain and disappointment.

Sandy knew she was grieving her mother's death. And he was a jackass for wanting her anyway. Taking her home, bringing her in here to his bedroom, it was a thousand kinds of wrong. But when she'd looked him in the eye and called him chicken, he couldn't figure out how to say no. She wasn't some ditzy production assistant with stars in her eyes. Quite the opposite. He'd spent the whole night wondering what she saw in him. He couldn't remember the last time he'd felt so nervous.

He unbuttoned the top two buttons of his shirt then pulled it over his head. His undershirt came next. Then he pulled her to him, and they were skin to skin.

"Sandy. Please." She whispered near his ear, and he felt the heat of her breath everywhere. "Make me feel something good."

"I can do that." He shoved aside the small lingering voice of guilt.

He kissed her, leading her toward his bed. Soon, their shoes and jeans met their shirts on the floor, and soon after that he stopped thinking entirely.

Chapter Seven

Miranda opened her eyes to the rising sun pouring over her. She looked around the room, at the tall lamps overhead, at the low chest of drawers against the far wall, at the glass doors leading out onto the deck. She glanced to her right. Sandy was still asleep.

He looked young. Like a little boy cuddled in his blankets.

She slipped from the bed. She located her panties on the floor and pulled them on. Then she pulled on Sandy's discarded undershirt, a black t-shirt that hung just past her hips.

She needed coffee.

She wandered out into the kitchen. Naturally he wouldn't have a normal coffee maker. Sandy was not a normal person. Standing here in his palace in the bright light of day was a brutal reminder of how much he was not a normal person. Nothing about her being here this morning—or last night—was normal.

She'd made a mistake, and she'd made it on purpose.

That didn't mean she couldn't have coffee. She just needed to decipher his espresso machine. As she fiddled with the knobs to see how they worked, she heard the front door open and close. The dogs jumped up, but they didn't bark.

She'd known this moment was coming, but she'd thought she'd have more time. And pants.

She looked down at her bare thighs, and she sighed.

"You up?" Marlon's voice called out from the foyer, getting closer with each of his footsteps. "Sandy?"

Marlon entered the kitchen, his eyes landing on her face, and for a moment, he looked confused. Then his gaze traveled down her body, taking in her state of undress, her general rumpled appearance. His eyes narrowed in suspicion.

She felt a twinge of sadness. Marlon was such a nice person, truly, if you overlooked his temper.

"What is going on here?" he demanded.

"I'm trying to figure out how to make coffee." She gestured at the machine. "But the sphinx won't reveal its secrets."

"Sandy!" Marlon called out.

"Ugh. Stop yelling, Marlon." She held up her hand. "It's too early."

"Don't tell me what to do." Wow, he sounded really pissed off. "Tell me what you're doing in Sandy's kitchen in your underwear."

"I'm wearing a shirt, too."

"That's not your shirt," he spat.

She looked down at Sandy's t-shirt. "Goodness! I didn't realize." She looked back up at Marlon. "Stop having a canary. Sandy and I are grownups. What's your problem?"

Marlon took a step toward her. She held her ground, but reconsidered how provoking she should be with him. Marlon looked like someone had stolen his teddy bear.

"What do you want from him? You must want something from him. So let's hear it."

"Dude. I already got what I wanted from him. Do you not know how this works?"

"Everyone wants something from Sandy. You're no different."

"Oh really? What do you want from Sandy?"

"This isn't about me."

"This is totally about you. You don't like me being here."

"You're right. I don't trust you. You show up on Daphne's doorstep, try to wreck Greta's wedding, try to keep her away from me—"

"That's not exactly how that went. Remember what you said to me last night?"

"And now you're here? Like this? You expect me to believe your being here isn't some sleep-away therapy for whatever mental problems you're having?"

Miranda bit her lower lip in thought. Marlon was on the right track, there.

He pushed on. "Sandy is my best friend. Me, Greta, Daphne, Timmy, Sandy—we're a tight group. When everyone else hears about this, I won't be the only one who's angry."

Oh good, she thought. *Save me the work.* "Do you get this uptight about all the women Sandy sleeps with?"

"Just the ones trying to weasel their way into our lives by using the only father I have."

Miranda cocked her head. "You don't trust Sandy to make his own decisions about girls? What if I'm the one who got taken advantage of here? He is a big, powerful man, and I'm just a nobody. I mean, that's what you're thinking right? I'm a nobody?"

"Yeah, right. I'm pretty sure that you can take care of yourself," Marlon said.

At that moment, Sandy came out of his bedroom in jeans and his button-down, untucked. His hair was sticking up in the back. Miranda smiled a little. He looked adorable. Too bad she'd never see him again.

"Sandy, what the hell is happening?" When Marlon spoke to Sandy, his voice held a tone of betrayal, not anger.

"Marlon, surely you're smart enough to have figured it out." Sandy sounded annoyed.

"But—why her?"

Miranda grinned half-way. She couldn't disagree with Marlon. Why her, indeed, when Sandy could have anyone? "If it makes you feel better, Marlon," she said, "I wouldn't have picked me, either."

"That does not make me feel better." Marlon could barely talk his jaw was so tight.

Miranda shrugged. "I'm just saying. I don't know what he saw in me. I'm unbearably average. And you're all so," she waved her arm around, "not."

"You are not average, Miranda," Sandy said. "Don't say that again." He sounded annoyed with her, too. Good.

"Come on, Sandy," she said to him. "You don't have to keep up with the compliments. You already got laid."

Both men looked at her with stunned expressions. She really wished she had on pants.

She pressed on. "I mean, we shared our dark secrets, drank your fancy booze, and worked out our issues in the sack. It was great. Really. You don't have to keep telling me sweet nothings." She tilted her head. "Do people still say 'sweet nothings'?"

Sandy grabbed her hand and dragged her back to his bedroom. She suppressed an inappropriate laugh. Once they were in private, he turned to her. "What are you babbling about?"

"Marlon's face. It's priceless. He is so pissed off at me."

"Miranda. Why are you acting this way?"

She located her jeans and boots from where they were crumpled on the floor and sat on his bed to pull them on. Once her body touched the bed, memories from last night flooded her mind. Sandy had treated her body like a sacred thing. He'd stripped her boots from her feet and her pants from her body, then laid her back and made her come twice before even thinking about reaching for a condom. She hadn't expected that ruining her life would be so mind-blowing.

She ran her hand across the comforter.

"Miranda?" His voice was gentler now.

She took a deep breath. No regrets.

After pulling on her pants and boots, she stood, placing her hand on Sandy's cheek. "Sandy. Thank you for everything."

"You don't have to go."

"Marlon is ready to murder me. Bravo to you for inspiring such loyalty, by the way. I'm not going to stay here and force you to defend me against the stupid things he's bound to say. You love him." She gestured at herself. "I'm merely a passing fancy."

She dashed from the room, scooping up her black silk shirt on the way. From the kitchen, she could see Marlon on the deck, ranting into his cell phone. She found her jacket and her helmet in the living room where she'd dropped them on the couch the night before. She stuffed her shirt into the pocket of her jacket—such a versatile garment, truly —and dashed outside. Her bike sat there with the key in the ignition. *Thank you, Manuel.*

Two minutes later, she was tearing down Laurel Canyon, preparing herself for what she'd find at Daphne's.

———

MIRANDA PULLED INTO DAPHNE'S GARAGE AND TURNED OFF HER BIKE. She left the garage door open, though. She had a feeling she'd be making a fast getaway.

As she was hanging her helmet on her handlebars, the gate to the garage at the top of the porch stairs banged open. Daphne stood there, looking both furious and hurt. "So it's true."

"Lots of things are true," Miranda said. "Care to narrow it down?"

"You slept with Sandy last night."

"True."

Miranda tried to climb the stairs, but Daphne blocked her way. Standing two steps above her, Daphne could stare down at her. "Why?"

"Seriously? Why sleep with a foxy movie star?"

"He's my friend. He's one of my best friends."

"You don't think I'm good enough for him?"

"No, that's not it."

But Miranda could tell—by the hesitation in Daphne's answer, by the flash of guilt in her eyes—that that was exactly it.

"Get out of the way." Miranda felt unexplainably hurt. She knew she wasn't good enough for Sandy. She shouldn't be surprised that Daphne felt the same way.

Daphne stepped back and let Miranda pass. But Daphne didn't let Miranda go. She followed her into the condo, dogging her steps all the way into Miranda's room.

Miranda stood in the middle of the room and paused. This was the moment when she had to make the choice. She'd thought the moment was last night, when she'd gotten in Sandy's car. But she could tell that Daphne was willing to forgive her. Why, Miranda had no idea. But she was. Miranda had tried to set this whole pretty world on fire, and somehow she'd failed. Daphne was willing to take her back.

Miranda looked at her black nylon bag on the floor, the one she could pack with everything she owned in less than five minutes. She looked over her shoulder at Daphne, who leaned against the doorjamb.

"Do you want something?" Miranda asked.

"Was it your idea or his?" Daphne chewed on her fingernail.

"I'd imagine it was both of ours."

"Marlon is really angry."

"I know. He let me have it at Sandy's." Miranda crossed her arms. "You know, Sandy thought I was good enough for him."

"I told you that's not the problem." There it was again, the flash of guilt.

That sealed it. Daphne was never allowed to be Miranda's partner at spades. She was way too easy to read. "I can tell that you're lying," Miranda said. "I hope you don't gamble."

Daphne looked miffed. "I'm a great liar."

Miranda laughed. "Maybe to other people. Not to me."

Daphne yanked on her ponytail in frustration. "I'm trying to figure out how you can be two totally different people at the same time. You're the jackass who brought my one-night-stand to Greta's wedding to humiliate me, and you're the hero who basically saved my life."

"It was more like your feet, but okay." The injuries to Daphne's feet the night of Greta's wedding had been pretty gruesome. She was still on painkillers and wearing Adidas sneakers instead of her usual high-heeled boots.

"I wrote off your bad behavior because you were grieving. I wrote it off because you were still mad at me from college. But now, I don't know what to think. It's like you're doing it on purpose, but I can't figure out why."

"Doing what?"

"Alienating everyone."

Miranda smiled. There it was. Daphne's intuition was always strong. Daphne was onto her, and that meant Miranda had to leave. Otherwise Daphne would ferret out all of her secrets. She'd try to fix her. And Miranda knew she was unfixable.

If Miranda stayed, she risked hurting everyone, in a very real way. She thought of the shiny gun barrel, of Charlie's face, of her mother's face, and of death. Miranda should be dead, but instead she was here.

Not for long.

The front door opened. Miranda jerked her head in surprise. She wasn't expecting anyone. Daphne looked just as surprised, striding into the living room to see who it was.

"Is she back there?" Marlon's voice. He still sounded angry.

"What are you doing here?" Daphne sounded sorely put out by Marlon's surprise visit. Miranda covered her mouth to stifle a laugh.

"She snuck out of Sandy's house before we could finish our conversation."

"The way I heard it, you weren't precisely having a conversation, you bully."

Miranda stifled another laugh. If Daphne kept up this adorable defense of her, she might relent and stick around. She stepped closer to the doorway so she could hear them better.

"I don't think Miranda is capable of being bullied."

"Did you yell at her?"

"Sure, a little. But she's like a goddamn natural disaster."

Miranda stepped around the doorjamb so Marlon could see her. "Agreed."

"Adding eavesdropping to your list of charming qualities?" Marlon said.

"Hardly a new addition." Miranda stepped closer, until the three of them formed a triangle in the middle of Daphne's living room. Daphne's eyes skipped nervously back and forth between her and Marlon.

"You've been a pain in the ass ever since you arrived," he said.

"Also correct."

He ran his hand through his sun-lightened brown hair, his expression tight. "Daphne, why are you letting her stay here?"

Miranda had had about enough. She didn't want to come between Daphne and Marlon any more than she'd wanted to come between Sandy and Marlon. It was time for her exit. "She's not," Miranda said.

"What?" Daphne asked. "Of course I'm letting you stay here."

"Marlon thinks I slept with Sandy to force my way into your little family," Miranda said to Daphne. She looked at Marlon. "Right? Isn't that what you said?"

"Yep."

She laughed. "Daphne, what do you see in this doofus? Please explain to him how wrong he is. I have to go pack."

She entered the bedroom and locked the door. Childish, sure. But effective. She heard Daphne try to turn the knob.

"Let me in, Miranda."

She didn't answer. She ignored Daphne's voice and packed as fast as she could. She figured she had three minutes before Daphne found the lock pick for the door. First, she packed her toiletries. Then, the clothes she'd stashed in the dresser. She looked down at what she had on, thought about where she was heading, and swapped Sandy's t-shirt for the silky halter top she'd worn the night before.

She laid Sandy's t-shirt on the bed for Daphne to find and return to him.

She grabbed the dress and shoes from the closet, carefully packing them in her bag. She might need a nice outfit where she was heading. She made two final checks. She verified the stash of cash in her jacket pocket and the three bottles of pills zipped into the interior pocket of her bag. Then she zipped up her jacket, slung her bag over her chest, and reached for the knob just as Daphne popped the lock. The door swung inward.

Daphne held the tiny metal lock pick in her hand. Marlon stood behind her with his arms crossed, his eyes still angry. Miranda sighed. Why couldn't they just let her leave?

"Where are you going?" Daphne asked, surprised.

"Out that door over there." Miranda pointed at the front door.

"We're not done talking."

Miranda raised her eyebrows.

"Just let her go." Marlon might as well have said *good riddance.*

Miranda stepped forward, and Daphne stepped out of her way.

"Are you going to stay with John?" Daphne asked.

Miranda paused for a moment, considering. She was not going to stay with John. But lying could throw Daphne off her trail, at least for a little while. Long enough. "Yeah. I guess so."

"Call me tomorrow?"

Miranda could tell what Daphne was really saying. *Come back tomorrow.*

Miranda wasn't coming back, ever.

Walking past Marlon and Daphne and out the door was even harder than walking out of her parents' house had been. She'd known her own family was unfixable. But this, this temptation was strong. Just as she reached for Daphne's doorknob, she glanced over her shoulder. The worry on Daphne's face almost broke her resolve.

And then she reminded herself why she was leaving in the first place. It wasn't for herself. It was for them.

In the garage, Miranda buckled her helmet under her chin. She felt one more time for the slender envelope zipped safely in the interior pocket of her coat. She started her bike and hit the speed limit before she was out of Daphne's driveway, not even slowing to merge with traffic. A risky move, sure, but she was ready to take risks.

After all, she really and truly had nothing to lose. She'd just made sure of it.

———

Daphne knew that when Miranda had left she'd been hurting. Her sadness had been palpable, even hidden beneath her smart-mouthed bravado. Marlon's anger had only made Miranda shove the hurt deeper.

Daphne was so annoyed with Marlon. She believed that Miranda might not have left if Marlon hadn't shown up. Daphne might have been able to get through to her.

She turned from her front door, which she'd been staring at for a full minute since Miranda's departure, and faced Marlon. "Are you done having your tantrum now?" she snapped at him.

Marlon looked sheepish. "That girl sets off all my protective instincts."

"Then your instincts are broken. You're right that Miranda can't be bullied. So why do you think she left?"

"I don't know." He rubbed his hand on the back of his neck.

"Because she didn't want us to fight with each other."

Marlon nodded, thoughtful. "She left Sandy's when he and I started fighting."

"She wasn't trying to drive a wedge between us, or force her way into anything. You have it all wrong." She poked him in the chest. "She was trying to get us to run her out."

"Trying to get me to run her out."

"Probably, since you're the one most likely to act like a troglodyte. But it wasn't just you. I screwed up too."

Marlon took a seat on the couch. "What did you say to her?"

"I implied that I didn't think she's good enough for Sandy."

Marlon raised his eyebrows as if to ask what the problem was.

"You don't think she is, either." Daphne shook her head. "No wonder she left. First, you laid into her—and I know what it feels like when you do that."

Marlon winced.

"And now she knows that we all think Sandy is too good for her. She probably believes we all hate her."

Marlon's look of guilt was starting to match her own. "Should I go after her? Try to convince her to come back?"

"No need. She's going to John's for the night. Tomorrow, I'll call her and tell her that her gambit didn't work and she needs to come home."

"I suppose you want me to apologize."

"Yes, I do." She dropped down next to him on the couch and took his hand.

"Why'd she do it, though? Why try to drive us away?"

"I don't know, not exactly. I suppose something happened to her recently that made her feel like she doesn't deserve love, or friends, or family. I know what that feels like." After all, it had been Marlon—with some help from their friends—who'd convinced Daphne that she deserved those things, too. And it had been Miranda who had been there when Daphne had tried to push everyone else away.

Miranda hadn't given up on Daphne, and Daphne wouldn't give up on her.

Chapter Eight

Miranda headed east on San Vicente, her bike growling at stoplights, launching forward when she let it, generally behaving like a poorly trained racehorse, the kind she used to ride when she was younger. Her trainer had purchased them straight from the tracks—horses who'd been destined to become dog food. The horses hadn't made it on the track, but given the right kind of love, they'd excelled over fences. She'd ridden horses in another time and place, another world, when equestrian events had been a regular part of her life.

She sighed, the sound echoing inside her helmet. She gunned her engine, the high-pitched whine drowning out her memories as she zipped around a Hummer.

When she hit the 405, she headed south to the 10. Once on the 10, she turned the bike loose, weaving in and out of traffic, even splitting lanes when the traffic slowed to a crawl. She was riding like a maniac, and she knew it. But she had to get out of there.

She didn't really care if she got hurt. Her fear peeled off of her along with the pain of leaving her friends—and family—behind. Exhilaration took their place.

She rode and rode, blazing past downtown and out into East L.A. She passed Pomona, and then she hit the 15 and headed north. Her bike screamed over the hills and into the valley.

In Barstow, she stopped at a gas station. She fueled up and drank a bottle of water, stuffing another in her bag.

The desert was next.

The sun was high when she pulled out of the gas station on the outskirts of Barstow and blasted into the Mojave. She settled in for the ride. She had two hours to go.

To her left and right, dry scrub plants dotted the sandy landscape. Low, dun-colored hills rose from the horizon, only to smooth out again into the endless brown flats broken only by the ribbon of road. She passed other cars periodically, but they were gone as soon as they appeared. Not many drivers were heading to and from Las Vegas this early on a Sunday morning.

She stared at the desert. She needed to remember why she was leaving so many good people behind. Daphne. Sandy.

John.

God, John was never going to speak to her again. Not after what she'd done with Sandy. She shook her head, seeking resolve, reminding herself that what she'd done she'd done on purpose. She remembered Friday afternoon, the rush of emotion she'd felt: Daphne's promise of family, how it had made her feel so full of warmth, and how the promise of something more with John had made her feel the same.

She needed to destroy both.

She pushed thoughts of John from her head.

Instead, she thought about Sorcha. But she didn't think about the Sorcha of last year. She thought about the Sorcha of her childhood.

WHEN MIRANDA HAD BEEN A CHILD, SORCHA HAD BEEN UNPREDICTABLE. Always beautiful—so, so beautiful—and smart, and full of love for her children. But unpredictable in her moods—or, as Miranda had called them as a child, her feelings. Miranda had thought that was how moms were. Dads were aloof, and moms were full of feelings. Sometimes, though, her mom's feelings seemed to wear her mom out.

When Miranda was in the fifth grade, Sorcha slept a lot. That's what Miranda could remember about that time. Sorcha sleeping. She slept and slept during the day. She hardly even went to work. She just slept.

When Miranda and Charlie got home from school, they tried to stay as quiet as possible so their mom could sleep undisturbed. It was a good thing that the George family home was so large—there'd been plenty of room for two young children to run around without bothering someone asleep in the master suite. But Charlie was only a third grader, and it was hard for him to stay quiet because he was so young. And unlike Miranda, he couldn't understand how important it was to be quiet.

One afternoon after school, Sorcha was asleep in her bedroom—the master suite was on the first floor of their parents' home—and Miranda and Charlie were playing upstairs in Charlie's bedroom. But then Charlie said he was hungry, and Miranda said she would help him make a sandwich. They didn't want to bother the housekeeper, who was busy in another part of the house.

When they arrived in their parents' cathedral of a kitchen, with cabinets that towered to the ceiling, Miranda realized that she needed to get out another jar of peanut butter. She also realized that she couldn't reach the top shelf where the housekeeper stored the extra jars.

Miranda dragged a bar stool over to the cabinet and climbed on top. She teetered on the edge and used her fingertips to pull the glass jar of gourmet peanut butter from the shelf. She almost had the jar in her grasp. But then, at the last moment, the jar slipped. It toppled from the shelf and down, down to the floor, shattering with a boom.

Miranda met Charlie's wide eyes. And then they heard the door to the master suite open.

They dashed into the hall to see Sorcha emerge. Her hair stood out from her head. The afternoon light through the windows cast sharp shadows across Sorcha's face as she approached them, passing the foyer, the dining room, the parlor, until she stood in front of her children. Faster than Miranda would have thought possible, Sorcha backhanded Charlie across the face, sending him flying backward and onto his bottom. Both of his hands flew to the side of his face, and he wailed in pain.

"Mom!" Miranda yelled.

Sorcha's eyes zeroed in on her. Good.

Miranda spoke quietly to her brother. "Run to your bathroom and lock the door."

Charlie didn't move. He was sobbing.

Miranda took another step back. Sorcha advanced on her.

"I just need sleep," Sorcha said. "Why won't you let me sleep." Her eyes fell on Charlie again, whose sobs were the loudest thing in the house.

"Why are you such a bitch!" Miranda yelled, trying to recapture her mother's attention with a word she was forbidden to use.

Sorcha's eyes whipped back to her again. That's when Miranda realized that Sorcha wasn't seeing her children at all. Her focus was somewhere else, somewhere far way, somewhere far more dangerous —to both Sorcha and the kids.

"The bathroom, Charlie!" Miranda screamed, and Charlie turned and ran, scrambling for his en suite bathroom. Miranda felt her body relax. When she heard the far-off slam of his bathroom door, she relaxed even more.

"Who are you?" Sorcha whispered.

Miranda had never seen her mother like this. At least, Miranda didn't think she had. Sorcha seemed angry, but not at Miranda and Charlie. Sorcha didn't know that Miranda and Charlie were in the house at all.

Miranda stood her ground. She was nearly as tall as Sorcha now. Sorcha was only average height, and Miranda, at age ten, was getting tall because of her dad's side of the family.

But Sorcha was her mom, and you didn't fight your mom. Despite everything, Miranda loved Sorcha dearly.

Charlie was safe. That's all that really mattered. Sorcha would get tired again, and Miranda would be okay. Eventually.

Two hours later, Charles George arrived home from work. He knocked on the door to Charlie's bathroom, demanding entrance. Miranda opened the door for him.

Miranda knew what her father saw when he examined her and Charlie. Charlie's jaw and cheek were swollen, and he had a fat lip. Earlier, she'd looked at herself in the mirror and cleaned up as best she could. But there was still blood crusted under her nostrils, and her nose was swollen, as was the right side of her mouth.

Her father stood in the doorway of the bathroom, staring silently at his children. Miranda waited for him to say something, to ask how they were, to ask what had happened, to ask how he could help them. She waited for him to open his arms for an embrace. But he didn't. He pressed his lips together and shook his head. "No school for the rest of the week," he said. Then he stalked away.

"Don't worry," Miranda said to Charlie, when he looked at her with brown eyes identical to her own. "I'll take care of you."

So she had. For over fifteen years, Miranda had done all she could to take care of her brother, to keep him safe. It had been her primary mission in life. Daphne's betrayal in college had hurt so much worse because the consequences had harmed Charlie. And when Sorcha had died—even then, Miranda had failed to protect Charlie again.

———

Sorcha hadn't always been lost in *episodes*, as Miranda called them. The only reason that Miranda had her job with the freelance agency at all was because of her mother. After college, Miranda had stayed in Winston-Salem, working as a paralegal in her parents' law firm because she didn't feel like she could leave her mother. Someone had needed to hold her family together, and that someone had been Miranda.

When Miranda had finally broken down and confronted her mother about her mother's illness, Sorcha had spoken with all of the honesty that Miranda could have hoped for, even though Sorcha must have known that lying would have made herself look better.

Miranda remembered that day with so much love, so much fondness. Sorcha had told Miranda to start making decisions for herself—to start being more selfish. Miranda loved her mother even more for it. She missed her mother even more. Despite all of the awful things that had happened the day her mother had died, Miranda could never hate Sorcha.

Miranda refused to think about that day. If she thought about that day, Miranda might do something stupid, like ride her bike into oncoming traffic in the middle of the Mojave.

She was planning on dying, sure, but she didn't want to be roadkill. What a mess. If she were going to have a George family funeral, she wanted couture and an open coffin.

The highway she traveled on had widened to six lanes. The traffic going the other way had picked up, slowing to a crawl at points. Angelinos were heading home after weekends spent gambling, dancing, drinking, fucking. She couldn't blame them. She, too, was escaping to Las Vegas to expend some extra emotions. Or perhaps she should call them *feelings*. God, she had so many feelings she didn't know what to do with them all.

Flying down a highway on a motorcycle helped. She had little space to think about anything but staying alive.

On her side of the road, there were few cars—mostly long-haul truckers whom she zipped around. Eventually, in the hazy distance, a surreal sparkle appeared against the desert mountain backdrop. When she saw the skyline, she knew she'd made the right choice. Her entire life had turned surreal back in January. Las Vegas seemed a natural end point.

Thirty minutes later—longer than she'd thought possible, but she knew distances in the desert were deceiving—the Strip emerged on the right side of the highway. She selected the first high-rise casino she came to, located at the southernmost tip of the Strip. At the massive interchange with I-215, she exited at Las Vegas Boulevard, then headed north. She passed McCarran airport on her right, then turned left in front of the gold-plated hotel. She turned left once more into the front drive, rolling slowly up the wide, nearly empty entrance drive to the valet stand. The entryway was covered by a massive roof, as massive in scale as the buildings themselves, three stories tall at least. Sconces as large as a man gripped the sides of support columns, and those were fifteen feet in diameter. Chandeliers the size of small cars hung from the coffered ceiling. The entry drive could handle ten vehicles across, easy. Palm trees sprouted from every available patch of sandy dirt, leading up to the wide, burnished gold doorway.

A young black man wearing a valet uniform and sporting a crisp Caesar haircut approached her. She set the kickstand on her bike and stepped off. She pulled her helmet from her head, tucking it under one arm. When the valet saw her—saw she was a girl, more like—he paused in his step. Then he gave her a grin.

She probably looked like crap, she realized. She hadn't even had time to brush her hair since waking up at Sandy's. She was wearing last night's clothes and eyeliner. She was hungover. She'd just spent hours riding through the desert without a break.

So what was this kid smiling about? Oh, right. He was about to get to ride her motorcycle.

"Welcome," he said to her. "Will you be checking in?"

"Yes. Y'all valet motorcycles here?"

"Sure we do." The valet's name tag read *Hamilton*.

She left the key in the ignition and backed away from the bike. "You need my helmet, too?"

"For this? Nope. I won't be taking it far. Wait at the valet station, please." He hopped on, flashing her a killer smile.

She raised her eyebrows. Hamilton was a hottie.

He started the engine like a pro, then rode her bike further up the drive, slowing on the far side of the main entrance. He put it in neutral, then backed her bike into a narrow space in between a Ferrari and vintage Jaguar, then kicked down the stand.

She met him by the valet stand. "Next to a Ferrari and a Jag. Couldn't you at least store it adjacent to a vehicle with a better service record?"

"Up here in the valet gallery? Unlikely." Hamilton gestured at the high-end cars arranged in front of the hotel like a car show. Gallery, indeed. "They're all overbred and defective."

Just like me, Miranda thought.

"Let me tag your key." He wrote her a valet ticket with her name and phone number. When he handed her the ticket stub, she handed him a twenty.

"The gallery cars park for free, just so you know." He pointed to a little symbol he'd drawn on the corner of her ticket stub.

"I thought valet was free in Vegas." It used to be, all the years she'd come with her folks.

"No longer." Hamilton shook his head. "Lots of changes."

She looked at the valet ticket, then back at him. "You know, most of the cars up here in the gallery are owned by people who can actually afford to pay for parking."

"Rich people expect more comps than everybody else."

"I'm not rich." *Not anymore.* She handed him her helmet. "Hang on to this. Take it for a ride if you want. If anyone questions you, tell them to call me."

Hamilton tucked her helmet under the valet desk. "Maybe I will, later." He raised an eyebrow. "Maybe we'll go together."

"I already tipped you. You don't have to flirt."

"I don't flirt for tips."

She drew her eyebrows together in a skeptical frown. "That is bullshit."

He laughed. "I do flirt for tips. But as you just pointed out, that's not what I'm doing now."

"What are you doing now?"

"Hoping."

She snorted. "Okay, Hamilton. Send me a text message so I have your number. We'll see what all that hoping gets you."

"Where are you from?" he asked.

"I thought a person got to be anonymous in Las Vegas."

"If you'd like. But I can tell you're not from L.A., not with that accent."

"North Carolina."

"Well, Mysterious Miranda from North Carolina," he said as he pulled his phone from his pocket and proceeded to type a text message, "I will continue to hope."

———

SHE ENTERED THE HOTEL LOBBY, AND THE SMELL OF CIGARETTES HIT HER like a brick. Miranda hated cigarettes. Somehow she forgot about the smoking every time she came to Las Vegas. Smoking and gambling, like steak and wine.

She headed over to the registration desk. There was no line. Sundays were slow; she knew that. April was pretty slow; she knew that too. This casino wasn't like the Bellagio, tricked out and filled with high-end shops, the only place her parents would ever stay— although, as her mother put it, the Bellagio was looking a little *shopworn*.

Miranda chuckled to herself. The only way to handle her parents' snobbery was to be amused by it.

Her father's snobbery.

She sighed.

She stepped up to the young Asian woman working the desk.

"Do you have a reservation?" the woman asked.

"No," Miranda said. "And I'm paying cash."

The woman didn't hesitate at all. "Do you have a room preference?"

"I just got here. I don't even know what kind of room to prefer."

The woman smiled. "In that case, might I interest you in a suite in our adjacent boutique hotel? We're running a special on room rates. It connects through the hallway just there." She pointed to her left.

"Sure." If anything, hiding out in the off-name hotel might make her harder to find. Not that anyone knew where she had gone. But Sandy had his ways. As did her father. Jesus, if the two of them decided to team up, she was done for.

"I'll need an ID, and a two-thousand-dollar deposit."

Miranda pulled the envelope from her jacket pocket and counted out twenty bills, placing them on the marble counter. Then she pulled out her driver's license. She hesitated.

They had no idea where she'd gone, she reminded herself. They wouldn't be able to find her.

Still. "I go by Sorcha," she said. "My middle name. Can we put that on the reservation?"

The woman paused, appraising Miranda. "I can put anything you'd like on the reservation, if you need me to."

Miranda hesitated. "Sure." Then she gave her a name to use.

The woman typed in the information. Then she handed Miranda her license back, along with a keycard. "Follow the main walkway through the casino to the stage. Then turn left. After you pass a Starbucks and a theater, you'll enter the other hotel. You'll know it when you get there."

Miranda thanked her. Then she picked up her bag from where she'd set it on the floor and headed through the main casino. She wanted a bath. She wanted a drink. She wanted to disappear.

Everything else could wait, at least for a while.

Chapter Nine

Monday, while she brewed her morning coffee, Daphne tried to call Miranda. The call went straight to voicemail. After lunch, she tried again, and she got the same response. She tried twice more, every hour—at two o'clock, and three. Then she started to worry.

At four o'clock, she stood on the sidewalk in front of her favorite place to work, a coffee shop called Uptown. The place was located in the heart of Brentwood and did not cater to a laptop crowd. But Tony Upton, the owner, liked Daphne, and he let her camp out and work for as long as she wanted. At the moment, her laptop sat on her regular corner table while she stood in the low-lying winter sun, trying not to worry about Miranda.

She failed.

She dialed John Wesley's number. Miranda might get annoyed with her for stalking her through John, but Daphne decided she didn't care.

"Daphne?" John said. "What's going on?"

"Can I talk to Miranda?"

"I haven't seen Miranda since Friday. She won't return my calls." He sounded oddly concerned.

The hairs on Daphne's arms raised. "She left my house yesterday morning. She said she was going to stay with you."

"You're worried about her." John's voice grew harder. "Tell me what happened."

"We had a disagreement, that's all."

John was silent for a moment. "It must have been a big disagreement."

Daphne considered what to tell John. John, a guy whom Miranda actually liked, despite what she said—and despite what she'd done with Sandy. Daphne decided to cover for her friend. "Yeah, it was big. I was a jerk. And now I can't find her."

"All right."

"All right? All right what?"

But John had already hung up.

Daphne hustled back inside Uptown. She paid her tab, packed her bag, and headed home. Her walk home was usually a time to greet neighbors and settle her mind after a day's work on her screenplays— she was a screenwriter, and a successful one. But this walk—past well-groomed lawns, succulent plants, and towering palms—did nothing to settle her. She knew, in her heart, that Miranda was in trouble.

WHEN SHE ARRIVED AT HER HOME, A TWO-STORY CONDO BUILDING WITH garages below and homes above, she found a black, late-model BMW 5-series, one she didn't recognize, parked in front of her closed garage door. She was annoyed—she would have to figure out which of her neighbors had a guest over who didn't understand the parking rules.

Or maybe she wouldn't. Sitting at the bottom of her porch steps was a person with a familiar face. Dark brown eyes, dark blond hair —he and Miranda could have been twins, really—except when Charlie George stood, he was six-four.

He gave her a smile, but she could tell he was only being polite. The smile didn't reach his eyes. "Hello, Daphne. What have you done with my sister?"

Daphne breathed deeply. "I'm really glad you're here, Charlie. You'd better come inside."

Daphne led the way up the stairs and unlocked the metal exterior door, then the solid wood front door. She slipped off her shoes.

Charlie, who'd always been courteous, did not do the same. He wasn't planning to stay, then.

Not yet. He'd likely change his mind, she knew. "We're going to be here for a bit," Daphne told him, nodding at the shoe pile.

"Is she here?"

"She was. I'm trying to find her."

He slipped off his leather shoes and followed her through her living room, eyeing her large, rectangular, orange couch—she was, for once, alarmed by how strange it was—and into her dining room.

Her condo, which had always been her haven, seemed to fall short under Charlie's assessing gaze. He made her uneasy, uncertain—her home felt messy and weirdly furnished. Charlie filled the space like a prince visiting a peasant's cottage.

Before he could sit at her kitchen table, she stopped him.

"Wait," she said. "Let me wipe down the table, just in case."

He stepped back while she grabbed a dishrag and wet it in the sink.

She felt so flustered. The last time she'd seen Charlie George, he'd been a senior in high school. Now he commanded the room. Yet, by her math, he couldn't be more than twenty-five years old.

She dried the table, tossing the rag into the sink. "It's clean now." She motioned for him to have a seat. "Do you want something to drink?"

He tossed his keys on the table and sat. "Do you have scotch?" The keychain was from a rental car company. Briefly, she wondered how much it cost per day to rent a BMW 5-Series.

"I have your sister's favorite tequila. She bought the bottle a couple of days ago."

Charlie frowned. "No thanks. Coffee would be good." He nodded at her coffee maker.

She pulled her grinder toward herself, along with a bag of beans. "How did you find me?"

"I had help from my parents' investigator." He pulled a folded piece of paper from his inside jacket pocket and laid it flat on the table. It was covered in typed notes. "He asked for a list of Miranda's friends from college. He pulled info from the alumni database and, well, other databases, and cross-referenced it with the places where she'd been using my mom's credit card. She was either staying with you, or it was a giant coincidence that she'd used the card fifty times within walking distance of your place."

Daphne set the pot to brew, and joined him at the table. "She's been staying with me. She came here the night she landed at LAX."

"Did you know I've been calling her?"

"I encouraged her to talk to you. She hinted that you'd been fighting."

Charlie laughed scornfully. "We haven't been fighting."

"Why was she ignoring your calls?"

"Don't you know how our mother died?"

"She lied to me at first, but finally she told me."

Charlie nodded. "I'm worried about her."

"I'm worried too. She was so upset when she left. She lied to me, told me she was going to the house of this guy she'd started seeing, but she never showed up at his place."

"What'd you do to upset her?"

Daphne paused, considering what to tell him. Miranda's secret wasn't really a secret. Sandy knew, of course. Marlon knew. She, herself, knew. But she hadn't felt right telling John on the phone, and she didn't feel right telling Charlie now. "She tried to pick a fight with me and my friends. But I could tell that she was doing it on purpose. It seemed like, just as I was about to tell her to cut it out, she did everything she could to make it worse." All of that was true. "Why would she want to drive us away? She's only been here a week, but she's already gained so much—a place to stay, job prospects."

"Twenty thousand in cash."

"What?" Daphne could hear the screech in her voice.

"She bought the bike, and the next morning she went to the bank and withdrew twenty grand. Right after, my dad called and told her he was cutting off the credit card."

"That was Friday."

"Yeah."

"She told me she spoke to your dad that day. She asked me to cut her hair."

"You cut her hair?" He sounded incredulous.

"I'm good at cutting hair." She knew she sounded defensive. "It's short now. To here." Daphne held her hand up to her chin.

Charlie leaned back, surprised, as though the rest—the

motorcycle, the money—were run-of-the-mill, but the haircut was the big shock. "Miranda has had long hair ever since she was a toddler. I don't think she's ever done more than have it trimmed."

"I didn't want to do it. It seemed drastic."

Charlie rubbed his hands over his face. "Any idea where she went?"

"There's someone I can call for help. He has—" How could she put it? "resources."

Charlie nodded. "Good. I'm worried. I need to call our investigator, but I can't call him until tomorrow—it's late back home. Not unless we think she's in imminent danger." He paused. "Do you think she's in danger?"

"She rides that motorcycle like a maniac."

Charlie nodded, smiling grimly. "I imagine that's true."

He was taking everything she said far more seriously than she'd expected him to. It was like he knew something she didn't. "I'll call my friend now."

"I'll make us coffee." The pot had finished brewing, and neither of them had noticed.

They both stood. Charlie headed into the kitchen, and Daphne into the living room where she could talk privately with Sandy.

Daphne dialed. When Sandy answered, she cut right to the problem. "Miranda's missing."

Sandy didn't hesitate. "Since when?"

"Since she came here straight from your place yesterday morning, packed her bag, and left."

"Any idea where she went?"

"She told me she was going to John's place, but she never went there."

"She lied to create a diversion. She didn't want you to come looking for her." Sandy sighed. "Smart girl."

"Can you help?"

"Of course I can help. I'm getting my keys now. Your place?"

"Yeah. And Sandy? Her brother Charlie's here. He just showed up."

"I'll consider myself warned."

"I haven't told him."

Sandy paused. "That's probably a good idea. I'll be there in twenty."

Daphne hung up as Charlie was setting two mugs of coffee on the table, along with the pint of cream from her fridge.

She joined him back at the table, picking up the mug to warm her hands.

"Our investigator can help, but he's got to have something to go on. Without the credit card trail, we don't have much." He dropped his fist on the table, nearly spilling his coffee. "My father is such an idiot."

"For cutting off the credit card?"

"It was the only way we had to keep track of her. But Charles Senior had to have a hissy fit because she withdrew some cash."

"Well, twenty grand is a little more than 'some cash.'"

Charlie scoffed. "Not to us."

Daphne rounded her mouth into a surprised O. Miranda had never seemed particularly wealthy in college. She'd seemed like everyone else at Cameron University—richer than the impoverished Daphne. But from what Charlie was saying, Miranda had grown up surrounded by the kind of wealth that was difficult to even imagine.

It was just another of Miranda's many secrets. How many more were there?

"His hissy fit might cause us to lose Miranda, too," Charlie said, looking so worried that Daphne wasn't sure whether he was going to hit something or cry. "She hasn't even been out of the hospital for two weeks yet."

The hospital? What was he talking about? "Charlie, I don't know what you mean."

"Miranda was in the hospital until a few days before the funeral. We waited to have the funeral until she was released."

"I didn't know she was in the hospital."

"She didn't tell you?"

"I don't think she told me the whole story." Daphne was afraid to ask, but she knew she had to know the truth.

Charlie pressed two fingers between his brows, his pain obvious. "If she had, you'd have never let her leave."

And then Charlie told Daphne what really happened back in North Carolina.

———

As Charlie George finished recounting the events of the past three months to Daphne, there was a knock at the door to her condo. He raised an eyebrow. "Are you expecting someone?"

"I am. The help I promised."

He followed her to the door, interested to see who this supposedly helpful person might be. He had his doubts.

When she opened the door, two men stood on her front porch. One was a young guy, in his late twenties maybe, only a little shorter than Charlie.

And the other guy was Alexander Martin. Charlie nodded to himself, understanding now what Daphne meant by *resources*.

"Oh." Daphne sounded surprised when she saw the men there.

"Weren't you expecting them?" Charlie asked her.

"Not him." She pointed to the guy who wasn't a movie star.

The guy spoke. "I'm not sure what you expected me to do after you called me and told me she was missing."

"I suppose you're right," Daphne said. "Come on in."

Charlie leaned against the arm of the hideous orange couch, making room in the entryway for the other two men. Everyone, including movie stars, seemed willing to remove their shoes for Miss Daphne Saito. He'd only done it because she'd forced the issue, and because he'd been wearing shoes that slipped off easily.

"You're her brother," the younger guy said to him. "You could be twins."

Charlie nodded. "We get that a lot. Who are you?"

"I'm John. The one she comes to when everyone else is annoying her." John glanced over to Daphne.

"I don't annoy her," Daphne said quickly. "Do I?"

"I'm Sandy," Alexander Martin said, holding out his hand. Charlie shook it, noting the nickname.

At that moment, Charlie's phone rang, and he pulled it from his pocket. He didn't recognize the number, but he answered it anyway. Desperate times.

"Charlie." It was Miranda. She sounded sad and apologetic.

His heart started to pound. "It's about time, sis." He kept his voice gentle, and he waved at the other three to get their attention. He held his finger to his lips to request silence. He did not want his sister to know where he was, or with whom. "You okay?"

"Not really. I miss you."

"You took off and then ignored my calls. So that pain is both self-inflicted and easily cured."

"I can't come back."

"Why not?" He worked very hard to keep his voice calm.

She didn't answer him. "I should have died. You and dad should have let me die."

"Don't be ridiculous. If you're dead, who will give me decent tennis competition?" He would keep things light. He would remind her how much they meant to each other. He wouldn't let her forget who they were—sister and brother against the world.

"Charlie. Please. You have to stop calling me."

"Where are you?"

"You are the only person in the world I give a fuck about. Promise me you'll stay away from me. If I hurt you the way mom hurt us—"

"Hurt *you*, Miranda. She didn't hurt me at all."

"She could have hurt you."

"You're not going to do what she did."

Miranda's voice dropped to a whisper. "But I'm just like her."

"You aren't. Don't say that." Fear clutched his gut. His whole life, his big sister had kept him safe. And that's what she thought she was doing now.

"Bye, Charlie. I love you. You are my Little B. Always."

She hung up.

Charlie turned his back to the others and covered his mouth with his hand. He forced every emotion he was feeling back inside himself —the frustration, the anger, and yeah, the tears. He didn't know these people well enough to show them anything besides determination. All he knew was that Miranda hadn't trusted them enough to stick around or to tell them where she'd gone.

He looked at his phone. He pulled up the unfamiliar number she'd called him from and dialed it. A man answered from the front desk of a casino resort in Las Vegas.

He looked at the group of strangers who'd gone silent. He looked at Daphne, the girl whom Miranda blamed for getting him arrested once, an event he'd always considered an adventure. But Miranda had considered Daphne's actions that night unforgivable. But maybe Miranda had changed her mind, given that she'd run here after Sorcha's funeral. That's why he'd told Daphne the truth about Sorcha's death. Miranda had come to her, so Daphne needed to know.

Charlie looked at the young guy, John. He probably had the hots for his sister. He'd seen this ailment before. Miranda was difficult to love, but once a guy fell for her, he fell like a brick dropped from a tenth-story window. She'd left enough of Charlie's friends in broken pieces over the years.

The last person was more of a mystery. Why, of all people, was Alexander Martin standing in Daphne Saito's living room? And why was he looking so worried about Charlie's sister? He couldn't have known Miranda for more than a week, and he couldn't possibly have a crush on her like the John fellow did.

Or maybe he did. Charlie appraised Alexander—no, *Sandy*—once more. What Sandy would feel wouldn't be a puppy crush like John's though. Surely he was too old for that crap. Right then, Charlie started to wonder just what Miranda had done to piss everyone off. He'd bet anything Sandy had something to do with it, and now the man felt guilty.

"That was Miranda on the phone," Charlie told them. "I know where she went."

"She told you?" Daphne asked.

"Of course not. But she called from a hotel phone. She's in Las Vegas, at a casino on the Strip. I'm going to call our investigator from the car and hopefully have a room number before I arrive. She doesn't know I'm this close, or she would never have let me know where she is by using a land line."

He realized then that she'd wanted him to know where she was. Charlie's gut clenched with fear.

He did the math, quickly. If he were back in D.C., it would take him about five hours' flight time to get to Las Vegas with their private jet company, depending on the jet he was assigned. Add about half an hour to get to the airport. Add more time to get the jet and crew to the airport and ready for a flight—another two to six hours.

It was just after five p.m. right now. If he were still in D.C., the soonest he could arrive in Las Vegas would be 1 a.m., but it would likely be later than that.

Miranda had a plan. She wanted him to know where to find her body.

Charlie turned his back to the others again, forcing the image of his sister toe-tagged as a Jane Doe from his mind. He couldn't break down now, not when he was so close to finding her. They had little time. They needed to leave L.A. immediately. He needed to focus.

He turned back around.

"I'll come with you," Sandy said. "I can help."

Sandy was probably right about being able to help. Charlie didn't particularly want anyone else with him because other people tended to slow him down, but he wouldn't turn down the kind of influence Sandy Martin had.

"Sure." Charlie said. "I'm driving."

"I want to come, too," Daphne said.

"And me," said John.

"No way." Charlie wasn't bringing a three-ring circus on what was essentially a rescue mission. Miranda had run away from Daphne. And John too, for that matter.

Daphne's expression turned stubborn. Charlie had to resist rolling his eyes, which would likely piss her off. He went for the gentle approach. "Daphne, you know what I'm dealing with here. She left you behind for a reason—probably because she cares about you. That's a good thing. And we can't freak her out by showing up with a posse."

Daphne chewed her thumbnail like a little kid, and she nodded. "Okay. I understand. Besides, she might decide to come back. I'll wait here just in case. And you have to tell him the truth." She nodded at Sandy. "He needs to know."

Charlie knew Miranda was not coming back to Los Angeles of her own accord, but he didn't tell Daphne that. She wanted to feel useful, and so he let her.

John, though, looked like a tougher nut to crack. He stood with his arms crossed, staring Charlie down. "I should be there."

"Why, dude? I don't even know you. You don't know us." *Us.* The George siblings. Miranda and Charlie. They were a unit, and this guy was not a part of it. He was just another guy who was hooked on his sister like she was some sort of drug. Charlie had seen it a thousand times before.

"You're right," John said. "I don't know you. But I know her."

"After a week?" Charlie scoffed.

"I might be wrong," he said, "but I think this has been a unique week in her life. And she chose to spend it with me."

"It's true," Daphne said. "She chose him over me this entire week."

"You must have great weed," Charlie said.

John looked stricken—he'd landed a direct hit.

Charlie almost laughed, but he resisted. "Look, man. My sister eats guys like you for brunch, with bloody marys and a side of cheese grits." Charlie knew he was being harsh, but he didn't have time to waste managing this dude's feelings. "She chose you because you were there." Miranda did the same with all of Charlie's friends, knocking them down like bowling pins. *Why are they all so incompetent*, she'd say the next day. Nothing worse than incompetence in the eyes of his sister.

"You're wrong," John pressed.

Charlie did laugh this time, shaking his head.

"Besides," John asked. "Can't you use another body? Las Vegas isn't exactly small."

Charlie paused, considering. He could indeed use another body. He ran his hand through his hair in frustration. There was the smallest chance that John wasn't just another guy crushing on his sister, addicted to the high that was Miranda George. Charlie did not want to bring the guy along, with his earnest face and earnest haircut. But maybe that was what Miranda saw in him—an escape from the endless stream of stylish, southern family scions whom Charlies Senior had lined up for her to meet and marry.

"Fine, come along. But we're leaving right now."

The guy smiled. "I'm already packed."

Charlie assessed him again. Maybe he wasn't worthless after all.

Chapter Ten

It was nearly five-thirty Monday night by the time Charlie took the driver's seat of his BMW. Sandy sat next to him in the passenger seat, and John sat behind Sandy after tossing his bag in the trunk. Sandy didn't have a bag, but he didn't seem concerned about it.

"I'm going to head to the hotel she called me from. But I'm also going to call my family's investigator to see what he can turn up." Charlie glanced at Sandy. "You want to give me directions out of town?"

After Sandy got them on the interstate, Charlie called Buckhold, the best investigator on retainer with his dad's law firm. He updated the guy with the new information about Miranda's whereabouts. "And Buck," he said, "I'm worried. Time is short."

As he hung up, he glanced at John in the rear-view mirror. John's jaw was clenched tight. Yeah, the guy was definitely in it for his sister.

"So what's this all about?" Sandy asked. "Did your mom killing herself spin Miranda out?"

Charlie shook his head. "Our mom didn't kill herself." He wondered if Miranda would strangle him for telling these men what she'd deliberately kept from them—and for good reason—but he had a feeling that they needed to know. He had a feeling that at the end of this drive this information might make a difference.

"Miranda's been lying to everyone," John said, and he didn't sound surprised, which was, in itself, surprising. No, he sounded like he'd been expecting something like a lie. "Is your mom even dead?"

"She's dead," Charlie said. "I killed her."

Sandy turned quickly to look at him. It seemed Charlie had managed to surprise even the jaded movie star. "I think you'd better tell us what happened," Sandy said.

Charlie smiled slightly. "Our grandfather fought in Korea, and when he died, my father inherited, among other things, his officer's sidearm. We all knew what it looked like—a big semi-automatic. No one seemed to question whether it was a good idea to keep a gun in a house with small children, or in a house with a woman who was often desperately depressed or psychotic. For smart people, my parents can be complete idiots."

Charlie blamed the whole awful day of his mother's death on his father. And now, if Miranda died, that would be his father's fault, too. He laid all of the fault at the feet of Charles George, Sr., right where it deserved to be.

He squeezed the wheel of the car to get his emotions in check.

"It was just a couple of days after New Year's. I was home for winter break. Miranda and I had been out watching a matinée. When we got in, our mother was waiting for us."

"Daphne said Sorcha shot herself," Sandy said.

"She pointed the gun at me," Charlie said. "I freaked out. Miranda didn't flinch. She'd been living at home ever since college trying to keep our family together."

Charlie had graduated from college, and then he'd taken off to D.C. for law school. He'd left Miranda at home with his parents, where she'd had to put up with Charles Senior's bullshit and care for Sorcha.

Right now, that decision haunted the hell out of him.

"I knew something was wrong with Miranda," Sandy said. "I asked her the last time I saw her. She said she couldn't talk about it. She said she'd fall apart, so I didn't press her."

No, Sandy hadn't pushed Miranda to talk, but Charlie wondered what Sandy had done instead. He wondered what a little guilt might reveal. So he continued his story. "The room we were in is like a glass box. It's technically one of the living rooms in our parents' house, but our mother had commandeered it for her office. She had a large, round marble table where she worked. She worked a lot of late nights there."

"Miranda told me she was a defense attorney like your dad." Sandy said.

"Sorcha George was a genius defense attorney. The only person who comes—came—close to her is our dad."

"You sound like you admired her," Sandy said.

"I do. Did. She was incredible. She's the reason I wanted to be a lawyer. But the reason I have these great memories of her—that's because of Miranda. Miranda did everything she could to protect me from the bad. But then, that day in January, she couldn't protect me anymore."

"If your mom died in January," John interrupted, "why was the funeral last week?"

"We had to wait for Miranda to get out of the hospital."

His words were met with silence.

"Here's the whole story." He fixed his eyes on the road. "While my mom was pointing the gun at me, it was like she wasn't even my mom. I could see how sick she was. I wanted to fight her and hug her at the same time. Her voice didn't even sound like her voice. She said, *Come closer, Charlie, please.* She actually used the word *please.* While holding a gun. It was weird. And then she whispered, *It's not safe here.*"

"She was psychotic," Sandy said.

Charlie nodded. "Yeah, and that was not the first time. Then she held out a medicine bottle toward Miranda and said, *Take it.* Miranda stepped close enough to take the bottle from my mom's hand, and in that moment she met my eyes. I was so scared. Maybe you guys get guns pointed at you a lot, but I don't. It's terrifying. But Miranda didn't look scared. She looked, I don't know, resigned. Ashamed. Like she'd worked so hard to protect me from Sorcha, and she'd failed."

That day, Charlie had wondered how many times over the past years Miranda had been in dangerous situations with Sorcha and never told anyone. He'd only witnessed one—one, while he'd been in college—and it had been horrifying. He'd watched Sorcha take a swing at Miranda, and he'd watched his big sister duck like she'd dodged her mother's punches a hundred times before.

That's when he'd known. Miranda had been protecting him for years. His entire life.

"Sorcha kept the gun pointed at me, but she spoke to Miranda. *Open the bottle*, she said. Sorcha knew Miranda's pressure point. If you wanted to get Miranda to do something, all you had to do was threaten me. So Miranda opened the bottle. Later I found out it was a strong dose of Diazepam—Valium. Sorcha took it for sleep, or when she was manic. It usually worked. But Sorcha handed Miranda a full fucking bottle."

"She hadn't been taking her medicine," Sandy said.

"Not for weeks. It was around four o'clock, so our dad wouldn't be home from work for hours. We were on our own. I kept trying to think of ways to talk Sorcha down. I kept looking at the gun, wondering what kind of moron left a loaded handgun in the house with a woman who had attempted suicide no fewer than five times before. It's funny the things you think about in a crisis. All I could think about was how much I wanted to kick my father's ass for hanging on to that gun."

"What happened next?" John said. He sounded stricken, like he already knew what was coming.

"Sorcha started to seem panicky. And her panic was not reassuring at that moment. She spoke really quickly—*Take the pills. Take them. Take the pills.* Miranda's face showed the first signs of worry. And also, you know, sadness. The moment she realized that her mother was trying to kill her."

He paused. It was harder than he thought it would be to tell this story. Telling the cops had been easy. He'd only had to tell them the surface facts. He hadn't had to tell them about how his big sister had broken down.

He continued. "Finally Miranda disobeyed. She said, *Why, mom? What do I need the pills for?* Even then, Miranda spoke in a soothing voice. She hid the fact that she was crushed inside. Sorcha said, *It's not safe here.* I told Miranda not to do it, begged her to throw the bottle across the room. But then Sorcha said, *Take the pills or I'll shoot Charlie.* And so Miranda didn't hesitate. She put a bunch of the pills in her mouth and choked them down. Sorcha told her to take more. Miranda said, *I'm taking them as quickly as I can without water.* Sorcha just screamed for her to take more of them, and the gun actually shook in her hand. I was scared I was going to die. So Miranda took more, choking as the pills got caught in her throat."

"I'm an old man," Sandy said. "But this is the worst thing I've ever heard."

"Seriously," John said. "I don't know if I can listen to this."

Charlie snapped then, tired of these men who claimed to care about a person who was his entire world. "Well, Miranda had to live it. So you can listen to it for her."

"MIRANDA, THROW THE PILLS AWAY," CHARLIE WHISPERED. "YOU DON'T have to take them. She won't hurt me." He turned to Sorcha. "You won't hurt me, Mom, right?"

"Charlie." Sorcha held out a hand to him, as though to caress his cheek. "My perfect boy. I've always loved you."

"Of course you love me, Mom. Put the gun down."

"It's not safe, Charlie." Sorcha looked over Charlie's shoulder at something no one else could see, then her eyes cut to Miranda. "Take the pills."

Miranda swallowed a handful, coughing and choking and gagging them down.

"Can't you take them faster, Miranda?" Her mother almost sounded normal, her tone annoyed with Miranda's underperformance.

"It's hard without water."

"Let's sit," Sorcha said, gesturing with the gun at her marble table.

Charlie sat in one chair, and Miranda in another. A bottle of his mother's favorite scotch sat near Miranda. That was hardly unusual. Sorcha usually got drunk as she worked into the night. She'd pass out on the table around four in the morning, and then get up mid-morning and keep going.

Sorcha preferred the liquid kind of medicine. She always had, even when she and the rest of her family hadn't understood just what it was she was medicating. It wasn't until she'd tried to kill herself the first time—with a running car in the closed garage, such a cliché—that doctors had figured out that there was more to Sorcha's moods than ordinary irritability and fiery burnouts.

Charles George, Sr., hadn't been pleased to have his wife committed for two weeks—that was two weeks of lost billable hours after all—but the cost-benefit worked out in the end. Sorcha had emerged more efficient, at least for a while, with drugs to replace the alcohol and a more regular sleep schedule.

But then, after a few months, the old patterns emerged. After college, Miranda had stayed in their house, working in the family firm—hardly a compromise, since law students fought like hell for an internship at George Law—but Charlie knew Miranda mostly worked to keep their fragmented family from falling apart.

Some days, Charlie wondered why she'd done it. Like, on days when their mother was trying to kill her.

Sorcha used her empty hand to push the bottle of scotch toward Miranda. "Use this."

"Use it for what?" Miranda said.

"Use this to take the rest of the pills. Drink it all."

"Mom, stop it," Charlie said. "You're killing her."

Sorcha pointed the gun like someone trained to use one. "Shut up, Charlie."

Over the course of ten minutes, Miranda choked down the bottle of scotch and the rest of the tiny pills. Her eyes turned glassy and unfocused. Her head tilted to the side.

"Miranda?" Charlie called to her. "Miranda?"

Charlie stood. Sorcha did as well. Miranda fell from the chair, crumpling to the floor. She tried to rise, pushing herself up on all fours like a dog. She looked out the large window into the enormous garden fenced in with the stone imported from a thousand miles away.

His sister was going to die in their parents' palace.

She tried to crawl toward Charlie.

"She's dying!" Charlie screamed at Sorcha, stepping closer to his mother. He tried to keep the two of them in focus, the sister he loved more than anything in the world, and the mother he'd tried so hard to understand.

Sorcha watched Miranda with an expression of fascination. She let the gun drop to her side. Charlie moved toward her like a flash.

Miranda's arms collapsed, her face hitting the floor, her body following.

Charlie ripped the gun from her mother's hand, and he fired.

———

THE CAR WAS SILENT FOR A LONG WHILE AFTER CHARLIE STOPPED speaking.

"Are you okay?" Sandy asked.

Charlie knew what Sandy was asking. It was odd, he realized. No one had asked him that question except Miranda, right before she'd left for Los Angeles. She was always thinking of others before herself.

"I don't want to talk about me," he said. "I want to focus on Miranda." He'd worry about himself later. The nightmares and nights without sleep. How he was haunted by the look on his mother's face right before he'd pulled the trigger. Those things didn't matter right now.

"What happened to Miranda?" John asked.

"She spent weeks in a coma. At first we thought she was going to die—not enough oxygen had made it to her brain. Then we thought she would have brain damage. Then she got better. It took months of rehab, though. When they finally released her, we had the funeral a few days later."

"And she arrived in L.A. that night." John said.

"I had no idea she was planning to take off. When she started using Mom's credit card, I figured she was okay, she just needed some time. But then she didn't call me back, and then our fucking father cut off the credit card. And here we are."

They were in the middle of the desert, making about ninety-five miles per hour. He knew what the desert looked like around Las Vegas—he and Miranda had often driven out to see it, during their family's many vacations to the city. Miranda had always found Las Vegas fascinating, a city sprouting from nothing except a man's vanity, a fleeting dream that somehow became permanent. Driving to find her now, he could see why she might like that. She'd never had anything permanent for herself.

He'd been off building his career, and she'd been at their parents' mercy. How had he not seen it? Even when she'd insisted he go to law school, he should have insisted she come with him to D.C., that they share an apartment. She could have gotten any job she wanted. She could have gotten out of their parents' house, and she wouldn't be broken now.

"What are we going to do when we find her?" Sandy asked. "We could do with some strategy."

The man was right.

"We'll tell her to come home." John sounded so stupidly naive. "That whatever it is that happened with her and Daphne, it'll be okay."

Charlie cut a look at Sandy, who kept his eyes pinned on the dark road ahead. The man looked uncomfortable. Charlie began to get an inkling about what was really going on. Daphne was a pain in the ass for not telling him. Did she think he wouldn't figure it out? He was a George. Georges made a living figuring things out.

He was surrounded by idiots, and those idiots might get his sister killed.

"No, it won't be okay. Because nothing happened between her and Daphne." He looked at John's face in the rear-view mirror, the guy's confusion apparent. "Daphne lied to you. Miranda didn't leave because she fought with Daphne. She left because she's protecting people she cares about." Charlie sighed. "Even you."

———

SANDY MARTIN KNEW REAL MONEY WHEN HE BUMPED INTO IT, AND Charlie George reeked of real money. What surprised him was that he didn't get that same sense from Miranda. Somehow, in the week he'd spent with her, she'd managed to keep under wraps that she came from the equivalent of royalty back home—that she could walk into a bank and withdraw twenty grand, that she could pay cash for a motor vehicle without thinking twice. These were the sorts of things that had an effect on a person's vibe—and Sandy was good at picking up on a person's vibe.

Take Charlie, for example. This child spoke to everyone around him as though he were the governor of the great state of California, and he likely didn't even know he was doing it. Or care. He was raised to be a king.

And that was that.

Perhaps the differences in the George siblings' demeanors

stemmed from the story Charlie just told: the big sister who used herself as a human shield so her little brother could grow up unscathed.

But Sandy was not only good at picking up on a person's vibe. He could also tell when someone was withholding information. Like right now. Charlie hadn't finished his story. Charlie had said Miranda left because she was protecting people.

From what, Sandy wanted to know.

He'd known something was wrong yesterday morning, when she'd picked a fight with Marlon at his house. Granted, Marlon could be easy to fight with, but Miranda could have let Sandy handle things. She could have waited in his room for Marlon to settle down and see things clearly. But that's not what she'd done. Instead, she'd said crazy things to Sandy, too. She'd called herself *a passing fancy*. She'd spoken of their night together in the crudest of terms.

In his experience, she'd been acting like a woman trying to drive him away. And if he'd had a little less experience, or a little less self-assurance, she would have succeeded.

But she'd failed, and now he was on the road to Las Vegas with her arrogant brother heading toward some sort of crisis, and he didn't know what the crisis was because her arrogant brother wouldn't tell him.

"What else happened in the hospital?" Sandy asked.

Charlie glanced at him, surprise on his face.

"I can tell you're keeping something back. We need to know what we're going to find at this casino."

"You're holding back too, aren't you." Charlie's words weren't a question.

Sandy nodded. *Touché.* He was suddenly very aware of John's presence in the back seat of the car.

Honestly. Sandy hadn't been a part of something as tacky as a love triangle in at least a decade.

"After she woke up, Miranda requested a psych evaluation." Charlie kept his eyes on the road as he spoke. "She didn't explain why. She said she had a feeling."

"But it wasn't just a feeling, was it?" John spoke up from the back seat.

"No," Charlie shook his head. "It wasn't. Bipolar disorder is genetic. But you have to understand. Miranda is completely capable of taking care of herself. She knows what medicines she needs—she has the medicines with her, most likely. They weren't in her bathroom after she left—I checked. She knows what happened when our mother didn't take hers. No one researched this illness more than she did, back when she was trying to save our mom."

"So what are you afraid of?" Sandy asked, feeling he already knew the answer.

"From what she said to me on the phone tonight, she thinks she's on some sort of unavoidable path that'll end with her trying to hurt someone she loves—like our mom did. That's why Miranda left me. That's why she drove y'all off."

Sandy only knew that Charlie was holding back tears because he was watching him very, very closely. John, in the back seat, would have no idea.

"That's why she doesn't care if she dies in a motorcycle crash," John said.

Charlie glanced over his shoulder. "That's why she doesn't care if she dies, period."

Sandy thought of Saturday night, of the sharp-tongued girl with the glittering skin, of the chance that that brilliant life might end too early. He said to Charlie, "Drive faster."

Chapter Eleven

B uck called as they were approaching the Las Vegas skyline, brilliant against the evening sky, and Charlie answered after one ring.

"Bad news, kid," he said. "There's no record of her with a room in that hotel. Of her, or anyone with your last name or any combination of your family's names."

"You tried nearby hotels?"

"Nothing there either."

"Suggestions?"

"Head to the place she called you from. Look for her vehicle. Ask for her at check-in. If you have a picture, use it. That's what I'd do if I were there. And if you don't find her in twelve hours, your father will fly me there."

"We'll need you in six."

"Done. Miranda is a great kid. Keep her safe for me."

Charlie dropped his phone in his lap, exiting the freeway toward the casino from which Miranda had placed the call.

"Our investigator can't find a record of Miranda checking into a room in Las Vegas. But that doesn't mean anything. She's paying cash, and she could be using a pseudonym." He relayed the rest of Buck's message as he pulled into the drive of the hotel, parking right in front of the tacky gold doors.

It was nine p.m. when he, Sandy, and John climbed from the car—

they'd made good time. Charlie left the keys in the ignition for the valet, while John popped the trunk for the luggage. John had put his things in a small nylon bag, like you'd use to carry your crap to sports practice in high school.

Charlie pulled his own leather duffle from the trunk and shut the lid. John joined Sandy near the entrance, where they waited for him to handle the car.

The valet was a handsome black guy around Charlie's age with an intelligent glint in his brown eyes. Maybe a college kid working part time, perhaps a graduate student. Charlie had a thought—if his sister had arrived at this hotel yesterday, the valets, especially this valet, would know it. She always underestimated the effect she had on dudes.

"Hamilton, is it?" Charlie asked, checking out the guy's name tag.

"Yes, sir."

"We're here because we're looking for someone important to us."

Hamilton looked over his shoulder to where Sandy Martin stood on the portico. "To all three of you?"

"My sister." Charlie could tell the moment when Hamilton recognized the resemblance between himself and Miranda—the kid might work in Las Vegas, but he couldn't out-poker-face a George. "Have you seen her?"

"We're really not supposed to talk about guests." He played up an aw-shucks tone.

Charlie gritted his teeth. "She's in trouble. It would help to know if she were staying here."

"Can't you give her a ring?"

Charlie didn't answer because the question was inane.

At that moment, John called from near the entrance. "Charlie— she's here. This is her bike."

Charlie left Hamilton and his car, striding over to where John stood next to some flashy Italian four-wheeled garbage. Sure enough, a motorcycle was tucked in between two cars. "You sure it's hers?"

"I'm sure. I was with her when she bought it."

Charlie glanced over his shoulder at Hamilton, jerking his head for the kid to join them. Hamilton jogged over.

"Did you park this bike?" Charlie demanded.

"I don't park and tell," Hamilton said.

"Jesus Christ." Charlie was about to strangle the guy.

"Charlie," Sandy said. "It's all right."

Sandy's voice was oddly soothing. Plus, he'd be lying to himself if he didn't find it a little intimidating to be spending time with the guy. Few people intimidated him, but man. Alexander Martin was in a class of his own.

Sandy turned to the valet. "I apologize that my friend lost his temper."

Hamilton just smiled, as though he were used to it. He probably was.

Sandy continued, "Miranda, our friend—his sister—she's in trouble. We love her, and we need to find her to make sure she's safe."

At the word *love*, Hamilton's eyes flicked around to meet the eyes of all three of them, assessing. Finally, he spoke. "She arrived yesterday, and I parked her bike for her. I still have her helmet too. It seemed like she was going to be staying here, yeah, but I don't know what room."

"We don't either," Sandy said. "She didn't use her real name, and she paid cash."

Hamilton's eyebrows shot up. "She's trying hard not to be found, huh."

At his words, Charlie had to turn his back. He was growing impatient, but he was also growing afraid. He didn't want these guys to see his fear. He couldn't. Because if they saw that he was afraid, then they would try to comfort him. And if they did that, then he might break down. And if he broke down, he might not be able to get himself back together again.

All he could picture at that moment was Miranda on the floor of their house, in a room full of glass, dying for him.

"She is," Sandy said. "But we need to find her."

"Did you hurt her?" Hamilton asked.

Charlie turned back. "No—Jesus. No."

Hamilton studied his face for a while. Charlie had no idea what he saw, and he didn't care.

Hamilton nodded. "Yeah, okay. Here's the deal. She gave me her number and said to text her if I wanted to hang out. I might be able to figure out where she is."

———

Miranda's phone blinked on the bar in front of her. The time read nine-thirty. The number belonged to Hamilton. She wondered, briefly, if Hamilton was his first name or last name or his real name at all.

"Do you want to meet up? Where are you?"

Did she?

She leaned back against the bar, scanning the top-floor club of her hotel. She took in the revelers with their cameras clustered around the tall windows facing north, the strip laid out before them like a banquet of light.

She wore her black dress and heels, the ones she'd bought for Greta's wedding using her dead mother's credit card. She felt like her old self in them, the princess who wore couture, not the reckless girl on the motorcycle.

She headed away from the crowds to an empty part of the club, to the windows facing south. Forty floors below her, traffic on Interstate 15 continued at its unrelenting pace. She stared as far as she could see in the darkness, the white headlights and red taillights guiding the way back to Los Angeles. They faded into the distance. Ten miles away, she estimated. That's all she could see, but those ten miles seemed like forever. Those ten miles were the way back to another world, a world she'd never be returning to. She turned and leaned back against the glass, resting her gaze on the groups gathered across the room, backlit by the lights of the Strip. She imagined them all happy, even though she knew they weren't. Happiness was for the very few.

However, as far as she could tell, on this Monday night, she was the only person in the bar without friends. She'd never felt more alone in her life.

Her phone flashed again. *"You ignoring me?"*

"I'm checking out the rooftop club. It's nice."

"Tell Domingo behind the bar you're my friend. He'll take care of you."

She knew that all she had to do was head to her room, open those pill bottles, and go to sleep. She knew that was what she should do, before she lost her nerve or tried to convince herself that she wouldn't, in fact, end up terrorizing the people she loved most.

Because that was the hell of it. She knew her mom had loved her, and she'd loved Charlie too. She'd loved them more than anything, but that love hadn't stopped her from trying to kill Miranda, or from pointing a gun in Charlie's face.

She thought of Charlie, of his voice, and she was glad she'd said good-bye to him. She was glad she'd let him know where to find her when she eventually opened those bottles.

A year ago, when Miranda had started suspecting that she, too, was sick like her mom, sick in a way that could never be cured, only "managed" as the hospital psychiatrist had put it, she'd wondered if she maybe had a shot at a normal life. Sorcha had tried for normal, after all. Law school, marriage, kids—all of it. She'd tried. And she was dead. And she'd almost taken her kids with her.

That horrible afternoon back in January, as Miranda had squeezed her mother's pill bottle in one hand and scotch in the other, she'd tried to remember if there had been warning signs that day, or the day before, or that week or month, that her mother had had an episode coming. If there had been signs, then Miranda could have told her dad that Sorcha seemed to be on edge. Her father didn't care much about Sorcha taking out her issues on Miranda, but he cared if Sorcha dropped the ball on a case.

When she'd looked at that gun in Sorcha's hand, it'd been clear that a ball was about to be dropped big time. Looking past the gun and into her mother's eyes, Miranda had seen a familiar distance from the present moment, as though something was riding her mother, pushing her mother down inside herself.

In that terrifying instant, Miranda had known that her mother loved Charlie. As Miranda had swallowed the pills and liquor, she'd hoped her mother's overwhelming love for Charlie would save him. As Miranda had blacked out, the bright windows turning dull, that had been her only thought. Saving Charlie.

Miranda rested her head against the glass. That day when Sorcha died, she should have taken Miranda with her. If she had, then Miranda wouldn't be leaning against a floor-to-ceiling window forty stories above the Las Vegas desert, wondering what it would be like to fall.

She headed back toward the bar. The bartender, Domingo, met her where she stopped, nodding at her empty glass. He seemed to take pride in his work. He mixed drinks, even the stupid vacation drinks, with flair.

"Another?" he asked.

"No thanks." She handed him the glass. "How far can you see from that window?" She pointed south, to where I-15 disappeared into the horizon.

"About seven miles at night. Twice that during the day."

She nodded. Only seven miles then. Seven miles toward a life she could never have.

Her phone buzzed again.

"Did you mean it about taking your bike for a ride?"

She smiled. Of course she'd meant it. Hamilton couldn't know that she wouldn't be coming back to reclaim her bike, ever. She composed a text. *"She gets testy without regular exercise. You'd be doing me a favor if you took her out."*

Miranda had been ignoring so many texts and calls from her friends and family the past two days that she hadn't realized until that moment that they'd stopped coming. Even Charlie had stopped texting her. She wondered if he'd accepted good-bye for what it was, and let her go.

More likely, he had hopped on a plane and was on his way to her. But she had time. Even NetJets couldn't get him here till morning, and then he'd have to find her.

"Can I pay my tab?"

"On your room, then?"

"No," she said. "I'm paying cash." Miranda knew how to leave no trail, and that included avoiding receipts with room numbers.

She left a hundred-dollar bill on the bar for Domingo and slipped from the club, dashing off another text message as she went.

THE THREE MEN HEADED DIRECTLY TO THE ELEVATORS THAT WOULD TAKE them to the rooftop restaurant and nightclub. Charlie was grateful to Sandy for calming the situation down, for using his charm to get the valet to help them. Charlie wasn't one to lose his mind in a crisis, but his sister was the exception—Miranda always took care of him, not the other way around. Without her, he felt like a scared little boy again.

He thought about law school back in D.C., where he was not in classes right now. He'd ditched out without thinking twice, hopping on a plane for L.A. as soon as he'd heard that his father had cut off the credit card. Up until that point, Buck had been keeping him posted on Miranda's location. But without the card, things got harder. Plus, after a week, he'd figured it was time to go get Miranda and bring her home. He couldn't have known that things were so much worse than they'd all imagined.

The three men stepped on the elevator, and John pressed the button for the rooftop bar.

John. This guy. He seemed so boring. So not his sister's type. Good-looking enough, he guessed, but painfully square. He was wearing jeans and Vans sneakers like a ninth-grader, and a t-shirt for some band Charlie had never heard of. Sandy Martin, on the other hand, was not painfully square. He also wore jeans, but they fit him right, and he wore a dress shirt that had obviously been custom-tailored to his body—a body that looked as fit as it had two decades ago, or more.

Charlie added more details to the theory he'd formed in the car as the elevator whooshed upwards. The doors opened, revealing a hostess stand. To the left was dining room seating. To the right was a nightclub. Charlie headed that direction, remembering the name of the bartender—Domingo—expecting Sandy and John to follow him.

"I'll take a walk around," Sandy said. "See if she's hiding in the corners."

"I'll wait by the exit," said John.

Yeah, three had turned out to be a good number to have. Charlie approached the bar. Three bartenders mixed drinks, while servers ran them to the dining room and to the groups of seats that filled the massive club. The tall windows gave a spectacular view. Miranda would have liked this place. She always enjoyed having a high perspective on things.

He strolled down the bar, checking name tags on the bartenders. There. Domingo. He approached, waiting, hoping Hamilton had come through.

Domingo finished pouring the martinis he'd been mixing into two glasses and slid them across the bar to the waiting patron. Then he turned to Charlie.

Charlie eyed him, waiting a moment, assessing.

"Thirsty?" Domingo asked.

"No," Charlie said. "My sister. She's here—Hamilton texted you."

"She was here. She paid her tab about ten minutes ago. You just missed her."

Charlie wanted to pound his fist on the bar, but held his frustration in check. The bar was Domingo's domain, and he needed the man's help. "Can I see the receipt?"

"She paid cash. No room number."

"Can I see it anyway?"

"Yeah, sure." He popped open the register and pulled the receipt out of the tray. "Here."

Charlie looked at the list of drinks—proof that his sister had been here—three top-shelf scotches, neat, and a thirty-dollar tip. He looked at the time stamp. Almost precisely ten minutes prior. "Can I keep this?" The receipt was a manifestation of Miranda's life. She was still here. She was still her.

Charlie still had a chance.

"No problem."

"Thank you."

After leaving a hundred-dollar bill on the bar, Charlie turned to find Sandy waiting a few steps behind him. "We just missed her," Charlie told him, not bothering to hide his frustration. "We were so close."

"We'll find her, Charlie," Sandy said. "We'll get everyone looking for her."

"That'll just scare her off."

"Not the way I do it." Sandy gave a small smile.

Charlie gave a half-smile back. He was beginning to understand what Miranda saw in Sandy Martin besides his blue eyes.

———

SANDY DIALED MARLON AS THEY RODE BACK DOWN THE ELEVATOR TO THE lobby. Charlie had also gotten on the phone, presumably with his family's investigator. Sandy could tell John was eavesdropping on both conversations, so he kept his words vague about Saturday night.

"What's up?" Marlon asked.

"I need the best person in Las Vegas for tracking someone down quickly and quietly. Someone who can bring a team and work well with a casino's security."

"Sure, okay. Right now, yeah?"

"Yeah. Just make the arrangements, and then have them call me as soon as they turn something up. I'll answer."

"I'm sorry I lost my temper at her in your kitchen."

"She didn't leave because of you." Sandy said. "She played everyone. She was hitting all the pressure points."

"Daphne filled me in on what really happened to her mom. Just in case I wasn't feeling bad enough."

"Maybe next time you'll learn to control that protective instinct of yours. Take a beat before letting loose."

"I can do that," Marlon said.

The elevator doors opened and the three of them stepped off. "We're about to check in at the hotel where we think she's staying. I'll send you the info once I have it. Whoever you think is best—have them call me directly. We don't have any time, Marlon."

Charlie didn't head back to the check-in desk at the main casino where they'd parked their car. After they exited the elevator, he led them to the adjacent hotel, the one with the bar atop it, the one whose lobby looked like a high-class East Asian spa—without a cigarette or slot machine in sight. He walked toward the check-in counter.

Charlie turned to John and Sandy to explain. "Miranda hates cigarettes. She's staying here."

Apparently drawing inferences ran in the family.

At the check-in desk, Charlie underwent an astonishing transformation. Gone was the stricken, fearful, angry twenty-five-year-old. Suddenly, he was a charming high-roller with enough good will to tame a lion. He approached a middle-aged man behind the counter.

"I'm here to check into my hotel room. My wife arrived this weekend. The last name's George." He passed over his ID.

After looking through the computer, the man made an apologetic face. "I'm sorry, sir. I'm unable to find a reservation under that name."

Charlie grinned, as though the man's words were a hilarious joke, and glanced at Sandy. "Sandy, jeez. She used a fake name on our reservation again. This is going to take forever. Got any guesses?"

Sandy knew how fake names worked on hotel reservations—after all, he did it all the time. Unless you had someone else make the reservation for you, the hotel kept your real name tied to the fake one. The man could easily have told them where Miranda's room was if she had used her own ID to make the reservation—which she must have done. But he wasn't going to share her room number unless they knew the fake name.

After Charlie drew the man's attention to Sandy, the man reacted in the typical fashion. His eyes bulged a little. He flushed. He grew mute for an overly long period of time. These were reactions Sandy was accustomed to. Charlie had brought Sandy into the game on purpose: *Yes, we know the fake name ploy. We do it all the time. See? I have the biggest star you've ever seen with me. We all know how this works.*

"Akane," John said out of nowhere. "It's under Akane."

Charlie looked annoyed at the interruption.

"Very good, sir. Room 3206. Would your friends like adjacent rooms?"

Charlie's annoyance changed to chagrin. "Yes, please." He passed over a credit card. "And you can use that card for my wife's room as well. I believe she paid cash."

Their room keys in hand, all three headed toward the tower elevators.

"Who the hell is Akane?" Charlie demanded.

"That's Daphne's Japanese name. The one she was born with. She changed her name for some reason that Miranda wouldn't tell me."

"And what made you think Miranda would be using that here?" Sandy asked.

"Don't you know how I met Miranda and Daphne?" he asked Sandy. "It's like the best joke between the two of them. Or the worst, depending on your perspective."

Sandy shook his head.

"The weekend before Greta's wedding—you know, like ten days ago—Daphne picked me up at a club on the West Side. She lied to me about her name and slipped out at dawn. I figured I'd never see her again."

Charlie snorted. "Daphne is cold."

John said, "She's not, actually. Anyways, the name she gave me was Akane. Then, the morning after your sister arrived, I ran into them at a restaurant in Brentwood. Daphne had just left, but Miranda stuck around, alone. I asked her if her friend's name was Akane. Miranda, being highly intelligent, figured everything out in like four seconds, but she and I became friends anyway. She teases me about my one-night-stand with Daphne, but it doesn't bother her." John paused. "It seemed like a name she'd use if she were feeling self-destructive and lonely, kind of like Daphne was feeling that night with me."

At those final words, Sandy felt a twinge of guilt. John really cared about Miranda, and he seemed to understand her, too. He understood a lot, actually.

Miranda could do far worse than John.

Once this mess in Las Vegas all worked out, Sandy would take himself out of the picture, he decided. He'd let her be happy with the right guy—with John.

Sandy pressed the button to call the elevator. "Moment of truth, gentlemen." The doors opened, and Charlie and Sandy stepped inside.

"Wait." John stopped, facing the open elevator. "I should wait in the lobby in case she comes down. If she isn't in her room, we should have a lookout. If she's there, though, text me and I'll come up."

Sandy nodded at him, and the elevator doors closed.

Chapter Twelve

Charlie slid the keycard into his sister's hotel room, praying she would be inside. He pushed the door open slowly, taking in the room—rooms. The sitting room had a couch, a desk, and a large flatscreen. There was a bar, too, and she'd already been at the small bottles of liquor, leaving the empty ones in the white ceramic sink.

He passed into the bedroom, Sandy following close behind. "Miranda?" he called out. He didn't hear any movement, and she didn't answer.

He was terrified he was too late.

The bed was made, the bedroom neat, except for a black dress strewn across the bed as though she'd just been there and changed clothes quickly.

A black satchel sat on the dresser. A pair of high heels were tossed together at the foot of the bed. He turned left into the large bathroom, toward the tub—whispering another prayer. The bathtub was empty, and so was the bathroom—no Miranda.

There, on the counter. Three prescription pill bottles. He knew those bottles. He'd filled the prescription himself.

He picked them up. Cradled them in his palm, reading the labels. They were full.

"What are those?" Sandy asked.

"They're Miranda's."

Sandy nodded, understanding without needing further explanation, and Charlie was glad. He didn't feel like giving further explanation to Sandy. What he wanted was an explanation from Sandy.

Charlie strode from the bathroom, clutching the pill bottles, until he stood in the middle of the sitting room. Sandy followed him, like Charlie knew he would. Charlie slammed the bottles of pills on the coffee table. They clacked loudly against the thick glass.

Sandy dropped onto the couch, a low-slung affair in black tweed fabric and chrome just on this side of tacky, and raised his eyebrows at Charlie.

Charlie grabbed a bottle of scotch from the minibar, cracking the small lid and pouring it into a glass. "So," he said, glancing at Sandy over his shoulder. "You slept with my sister?"

Sandy nodded slowly. "I did. Saturday night."

Charlie laughed, the entire fragile situation seeming to spin further out of his control. He pulled his phone from his pocket and dialed John. The guy answered after one ring. "She's not here," Charlie told him.

"I'll wait down here, then."

Charlie hung up.

"I guess sleeping with girls half your age is pretty normal for you," he said to Sandy.

Sandy's face remained placid. Charlie wanted to punch it, to break the man's camera-ready nose. "No, actually. Most girls her age are boring."

Charlie chuckled. "Miranda is not boring." He threw back the whole glass of scotch, then opened another bottle, refilling his glass. "You don't seem like an idiot."

Sandy raised his brows again. "Most of the time, no."

"What were you thinking? You couldn't tell something was up with her?"

"I could tell something was up, yes."

"And you fucked her anyway."

At Charlie's words, Sandy leaned back and crossed his arms, anger marking his face for the first time since Charlie had met him earlier that day. He'd seen Sandy worried, but not angry.

Charlie was glad. He wanted the man angry. Charlie was angry. No—Charlie was fucking furious. If Charlie were honest with himself, he wanted the man to take a swing at him so they could work it out like animals.

Sandy tilted his head, his eyes narrowed in a way that Charlie had seen before, in old movies that he and Miranda had watched together at home late at night, eating pizza and giving each other shit. The feeling of dissonance knocked him off balance for a moment, but thinking of Miranda helped him regain it.

"I didn't *fuck Miranda*." Sandy said.

"You'd prefer to dress it up in pretty words?" Charlie laughed. "You can try."

"Can you not see her as someone who makes her own choices?"

"I can see her as someone who had just come out of a coma and then buried her mother."

"So can I. I knew there was more to it than her—your—mother dying. It was obvious. And I knew that she was sleeping away her sorrows. That was obvious, too. But there's nothing wrong with sex. When you get a little older maybe you'll understand."

Charlie bristled at the crack about his age, but he let Sandy talk.

"I like your sister. She's incredible." Sandy shook his head. "Do you not see that?"

"Of course I see that!" Charlie screamed. He threw the glass in his hand at the wall, and it dented the drywall before falling to the carpet.

He turned his back on Sandy and rested his hands on the bar, breathing heavily, tears burning his eyes.

"We're going to find her," Sandy said, quieter now. "I'm sorry I lost my temper."

"That's what it looks like when you lose your temper?" Charlie said, incredulous.

"Doesn't happen very often. You should be flattered."

"Piss off."

Sandy picked up the glass Charlie had thrown, cleaning it in the sink and setting it on the bar. He grabbed another, filling them both with another round of booze. He lifted a glass to Charlie, kindness in his eyes. "You, too."

John chose a seat at the corner of the bar so he could see the lobby exit and the elevators at the same time. He drank a cola, but added a lime and a small straw so it looked like a cocktail. He watched the elevator doors, hoping. And then, suddenly, there she was, dressed in her tight jeans, her tall boots, and her motorcycle jacket. She didn't have her bag, and he remembered that her helmet was with her bike. Her hair was loose about her chin. She was heading toward the passageway that led back to the main casino.

John leapt from his chair to intercept her. She was moving fast, like she always did, her long, curvy legs eating up the patterned carpet. He broke into a jog. Desperation flickered down his spine, making his legs feel weak.

"Miranda," he called, when he was close, almost close enough to touch. But he didn't dare touch.

She whipped around, a catapult unloosed. She examined him for a moment, arms crossed over her chest.

"John." Her voice was low, sarcastic even. She sounded just like herself, as though nothing were wrong, as though they were standing on Montana Avenue in Los Angeles, not in a brightly lit corridor in Las Vegas at some late hour.

He glanced at his watch. It was after ten o'clock.

"Got someplace to be?" she asked.

"What? No. Not at all."

"How'd you find me?"

"I guessed the name you used to make your reservation."

"You did?" She sounded impressed.

"Daphne did bring us together." He gave her a grin. He'd missed her the past few days.

She nodded. "True."

"Have a drink with me before you go out."

"Where's Charlie?"

"He's here. Probably in your room."

"Alone?"

"Sandy's with him."

She eyed him. "Sandy came?"

He felt like he was missing part of a bigger picture, but he didn't want to worry about that right now. Right now he wanted to stop her from running out the door. To get her to listen to him. Or to sit with him, for a little while. "We're worried about you."

She pressed her lips together, aggravated.

"Just one drink."

"On one condition."

"Anything."

She shook her head. "Don't say that."

"What?"

"Never offer a person *anything*. You're not Faust."

"I don't care." And he didn't. At that moment, given the story Charlie had told them in the car, he'd make a devil's bargain for her. "What do you want?"

"You can't tell my brother I'm here. Or Sandy. You and I will have a drink, I'll leave, and that's it."

John considered. "I'm allowed to tell them after you leave."

Miranda eyed him. She nodded, then gestured with her hand toward the bar.

John led the way back to his corner seat. She leaned against the bar next to him, refusing a stool, as though she didn't plan to stay long.

John knew he had only minutes. He didn't have time to take the slow approach like he usually would. So he didn't. "Charlie told us what really happened with your mom."

Miranda glanced at him, then away, flagging down the bartender. She'd only looked at him for a moment, but he'd seen her eyes. The fear in them.

Of what? "I'm sorry that happened to you. You could have told me."

She snorted. "Yeah, sure. I can't even believe Charlie told you."

"Why not?"

"Because my mother's autopsy report states that she died by suicide. Don't you see?" She ran her hand through her hair. "Charlie lied to the police about what happened, and our father helped cover it up."

"He lied about shooting your mom?"

"What he did—when he shot my mom—could easily be construed as criminal homicide. She wasn't an armed threat once he'd gotten that gun from her."

John thought of the police procedurals he used to watch with Turbo when they were high. "But what about powder residue? Fingerprints? The physical evidence?"

Miranda laughed out loud. "Please. We're *defense lawyers*." She paused. "Well, they are." At those words, she looked incredibly sad. "The point is, he shared something with you—a total stranger—that he shouldn't have shared with anyone." She paused, covering her mouth with her hand, her eyes anxious. "Why would he do that?" She seemed genuinely worried about Charlie.

"Because he thinks you're going to kill yourself."

She looked away and waved for the bartender again. The bartender was busy with a group of men at the end of the bar—a bachelor party, perhaps—and she didn't see Miranda trying to get her attention. Perhaps it wasn't a bad thing that Miranda wasn't getting another drink. John could smell the whiskey on her breath.

"Is he right? Are you going to kill yourself?" John asked.

She stared up at the light fixture suspended above them, a complicated sequence of flat metal cut-outs shaped like birds interspersed with tiny bulbs. "I don't know."

John sucked in his breath, suddenly unable to get enough oxygen. Then, from his pocket, his phone rang, and the sound and vibration jolted him out of his shock. "Hold on a second," he said to her. He glanced at the screen. It was Charlie. "Hello?" Charlie told him what John already knew—that Miranda was not in her room. "I'll wait here then," John said to Charlie, feeling guilty for the lie. Charlie hung up in his ear. John set his phone on the bar.

"Who was that?"

"Your brother."

Miranda narrowed her eyes. "You told him I'm here?"

"Nope."

"Why not?"

He sighed. "Because I told you I wouldn't. Although right now I'm not sure why I agreed to that. He's upstairs in your room, freaking out with worry. And you're down here acting like what you do has no effect on anyone else."

Her face went blank. "You're wrong."

She stepped away from the bar.

"Wait, Miranda. Don't go yet." He felt every important part of him —his gut, his goddamned heart—compress and compress, ready to combust.

"I know exactly what effect I could have on other people." She shook her head. "Why can't y'all see that?"

She spun and dashed from the bar, nearly at a run. John considered his best move. He stood, and headed toward the elevators.

———

Miranda dialed Hamilton as she dashed down the long hallway toward the big casino floor. He answered quickly.

"Hey biker girl. What's happening?"

"You told them I'm here," she said.

He paused. "Did they tell you that?"

"You just did."

He laughed. "You'd think, living here, I wouldn't fall for tricks like that. Are you angry?"

"Not really, not at you. At least two of those three can be persuasive."

"How do you know Alexander Martin? That's some serious star power."

"I don't know him that well." As she talked, she passed slot machines and table games, the main entrance ahead.

"You're lying," he said.

"Do you want to go for a ride or what?"

"Meet me out front in two minutes," he said, then hung up.

As she approached the valet stand, she almost didn't recognize Hamilton. He was out of his uniform, wearing slim jeans and a black t-shirt under a red leather jacket. He was standing next to a black Ducati, holding a matte black helmet in his hand. Her own bike was parked by his, the helmet on the seat, the key in the ignition.

"You ride a Duke?" she asked him. "You didn't tell me?"

"A valet isn't supposed to talk about himself."

She rolled her eyes. "Tell me what you do when you aren't here."

"I'm a law student at UNLV."

She took a step back. "Seriously?"

"Yeah. I grew up here—I'm a local. But I'm in school here, too. Just working my way through with three shifts a week." He paused. "Why do you look so weird about it?"

"I really can't explain." She picked up her helmet. "Where are we going?"

"Desert?"

"Sounds amazing. Can we go fast?"

"Once we get out there, as fast as you want. Follow me." Hamilton pulled his helmet over his head and slung his leg over his bike. As he buckled his helmet under his chin, he nodded at her. Then he turned the key in the ignition and all nine hundred and fifty cubic centimeters exploded into forward tension. She shivered.

Okay. Fine. His bike was way faster than hers.

She hopped on and followed him out of the wide casino entrance, south out of town on Las Vegas Boulevard, and then out into the Mojave on a two-laner.

At night, away from the highway, the desert transformed into a windswept, starlit dome. She zipped along behind Hamilton, barely feeling the speed on the immense straightaways, her headlight and the moon showing her all she needed. If Hamilton hadn't been in front of her, she would have gone as fast as her bike could go.

But she didn't know where she was going, so she let Hamilton lead. They kept it around sixty in the curves, venturing toward a hundred in the straights. At a hundred her bike screamed, and she wanted to scream too. But her bike never wavered. Never hinted that it would blunder, lose its traction.

Lose its way.

Harm her.

No, if something went wrong, it would be operator error. Her fault.

They took a curve around a rocky outcropping covered in scrub, and then he slowed. She slowed too, pulling up beside him as he pulled off the road next to the rocks.

He flipped up his visor. "OK, I see you have no trouble going fast."

She flipped up hers, too. "Wanna race?"

He eyed her, pulling his mouth to the side in consideration. "Not really."

"I'm heading back to town, taking that turn north. First person to the Stratosphere wins."

"You want to race up the Strip? At prime time?"

"Why not?"

He shook his head. "I'll give you a 20 second head start." He flipped his visor back down.

She took off like an RPG, so fast that she wobbled a bit, causing her heart to race. Once her bike settled down, she refused to look at the speedometer, keeping her eyes on the road ahead. She ignored the terrain in her peripheral vision, ignored everything but the wind pressing against her chest, trying to rip her off of her bike. She clung, focused completely on operating the motorcycle properly—she had experience riding, but not at these speeds, never at these speeds.

She let her competitive nature take over—she wanted to win, to show Hamilton what she could do. To show herself what she could do. So she rode faster, as fast as she could tolerate, and when she turned left, she took the turn wide, the proper racing line, and leaned low, her knee nearly touching the ground, her heart racing again, Jesus she could really die out here. And then they were heading north, and the lights of the Strip were ahead.

Then they passed their first car, her to the left, and Hamilton—he went *right*—squeaking by between the car and shoulder, ending up next to her, and then they were together, and there were many cars, and stop lights—and the light turned green on their approach and they didn't slow a bit. Instead she split the lane between the cars just starting to go, Hamilton right behind her, and she burst out from between the cars into the clear road in front, and she darted between the cars, weaving, splitting lanes—there, a red light—she glanced right, then left, and boom. She was through, and Hamilton made it too, and she continued, and she could see the Stratosphere tower in the distance, the marker of her victory.

She slowed a bit to weave through stopped traffic at the next light, and then she was through it, and then—a burst of rolling lights. The wail of sirens. The police had been waiting. Two patrol cars. She considered, for a moment, trying to outrun them.

But why bother? She was a George. And her brother Charlie was in town. She pulled over. Stopped. Her body was slick with sweat. Her hands shook. Her teeth clattered. What was wrong with her?

As she came back to herself, she sucked in a breath. Hamilton. She'd gotten Hamilton in trouble.

She kicked down the stand and pulled off her helmet. At least the cop had enough manners to try to hide his surprise that she was a girl.

Chapter Thirteen

At the knocking on the hotel room door, hope lit in Sandy's chest, and that hope surprised him more than he thought possible. He stood, and he hoped that Miranda would be on the other side of that door.

He hoped hard.

Too hard for someone who'd just decided to walk away from her for good.

The reasonable part of his brain knew that she wouldn't be knocking on her own door. She'd be using her key, storming in, and tearing them apart with her fierce mouth.

But he hoped, regardless.

Charlie opened the door, and John stood there looking a little nervous.

Actually, John looked a lot nervous.

"What happened?" Sandy asked.

"I saw her." John entered, the door falling closed behind him.

John dropped into the chair across from Sandy's spot on the couch. Charlie took the other chair, the one in between them, facing the windows.

"You saw her?" Charlie said. "When?"

"I was with her when you called."

Charlie rose part-way from his seat as though he might attack

John with his hands. John didn't react at all. He seemed too defeated to defend himself.

"Why didn't you tell us?" Sandy asked.

"She and I made a deal. She'd talk to me if I wouldn't tell you she was with me. It seemed like a good idea."

Charlie fell back in his chair, considering. "Yeah, okay. Where is she now?"

"I don't know. She was leaving the hotel. She looked like she was dressed to ride her bike."

Charlie grabbed his phone from the coffee table and dialed. When no one answered, he swore. "Hamilton. The valet. My money's on him."

Sandy agreed. But he was also expecting a more reliable, well-paid confirmation.

"I asked her if she was planning on killing herself," John said.

Charlie raised his eyebrows in surprise.

"She said she didn't know." John looked, in a phrase, torn up. His eyes were red-rimmed. His hair disheveled. His posture slouched as though he couldn't find the strength to sit upright any more.

Could it be possible that John had fallen in love with Miranda in a week? Sandy thought back over his life, thought of the relationships he'd tripped into and crashed out of. Of course it was possible. When it came to love, anything was possible.

Look at himself, right now. He was about to do something very stupid.

"I think we all need to be completely honest with each other," Sandy said. "We've all been keeping secrets."

"Sandy," Charlie said, his tone a warning.

"It's fine," Sandy said. "He should know. And you've got to be honest with us, too."

"I'm not keeping secrets," Charlie said.

"Yes, he is." John said. "Miranda told me."

Sandy turned to John. "Miranda spent the night with me on Saturday. The night before she left."

John's brown eyes seemed to darken in pain, even more than he'd been in before. Sandy hated putting the pain there. He could tell that John was a good kid.

"I think she did it to alienate the people who care about her—people like you. And Daphne and Greta. All of you."

John nodded, considering his words. "Thanks for telling me. I would have looked like an ass being the only one left in the dark."

"That's not why I told you. I wanted you to know what happened, sure, but I also wanted you to know why."

John laughed sadly. "You let a twenty-something girl manipulate you into bed. Sure thing, Mr. Martin."

Sandy nodded, taking the hit. He deserved it. Even if John's assessment was more accurate than John could possibly know.

Sandy's phone rang. He looked at the screen, seeing an unfamiliar number with a Las Vegas area code. He answered.

"She just left the hotel, Mr. Martin. She was on her motorcycle, which we were surveilling outside the hotel. Another rider on a motorcycle joined her, and they headed south."

"On the highway?"

"No, on Las Vegas Boulevard, and then into the desert. We were," he paused. "We followed but were unable to keep up."

Sandy shook his head, wondering just how fast Miranda and Hamilton had been traveling. "Keep me posted."

"We have lookouts at the hotel and south of town where we lost sight of them. We'll find them again."

Sandy hung up. Marlon had texted earlier that the security firm was the best in town, that they interfaced with the police and with casino security, and that they, in Marlon's words, "weren't creepy." Apparently not being creepy was what made them so expensive.

Charlie looked at him expectantly.

"She did leave with Hamilton. They were both on motorcycles. The security firm lost track of them."

"She rides that thing like she's being hunted," John said. "It makes me crazy." John turned to Charlie. "Miranda was pissed that you told us about killing your mom. She said that your family had covered up a murder to protect you."

Charlie looked surprised. "That's partially true. I probably would have been charged with voluntary manslaughter, not murder—not that they would have had a chance of winning the case."

"Are you always so smug?" John asked.

Sandy nearly laughed.

Charlie smiled. "Miranda gets pissed when I do things she considers risky. Obviously there's a double standard. She gets to do whatever she wants." He waved his hand out the window toward the desert where she was risking her life on a motorcycle. "And telling you what I did wasn't actually a risk."

"You don't think that telling us that your family covered up a felony is risky?" John asked.

Sandy smiled, anticipating the answer.

"Nope." Charlie didn't hesitate a moment. "You're both here, for her. You wouldn't betray Miranda like that. And besides, no one would believe y'all over us anyway." He looked at Sandy. "Not even you."

Sandy was really starting to wonder who these Georges were. He was going to have Marlon look into them as soon as they returned to L.A.

With Miranda.

"I'm hungry," Sandy said. He turned to Charlie. "I'm guessing you're not willing to leave the room."

Charlie shook his head.

"Let's order up, then. Who knows how long we have to wait for her to get tired of tearing around the desert."

————

Two hours later, their food had come and gone. It was after midnight, approaching one a.m. Sandy was reading a magazine. John had his laptop out.

Charlie was standing by the window, tapping his foot. He couldn't sit still. He wanted a drink, but he needed to stay sharp.

Sandy's phone rang. Charlie turned, watching him closely. First, his face showed an expression of pleasure. Then one of frustration. But the pleasure remained, too.

They'd found her.

"Where is she?" Charlie asked when Sandy hung up.

"Metro has her."

Metro. The Las Vegas police.

"What'd she do?" Charlie demanded, grabbing his own phone from the table.

"Street racing. She's been charged with a misdemeanor, along with our friend Hamilton."

"If anything will get her to call me, it's getting arrested."

"She hasn't called you yet, though, has she?" John closed the lid to the laptop, not bothering to hide the snark in his voice. "Why not?"

Charlie didn't have an answer for John, and he was pissed at John for pointing it out. Instead of showing his anger, he made a call of his own. His dad answered after two rings, impressive given the late hour back home.

"I've found her. She's been arrested in Las Vegas. Who do we have here?"

"Simone Dorton." His father didn't even have to think about it. Over the years, the Georges had spent a lot of time in Las Vegas, and in that time, they'd made a lot of friends. "Do I need to call?" his father asked. Implied in the question was a follow-up: *Or can you handle it?*

"I've got it."

Charles Senior merely grunted.

"I'll keep you posted."

"I'm sure you will have no problems. I'll text you Simone's mobile and text her to expect your call."

Charlie hung up, not at all surprised by his father's reaction—or rather, his lack of reaction. Charles George, Sr., was cold, distant, calculating, and efficient. His daughter inherited only the final two traits. Her warmth, and her presence, kept Charlie sane. He needed to see her now. He needed to know that she was okay.

"Do you know where she's being held?" he asked Sandy.

"Yeah." Sandy held up his phone with an address in a text message.

"Let's go."

———

Twenty minutes later, they arrived at the block-shaped, bunker-like building with tall, narrow windows and bullet-proof glass doors. John, riding in the back seat again, had considered asking to be left behind. After all, what did he have to offer here? Back in L.A., he'd believed he had something special to bring on this trip—a connection with Miranda that none of these people had—but he'd been wrong. Sandy had made that clear in the hotel room, even if that hadn't been his intent.

But in the end, John hadn't had a choice about coming along to the police station. They'd checked out of the hotel, bringing their bags and Miranda's things, too. There was no being left behind. According to Charlie, they were leaving Las Vegas tonight.

They arrived at the station and parked. As they walked toward the entrance, Charlie was on the phone with the lawyer, getting some sort of run-down. The lawyer was on her way, but Charlie had been deputized somehow. His job was to get himself in the room with Miranda and to get her to shut up if she was talking. Charlie had said something like, *As if my sister would be that stupid*, but then he'd listened some more. He hung up before they entered the station.

They passed through the glass front doors, Charlie first, Sandy second, and John last. Charlie approached the officer manning the desk and gave his sister's name. "I'm part of her legal team," he said, passing a business card. "I need a consultation with my client."

"Just a moment," the desk officer said, typing into a terminal. "Please wait there." She nodded to an array of chairs.

They waited.

After twenty minutes, a tall Latino officer emerged though a metal door. He carried a folded piece of paper in his hand. "Counsel for Miranda George?"

Charlie stood. The officer approached, handing Charlie the paper. Handwritten on the outside were the words *"Confidential: For Eyes of Counsel."*

"Excuse me," Charlie said to the officer. "Private business. I'll be right with you." The officer stepped back and waited by the metal door.

Charlie read the note. He looked annoyed.

"What does it say?" Sandy said.

"It says," Charlie said, sighing, "that I have to take Hamilton on as a client, too, and furthermore, I have to guarantee that he gets off with no charges whatsoever, not even an arrest on his record, or she'll confess to something catastrophic and go to prison on purpose."

"I guess you have two clients, then," John said.

"I guess I do." Charlie turned back to the officer. "I'll meet with my clients now. This note informed me that I have two clients here—you arrested two individuals together. My team represents them both."

The metal door buzzed, and Charlie passed through it as though he'd done it a thousand times before. John was left in the waiting area of a Las Vegas police station with Sandy Martin, the person he least wanted to be with in the world right then.

They sat in silence, with one empty chair between them. After a while, a small, dark-haired woman came barreling through the glass front door and nodded at the desk officer. She didn't even pause as she reached for the metal door—which unlocked before her hand hit the handle.

Sandy nodded at the closed door. "My guess—that's their local counsel."

"Seems right." John did not want to make small talk with Sandy. He wanted to punch the wall and leave. He'd never wanted to punch a wall before in his life.

"I'm glad she's safe," Sandy said.

"Please stop."

Sandy paused. "Stop talking?"

John nodded, keeping his eyes on the beige wall across the way.

Sandy did.

Half an hour passed. Waiting like this—with Sandy, for Miranda—was torture. And he was hungry again.

John stood. "I'm going to get food."

"Mind if I join you?"

"Of course I mind." He rubbed his face with his hand. "Whatever. Come on. Charlie left you with the keys anyway. You have to come."

"I can give you the keys."

"Let's just go and not make a thing about it."

Sandy nodded and led the way out to the car. They were well off the Strip here, and fast food was easy to locate. They picked the first spot they came to. As John ordered a burger, he watched the young man taking the order do a double-take at Sandy. He could tell that the kid wasn't sure if he was seeing what he thought he was seeing. After all, what would Alexander Martin be doing at a hole-in-the-wall burger joint in middle-of-nowhere Vegas at two a.m.? It didn't make sense.

"It's him," John said to the kid. "You're right."

"Oh," the kid said.

"You should ask him what he's doing here. It's a great story."

The kid shook his head. "I—I'll get your drink."

Sandy whispered to John. "What are you doing?"

"Fucking with you, obviously." He grabbed his tray and headed to a table.

Sandy joined him a moment later, holding no tray—only a cup of coffee. He sat across from John. "OK, let's have it," Sandy said. "Charlie already laid into me back at the hotel. You can have a go. I don't mind."

"No thanks." John was rapidly losing his appetite.

"Really. I insist. In fact, we can take turns." Sandy had a strange gleam in his eye, like he was taking aim with a weapon. "I'll go first." Sandy sipped from his Styrofoam cup as though the coffee were the finest brew. "You're pissed that I got there first. I mean, what guy wants to be second, right?"

John coughed like he'd been punched. No. That wasn't it at all. Sandy was crazy. John shook his head.

"Oh, good," Sandy said. "I'm glad that wasn't it. If you were being territorial, or had some hang-up about a girl's virtue or some nonsense, I'd have run you off."

John looked at him, feeling sullen. He knew Sandy could have run him off. Sandy had made a single phone call and raised a small army in a city that wasn't even his. In like ten minutes.

"Was that some sort of stupid test?" John said.

"I don't think it was stupid." The gleam was gone from Sandy's eyes. All that was left was the familiar kindness. "Miranda came to me. She was everything you know her to be. I explicitly asked her about you."

"You did?"

"Yes. I did."

"This isn't making me feel better."

"And then that was that. I'm not telling you anything more. She can if she wants to. The next morning, she picked a fight with Marlon, then with me, then with Daphne, and Marlon again. Then she blew out of town. The only person she didn't pick a fight with was you."

"But she slept with you."

"On purpose, as a ploy."

"I refused to sleep with her," John said. "Every time the opportunity arose, it was so obviously not the way to her heart."

"And you wanted her heart."

John nodded, feeling more clearheaded than he had since they'd gotten in the car yesterday afternoon.

"It seems like you're the only one who has been making smart decisions where Miranda is concerned. She's lucky to have you in her life."

"I know you're only saying these things to make me feel better, but it's also working."

Sandy took another sip of coffee. "I'm not saying them for you. I'm saying them for her."

John felt his appetite return. He grabbed his burger and took a bite.

Chapter Fourteen

Miranda stood next to Hamilton in the parking lot of the police station, plotting the murder of her brother. Arrayed in front of her were Charlie, Sandy, and John. She could not believe what she was hearing.

She would miss Charlie when he was dead, she thought, but it would be worth it. He would join all the other dead bodies hidden in the Las Vegas desert.

Her temper rose even higher. He'd brought Sandy and John to the police station in the middle of the night? And he hadn't warned her? He'd let her find out by stumbling out into the waiting room and just finding them there? Together? Like they were the best of friends? She'd just spent hours in jail. She was filthy and smelly and pissed off.

Charlie was a dead man, and that fact had nothing to do with her diagnosis. It had to do with revenge. He should have warned her. But he hadn't. He knew she hated surprises, and he'd surprised her with this. She knew him well enough to know he'd done it on purpose to get back at her.

Fine. She'd bide her time and then—poison? Poison seemed too kind.

Hours ago, after she'd passed her scribbled note to Charlie via Officer Alvarez, Alvarez had brought her to the meeting room from her holding cell. Ever since her booking, she'd been in a holding cell with a sex worker named Janie. Janie was about Miranda's own age, and she'd been arrested four times for solicitation or suspicion thereof, but never convicted. Miranda had almost insisted that Charlie get Janie out too, but Janie assured Miranda that she didn't need help. One of her regular clients was a big time lawyer, she said, and he was already on his way.

When Alvarez called Miranda's name, she high-fived Janie and headed out to meet Charlie. She had no doubt that she was seeing the holding cell for the last time. After all, this is what Georges specialized in: getting people out of trouble who deserved to be in trouble.

She felt an immediate rush of fear for Hamilton. He did not deserve to be in trouble. She'd meant what she'd written in her note. If he didn't get off clean, completely clean, including the arrest record, then she wasn't leaving this jail. She knew that law students were required to report all recorded arrests on their bar applications, so this arrest needed to have never existed at all. She owed him that.

Miranda was from the American South. She knew all about black men getting in trouble for white women's crimes.

Not this time.

She entered the room, and Charlie stood from the table.

Seeing him, even after only a week, made her lose her balance. She gripped the edge of the metal table as her knees wobbled.

"Little B," she said, covering her emotions as best she could, knowing that Charlie would read them anyway.

He didn't say anything. He just looked at her. She read his emotions, too—the fear she'd put him through, the worry, the gut-wrenching sadness. All of it was there, all of it caused by her.

She wanted to hug him, but now was not the time.

Instead, she sat in the chair next to him. She knew the drill. The chair across the table from them was for the other side. The police. The prosecutor. They'd be cutting a deal tonight.

"Are you done with your escapade?" Charlie masked his fear with sarcasm.

"Oh my god." She raised her eyebrows in false surprise. "You sound precisely like Dad."

He banged his fist on the table. "Jesus Christ, Miranda. I was scared."

She frowned. "Much better. That doesn't sound like Dad."

"Will you please take this seriously?"

"Which part? The arrest? I am taking it seriously. I called you."

"You didn't call me, actually. Sandy's security firm did."

"Sandy has a security firm tailing me?"

"He has since we arrived last night."

"I would have called you if you hadn't come." She rested her elbows on the table. "And I passed you a note. That counts."

"I'm not talking about the arrest."

"Well, we should be talking about the arrest, since that's what we're here for, and we don't have much time."

"One of our people is coming to join us."

Miranda rolled her eyes. "Please don't say *our people* around anyone who knows me. It's embarrassing."

"Why, Miranda? It's who we are. We're people who have people. It never used to bother you."

"It always bothered me." It was true. Just after college, with her first and only boyfriend, Matthias, she'd hidden her identity from him at first. She hadn't let him come to her house. She hadn't wanted him to know that she lived in a house with *wings.* She'd been afraid Matthias would hate her. After all, she hated herself.

It turned out Matthias hadn't hated her. They'd spent nearly five years not-hating each other. But after he'd moved to Raleigh to work for a federal judge, their relationship couldn't withstand the distance. Or rather, she felt guilty holding him to it—he'd been perfectly happy driving back and forth to Winston-Salem on the weekends.

One day she broke it off. Six months later, her mother was dead.

And now she was in a Las Vegas Metro police station waiting to hear what kind of deal *her people* could cut.

What would her ex-boyfriend Matthias say if he could see her now?

The door to the room busted open and a short, dark-haired woman stormed in. Charlie stood. Miranda merely raised her eyebrows.

"Simone?" Charlie asked.

"The George children. Hello."

She dropped a paper file and a leather portfolio on the metal table. "Here's what they have on you. It isn't much."

They'd charged her with street racing, a steep charge, but really all they had was enough for a reckless driving charge. "The aggravating factor was that you two were racing around other vehicles. And pedestrians, most of whom were tourists."

Miranda kept her face blank.

"So what's the deal?" Charlie asked.

"The deal is this: They wanted a $5000 fine, one year suspended license, and to impound the vehicle. I countered with a $2000 fine and six months suspended license. They accepted."

Charlie pulled out his checkbook and slapped it on the table in front of Miranda. "I'll meet you outside," he said. Obviously he expected her to accept the deal.

Obviously.

The door slammed shut behind him.

"You have any questions?" Simone asked once they were alone.

Miranda shook her head.

"You have someone who can tow your vehicle?"

"I'm sure we'll figure something out."

Simone paused, her brown-black eyes assessing. "Why is Miranda George street racing a motorcycle up Las Vegas Boulevard?"

"Perhaps because she's Miranda George."

Simone's brows pulled together. She wasn't satisfied with Miranda's answer. But she wasn't being paid to be Miranda's therapist, and Miranda wasn't interested in being her patient. So Miranda kept her eyes on the metal table and waited for the most important part.

"Shall I tell them you accept the plea?"

"Not yet." Miranda glanced up.

Simone drew her eyebrows together, suppressing her frustration. "Why not?"

"What's happened to Hamilton?"

Simone's expression softened, so much that Miranda almost didn't recognize her as the same person. Simone extracted a piece of paper from her leather portfolio—Miranda's note to Charlie from earlier. "Are you in love?"

Miranda scoffed. "No."

"Why do you care?"

"He's a good person."

"He's being released unconditionally and the arrest won't appear on his record. I've requested to be kept out of the loop on that particular negotiation."

Ah, Charlie handled it, then. With a donation to the Las Vegas Police widow's fund, perhaps. Those always worked, if they were big enough.

"Tell them I accept the plea."

Simone stood, tucking her portfolio and Miranda's file back into her brief bag. When she opened the door, she nodded to Officer Alvarez who was standing outside. The metal door slammed, and Miranda was alone once more.

After another hour of waiting, Miranda wished she were back in her holding cell with Janie. She wanted someone to talk to. She wanted advice for how to explain things to her brother. Now that Charlie was here, now that she'd seen him, she was embarrassed. Her whole life had been a study in control. But now she was so out of control. The death of her mother had snapped her leash that tied her to her family, sure, but there was something more.

It was the other thing, the thing she didn't want to think about. The thing that killed her mother, the thing that pulled the throttle on her motorcycle and pushed her over one-twenty coming back through that desert, pushed her faster and faster, harder and harder, higher and higher.

And she was letting it push her. She couldn't stop it.

That thing had killed her mother. Not Charlie. Sorcha's autopsy report bore no lies, no matter who pulled the trigger.

The metal door squeaked open. Officer Alvarez nodded to her. "Come with me."

He led her to the processing desk where Simone met her. Simone gave her back her personal effects. Miranda had to sign some papers, too, which she carefully read, stipulating that her license suspension crossed state lines—but she knew that already.

"My job is done," Simone said. "Should I bill your dad?"

"Probably not. Text Charlie. He'll handle it."

"Already stepping into your father's shoes, is he?"

Miranda didn't answer. The thought made her both sad—she hated the idea that her brother would become anything like her father —and resentful—she was jealous that Charlie had been building a profession while she'd been babysitting their family.

"I'm going to use the bathroom," Miranda lied. "Thanks for your help." She needed a minute to get her head around the conversation Charlie was going to want to have with her. He was probably already arranging a NetJet to take them home from McCarran. She wondered how long it would take them to have a plane ready. And then she'd have to sit next to him in that tiny fuselage for hours while he grilled her about everything she'd done over the past week and a half.

She resolved right then—she was not getting on a plane. She was not returning to North Carolina.

After Simone left the bustling hallway, Miranda slipped on her white leather jacket and ran her fingers through her short hair to loosen up the tangles that still clung after her nighttime ride. She looked at the people working the desks—booking arrests, releasing others—and she knew, despite anything Charlie might say, she was no different than they were.

She headed out, the desk officer buzzing her through the large metal door into the waiting room, where Charlie sat with Sandy and John.

Why hadn't Charlie told her Sandy and John were at the station with him? Why did he bring them? She hadn't been expecting to see them. She'd been expecting time. A shower first, at the very least. And John had been with Sandy this whole time. What had they been talking about?

Seeing them all together, here, was too much.

They all stood when she emerged, the three of them looking bizarrely happy to be sitting in a Las Vegas police station in the middle of the night.

"No," she said. "I can't handle all of you right now. Go outside."

"What?" Charlie said.

"Has Hamilton come out yet?" she demanded.

"What? No." Charlie said.

"Go outside. I'm not leaving till Hamilton does." A part of her still needed proof.

She thought they would argue with her. But then Sandy walked out the door, and the other two followed him.

She sat in one of the plastic chairs and waited, her helmet on the seat next to her. Not long after, Hamilton came through the door. For a moment, she feared he would hate her. But then he smiled and sat in the seat next to her.

"Hey, speed demon," he said.

"I'm so sorry."

"So, my charges were magically dropped, and the arrest struck from my record. I'm clean as a whistle."

"I got fined and lost my license."

"Ouch. I'm sorry."

"Why? It was my fault we got caught."

Hamilton, thankfully, didn't argue with her. "I guess if a person is going to get caught doing what we did, it's good to get caught with you."

"I guess." She frowned. "It's better to not get caught, though."

Hamilton laughed. "Then you are off your game, girl. You don't race up the Strip. You do that out in the desert. It's what the desert's for."

Hamilton said something about getting food, but she didn't hear him. She could only focus on what he'd said, and how right he'd been. *She was off her game.* Everything was off. Her precision focus. Her running of the odds. Her goddamned ability to make decisions. She was off. And that scared her.

Hamilton stood. "Come on, Speedy."

She followed him outside, where her annoying entourage waited by a black BMW with Ohio plates. A rental car then. Charlie's.

Hamilton nodded at the guys, and they all greeted him. They were best of fucking friends. She rolled her eyes. Between Charlie and Sandy, they would have been able to get anyone to sell her out, even someone as cool as Hamilton.

So she began to plot Charlie's murder. Poison was definitely too kind. He deserved something painful, and unexpected.

John hadn't sold her out, though. Even when she'd been sitting right there with him at the bar earlier that night. Charlie had called, and he'd lied to her brother for her. John was someone she could count on.

She shoved the thought from her head. She didn't want to feel warm toward John right now. She didn't want to feel warm toward anyone.

She shook her head to clear it. "One of you call a cab for Hamilton, and then pay for it. Preferably one of you rich people."

John coughed to cover a laugh.

Hamilton started to say that he'd be okay calling a friend. She interrupted him. "Please let me abuse these assholes a little bit. They're going to give me hell for four hours in that tiny car."

Sandy pulled out his phone and dialed a number. He spoke for a few moments, and then hung up. "A car will be here shortly to take you where you need to go."

"Well, our bikes are way the hell out in an impound lot near the Air Force base. And they don't open for pickups till tomorrow. So I guess I'm heading home."

"Wait," Miranda said, fishing around in her bag. She pulled out a black ball point pen and the title to her bike. She flipped the title over, leaning on the hood of her brother's car. "What's your last name?" she asked Hamilton.

"His last name is Hamilton," her brother said. "His first name is Sam. Samuel."

She scribbled on the back of the title. Signed her name. Handed it to him. "I know this seems crazy," she said to him. "But it really isn't if you know the bigger picture."

Hamilton grinned at her. "I live in Las Vegas, Miranda. This isn't crazy at all." He folded the title and tucked it inside his jacket. "I'm going to give you six months to change your mind, though."

"You should pay off your student loans now. They're accruing interest."

"Who says I have student loans?"

It was Sandy who coughed to cover a laugh this time.

"You know what? Every one of you can go to hell." She turned her back on them and walked to the edge of the parking lot. She could hear Hamilton's voice, joking with her brother, her kind-of boyfriend, and her one-night-stand as though they were all jolly good friends.

She hated them all.

She needed Daphne, she realized. Daphne would tell them why they were being assholes. She'd be able to explain it clearly, so that their small man-brains could understand. They would listen to Daphne. None of this was funny. They thought they'd saved her. They thought they'd won. They hadn't won anything.

But she'd lost.

No. She *was* lost.

She crossed her arms, feeling cold now in the nighttime desert air. The breeze blew across the back of her neck, raising the small hairs there, and she started to feel light-headed. She looked up at the stars, the ones that were still visible despite the bright lights of the casinos, and they spun for her.

A few minutes later, a black Town Car pulled into the lot. Sandy spoke with the driver.

Hamilton came over to her. "I guess that's my ride."

"Most people have loans for law school."

"I do have loans. I was just messing with you."

She looked away from him. She felt brittle.

"I meant it about keeping your bike for six months. You might want it back."

She looked at the three dudes waiting for her. "You should sell it." She didn't say that she could always buy a new one if she wanted. She didn't say that maybe next time she'd get a Ducati like his. She didn't say that she most likely wouldn't be buying another motorcycle at all. She didn't say so many things.

Hamilton nodded. He took her helmet from her outstretched hand, and headed to the Town Car. The car pulled slowly from the lot. As it did, she felt her temper flare. She was grateful. The anger fused her broken bits back together, energized her.

She strolled back over to her brother. Sandy and John were leaning against the trunk, waiting, it seemed, for a George sibling showdown.

They weren't wrong.

"Getting rid of that bike was the smartest thing you've done all day," Charlie said.

"Fuck you, Charlie."

"I'm surprised you're not more grateful for my legal assistance."

"You were doing your job, you moron." She crossed her arms. "And not very well. How am I supposed to live in L.A. without a license?"

"Get in the car, and we'll talk about it."

She shook her head. "I don't want to ride with you people."

"Like you just said, you can't exactly rent a car."

"I'll take the bus. It runs every thirty minutes. Even you know that." They'd taken it together once, a day trip from Las Vegas to L.A., when they'd been in high school. Their parents had never found out.

"That bus was disgusting. Stop being difficult."

She cracked up laughing. "This—this is the difficult part? The fact that you can't get me into your car?" After everything else—her disappearing, the cross-country flights, his teaming up with strangers, Sandy's security firm, the getting her out of jail?

Arguing was easy. It was familiar. They'd been doing it for decades.

That was, perhaps, why she wanted to do it.

He turned his back on her and ran his hands through his hair, pain evident in every line of his body.

In that moment, watching his suffering, the realization hit her. She didn't want to hurt Charlie. Her anger flooded from her body, leaving her weak.

She loved Charlie. He was her Little B. He was annoying, and arrogant, but he was her best friend. Seeing him tonight, she knew there was no way she could hurt herself, not on purpose, anyway. Not the way she'd been planning to on this trip to Las Vegas. If Charlie hadn't come, she might very well be dead. But he had come, and she'd seen him, and he'd reminded her of how much they both needed each other.

She'd try, for him.

She stepped up to him and put her hand on his shoulder. "I'm sorry. I'll get in the car."

He looked down at her, his eyebrows raised with relief.

"I get shotgun," she said. There was no way she was sitting next to John or Sandy, not when it was so clear that John knew about her night with Sandy. And not while she was smelling like jail.

Chapter Fifteen

Just as the sun was rising on Tuesday morning, they traveled down the 10 heading west into downtown L.A. One week ago, Miranda had arrived in Los Angeles. And here she was, arriving again.

Miranda watched the sun's reflection ticking off the tops of the tallest glass buildings ahead of them, the sky slowly turning pink. It was early enough that traffic was still moving fast, so Charlie was able to blaze past the downtown exits, making his way toward the West Side.

"Wait," she said. "Where are we going?"

"Back to Daphne's," Charlie said.

"Why? I don't want to go there." She'd spent the last four hours thinking about the look on Daphne's face when she'd told Daphne that she'd spent the night with Sandy—the look of guilt when Miranda had accused Daphne of believing Miranda was not good enough.

Miranda had been thinking about how she agreed with Daphne.

She wasn't good enough.

"I'll get us a suite at the W," Charlie said. "We can shower and sleep and then fly home."

Miranda choked on a laugh. "I'm not going home."

Charlie pressed his lips together as he passed a slow-moving G-Wagon. "What do you propose, then?"

She didn't know. She just knew that Daphne's house—in part due to the ever-present Marlon—was out of the question. She knew that going home to North Carolina was certainly out of the question. She could go someplace else entirely. She could pick some small town and disappear.

But there was the matter of the three bottles of pills in her bag. She didn't know if she could make this next part of her journey alone.

As they passed the exit for La Brea, Sandy spoke. "Let's head to my place. We can make a decision while drinking coffee."

"There is no 'we' in this decision," Miranda said. "Just because you all fancy yourself some kind of douchebag cavalry doesn't mean you can tell me what to do."

"I, for one, would never tell you what to do," John said.

"I hate you too, John," she said.

Damn, she was grumpy.

Sandy gave Charlie directions north to Sunset, north again to Laurel Canyon, then to his midcentury cliff-side palace. Charlie parked in the drive out front.

Miranda climbed from the car, eyeing Charlie as he took in Sandy's house, its sprawling façade of pale stucco, dark wood siding, and impossibly large windows. The house stood three stories tall, and then tumbled down the canyon beyond. To the left, she knew from her experience Saturday night, were Sandy's rooms. To the right were the myriad first-floor guest rooms. In the middle were the living areas, kitchen, and dining room, enough public space to host over a hundred people for Greta's wedding without things feeling crowded. And that was just on the first floor. Too bad she'd never see what was upstairs, or what was in the walk-out level below. She had a feeling there was a pool.

Charlie nodded, his eyes narrowing in a way that Miranda knew echoed a look Miranda sometimes made, and she could tell he was impressed. The expression on Charlie's face was the most you'd ever get from a George.

Sandy opened his unlocked door and headed inside, greeting his dogs and sending them to their beds.

Miranda took in the familiar gray leather furniture, the large painting in the foyer that she knew had been done by Marlon, even though neither he nor Sandy would ever tell you. Straight ahead were the floor-to-ceiling sliding glass doors that opened onto the deck overlooking the city where she and Sandy had had drinks only a couple of nights ago.

How was she back here already?

In the kitchen, Sandy invited everyone to sit at his table, an overly long affair of thick boards bolted to heavy trestles. It could have sat twenty people. The four of them crowded at one end. Sandy pulled out his phone and placed a call for food to be delivered.

"Breakfast will be here in ten," he said.

Miranda stood. "I'm taking a shower. I smell like I've been incarcerated." She headed for the guest wing. "If someone wants to bring me my bag, that'd probably be a good thing." She didn't wait for an answer though. She figured there'd be a bathrobe if no one showed up with her stuff.

She entered the first bedroom she came to, done up in shades of blue. It faced the back of the house, so it had doors that opened onto the deck. She opened the doors. There was a breeze, and it felt good. She stood in the middle of the room, letting the air waft around her. She started stripping, throwing her dirty clothes on the floor—her jacket, her shirt and bra, then her boots, socks, and jeans. She stepped closer to the open door, resting her hands on either side of the doorway, not caring if anyone saw her nakedness, and the breeze became a live thing rushing over her body, dancing over every tiny hair on her arms and legs and back. She shut her eyes and let the air wash over her, imagining it lifting her, carrying her over the edge of the deck and into the air above the valley. She could drift away on an updraft. It would be so pleasant. So—relaxing. She stepped forward onto the deck, closer to the railing. Her hands gripped the top rail. She set a foot on the bottom rung. Then another foot on the next rung. Another. She let go with her hands, the breeze lifting her, holding her.

"Miranda, what are you doing?" Charlie's voice snapped her out of her reverie.

She turned, hopping onto the deck. He grabbed her arm and dragged her back into the bedroom. She jerked her arm free, taking her bag from him. He hadn't seen her naked in years, but she didn't care. There'd been a time when they'd had little modesty between them. What difference did it make now? Now that she was so close to the edge of everything? When a breeze could blow her off of Sandy's deck?

"Thank you. Now get out."

He sat on the bed with his back to her. "I'll wait."

"I'm not a child."

"I'm not treating you like a child. I'm treating you like the sister I can't bear to lose." His words held both pain and persistence.

Both caused her to relent. "Fine. I'll probably be a while."

"I don't know why. You cut off all your hair."

"I did, didn't I." She smiled. She liked her short hair. She felt weightless. She thought of the tempting breeze, and she shivered.

After her twenty-minute shower in Sandy's decadent grotto of a bathroom, she emerged in the bathrobe she'd expected to find. She grabbed her toothbrush from her bag and brushed her teeth. Charlie had reclined on the bed, arms behind his head.

"If you stay in L.A., I'm staying too. I'll get an internship at a firm here."

"You have to finish law school, you dodo."

"I can do that easy. I fly back for finals, and I'm done. Believe me, I can miss the final few weeks of my 3L year. It's no big deal."

"Why would you stay here to babysit me?"

"Why wouldn't I? You're acting like a baby."

She frowned. "Not a baby."

He paused, and then nodded. "Not a baby."

"I don't want to get dressed. This robe is comfy."

"Leave it on then."

"Sandy told John about Saturday, didn't he." She already knew the answer, but confirmation would be helpful.

"Yep."

"Did John freak out?"

"Totally. I think he's in love with you."

Miranda rolled her eyes. "You always think that."

"And you never do. You constantly underestimate yourself. Why is that?"

"I don't know." She'd never thought about it before. Another thing to add to her list of problems to solve. Did she not believe in love? Or did she not believe that she could be loved?

"Don't fool around with Sandy again. That's not a good idea."

"Don't tell me what to do. I fuck whom I feel like."

Charlie started to get annoyed, and she watched as he visibly restrained his emotions. "Please, Miranda. Cut that off."

"Are you going to tell him the same thing?"

"Yes. And in a more threatening fashion."

Miranda scoffed. "Sandy's not afraid of you."

Charlie paused. "When it comes to you, maybe he should be."

Miranda put her hand on Charlie's arm. "At some point you have to stop being so protective."

"Five minutes ago you were about to jump off the deck!"

Miranda tapped her lip, thoughtful. "I'll take your words under advisement."

"Fine," he said. "Lead the way." He gestured out of the room.

"Lost already?"

"Please," he said. "This house is smaller than ours."

"But the garage is way better."

"Granted."

She padded out of the bedroom on her bare feet, Charlie following behind. They'd reached a truce, and Miranda felt relief. Together, over the decades, she and Charlie had been able to face anything. And he'd come for her. He wasn't letting her go. He was her Little B. And she loved him.

After changing into clean clothes, Sandy answered the door when the bell rang. He greeted the delivery kid from the café down the street, taking the bag with the four meal boxes and four cups of coffee. He tipped the kid in cash and then turned back to the kitchen.

He refused to think of Miranda George, naked in one of his showers. Would she have chosen the green room, with its speckle-glazed, terra-cotta tile he'd found on a trip to Mexico and laid himself around the cast iron tub? Or the yellow room, with the clerestory windows in the shower? Or the blue room, with the largest shower of them all, a travertine cavern with four shower heads?

She would have chosen the blue room.

In the kitchen, alone once again with John, he set the food boxes on the table along with the coffees. John dug in. Sandy waited for his guests to reemerge. Charlie had grabbed her bag from the car and joined her in the room. He hoped that Charlie would be able to mend whatever had torn them apart. He could tell that their sibling bond was strong, no matter how much Miranda tried to act like it wasn't.

A few minutes later, Miranda and Charlie entered the kitchen. Miranda looked more relaxed than he'd ever seen her. Charlie looked relaxed as well, as though things were turning back to right in his world. Sandy took that as a good sign.

Miranda, however, was in a bathrobe, with presumably nothing underneath, her bare feet and ankles poking out, daring him to look.

Sandy fixed his eyes on John and tried to remember the promise he'd made to himself in Las Vegas. He would step back. He would give Miranda and John a fighting chance.

"Food." Miranda sat down in front of a box. "Coffee." She dumped in cream and then took a guzzle, unbothered by the hot temperature. "Sandy, you always know how to make a girl happy."

Sandy coughed. John shook his head, looking uncomfortable.

Charlie, the asshole, laughed.

"So I'm not staying with Daphne. I'm not going back to North Carolina. Charlie, apparently, is moving to Los Angeles to babysit me. I guess I'll have to get a job and a cheap studio apartment."

"Why don't you want to move back in with Daphne?" John asked, seeming to find that option the most palatable.

"It's obvious that she and Marlon are on the verge of moving in together. She'd take me in because she's a good person. But I don't want to be in their way."

It wasn't obvious to Sandy that Daphne and Marlon were thinking about moving in together. Miranda had said the same thing on Friday night—she must be seeing something he wasn't when it came to Marlon and Daphne. He filed that information away to discuss with Marlon later.

"Why don't we just get a suite at the W like I said?" Charlie asked.

Miranda pressed her lips into an angry line. "No."

"I thought we were past our little spat, sister."

"We are. But I'm not living on Charles Senior's dime anymore."

Charlie looked thoughtful. "One could argue that you've earned it after all these years."

"One could agree with you. My answer remains no."

Sandy's words flew out of his mouth before he could stop them. "You could stay here. Just till you get on your feet."

Sandy never spoke without thinking. He thought it was one of his best qualities. He was careful. Deliberate. Miranda George broke all that down. He couldn't decide if that meant he should run toward her, or away from her.

"No," Charlie and John said, nearly in unison.

"Absolutely," Miranda said. "That is, if you don't mind." She turned to face him. "It's the first thing I've heard that doesn't make me want to run away again."

"It also probably helps that you'd be stuck up on an isolated hill with no car." Sandy chuckled, trying to lighten the mood after his serious offer.

"Don't take her lack of license for granted," Charlie said. "She'd hitchhike."

Sandy raised his eyebrows. "Really?"

"She did it when we were younger, after our parents took her car away as a punishment."

"Only a couple of times. It wasn't that big of a deal." Miranda crossed her arms in the too-big robe.

"What'd she do to lose her car?" Sandy asked.

John shook his head, standing from the table. "This conversation seems to have moved on without me. I'm going to need a ride."

Seeing John's stricken face, Sandy remembered the promise he'd made in Las Vegas, and how he'd just broken it. He hated himself a little bit.

Charlie stood, speaking to Miranda. "I have not agreed to this. I'm going to take him to Daphne's, get a suite at the W, and then I'm coming back for you."

Miranda stood, following him to the front door. "I'll lock the gates to keep you out."

Sandy followed Miranda. He hadn't locked the gates in a decade. He wasn't sure if they even worked.

"Damn it, Miranda," Charlie said, facing off with her in the foyer.

"Cool it, Little B. It's just for a little while. I'd think you'd be happy knowing where I am all the time."

"What I want is for you and me to be together. I'll work at the firm. I'll study for finals this spring, and for the bar exam this summer. We can play tennis and go to the pool—it'll be like home, but better, because we're in Los Angeles instead of crappy Winston-Salem."

"We can still do those things. But I'm living here." She glanced over her shoulder at Sandy, her brown eyes imploring, begging him to stand up for her. This girl had never begged for much in her life, Sandy was sure of that. "Right?"

Sandy could think of nearly a hundred reasons why Miranda George shouldn't stay with him. First, she was vulnerable. Second, she was sexy. Third, despite her vulnerability, he still wanted her badly. Fourth, he did not know, if she made the kind of request that she was making right now, with those eyes of hers that seemed to slice him wide open, whether he'd be able to say no. Like, to anything. Fifth, he definitely would not be able to say no. Sixth, Marlon was going to kill him. Seventh, he would deserve it, just not for the reasons Marlon believed. Eighth, Charlie George would kill him, and he would deserve it for exactly the reasons Charlie George believed.

"Right," Sandy said to Miranda, and her shoulders relaxed.

John was staring at Miranda, looking like someone had just wrecked him. She didn't even notice. She just looked relieved.

"I'll come see you tomorrow," Charlie said.

She nodded.

Charlie grinned, grabbing his sister in a smothering hug, and she hugged him back, arms wrapped around his waist.

Then Charlie and John left, and he and Miranda were alone in his quiet house.

———

Miranda watched her brother and John—she wasn't going to think about John right now—depart. Charlie closed Sandy's front door behind them.

She rested her hand against the back of the sofa and felt immense relief. She couldn't have gone to Daphne's and lived with her anymore—she didn't want to be Marlon's roommate. Even if Marlon didn't officially move in, he would've been there all the time. And staying with Charlie, as much as she loved him, would have meant allowing her father to support her. Living on Charles Senior's dime was too unbearable to even think about. She felt safe at Sandy's house, isolated from everyone who wanted to pull her in different directions. And, if she were being honest, from the people she would be embarrassed to see after the scene she'd made. Sandy's house was luxurious, sure, but she also liked him. Leaving him on Sunday morning had hurt more than she'd thought it would have. And when she'd learned that he'd come for her in Las Vegas, her heart had turned over.

She turned to Sandy. He'd changed while she'd showered. He wore a tight t-shirt and jeans, and his feet were bare.

She reached for him, taking his wrist and pulling him to her.

"You look great dressed down," she said close to his ear, just before she kissed his neck.

He sucked in a breath. "Miranda."

His hands hovered near her arms, as though he weren't sure what to do.

She took the last step forward, pressing her body to his. "I'm here. I'm safe. I'll follow whatever rules you want to set." She smiled. "No hitchhiking." She kissed him. "But please don't make up some bullshit reason that we can't do this."

He wrapped his hands around her upper arms and kissed her back. She shut her eyes, *finally,* relaxing completely for the first time since she'd been dragged into that Las Vegas jail. She might not get any more weed for a while, but she'd get this.

This.

She put her arms around his shoulders, running her fingers up through his hair threaded with silver but still thick, and getting scruffy on the back of his neck. "Come on. Let's go to your room."

"Let's talk first. And you didn't eat any breakfast."

"Talk after."

He pulled his face from hers. "Promise me."

She stepped back from him and untied the robe, letting it fall to the floor.

He rubbed his hand down his face and sighed.

"We can talk after. You can even feed me. I promise I'll eat anything you put in front of me." Miranda frowned. "Except tomatoes. I hate tomatoes."

Sandy turned as though to walk away from her, to leave her standing in his foyer naked, but then he reached back with his hand, *thank god*. She took it and followed him to his room.

An hour later, she was leaning back against his headboard. She stared through his bedroom window at the mid-morning sun and the smog blanketing the city below.

"If you want your privacy," he said, "you can have your pick of the guest suites."

She kept her eyes pinned to the windows, unable to look at him. "I'll sleep in a guest suite if you prefer." She was waiting for him to tell her to take a hike. She was waiting for rejection. She was used to it. Her father had been rejecting her—and Charlie—since forever.

"You can sleep wherever you'd like. I'd be a fool to relegate you to the guest wing."

"Sometimes I can't tell if you're serious." She couldn't, even though she knew that his actions—coming for her in Las Vegas—should have convinced her that he felt perhaps a little more than a passing fancy.

He reached over and put his hand on her chin, forcing her to meet his eyes. "I'd be a fool."

She looked away. "Sure. Fine. I believe you." She didn't believe him, though, not about their sleeping arrangements. Sandy had probably grown accustomed to his own space over the past years. She wouldn't stay in his suite.

She might drop in now and then, but she'd stay in the room she'd showered in. She knew better than to overstay her welcome. She also knew how to make sure that her stock remained high.

She slid from the bed.

"Where are you going?" he asked.

"I thought you wanted me to eat something. You wanted to talk."

He gave her a skeptical look, as though he knew that she was trying to escape anything resembling intimacy. "Right."

"Meet me in the kitchen." She strolled out naked to find the bathrobe.

In the kitchen, she corralled all of the half-full cups of coffee from breakfast that morning and poured them into one ceramic mug, then she put that mug in the microwave to heat it up. After the timer beeped, she pulled the mug from the microwave and took a sip.

"You know, for a princess, you really aren't that picky. We could have made fresh coffee."

She hadn't known he'd been watching her. He was wearing his jeans and t-shirt again, his bare feet moving silently on the floor as he joined her near the cooking area.

"For a king," she said, "neither are you."

"You're referring to yourself?"

She nodded.

He sighed elaborately. "Sit."

She sat on one of the barstools that lined the enormous granite counter, and he sat next to her. "Spill. Everything."

"You already know everything. Don't lie. I can tell Charlie told you. You're looking at me with just enough pity hidden behind the effort to not look at me with pity."

"What happened with your mom was awful. What your life has been like for the past five years—hell, twenty years—has been awful."

Miranda felt a wave of defensiveness. "My mom is amazing." She paused. "Was." She dropped her face in her hands. "She was amazing. She was just sick."

"And now you know you are too."

She couldn't speak. She nodded.

"What are you going to do about it?"

"I don't know," she whispered. "I'm scared."

"Why'd you come to L.A. the day of your mother's funeral? It seems like a strange choice—but you don't seem to do things by accident."

Miranda stood, suddenly unable to contain her emotions. Sandy had just prodded the pressure point that had launched her ill-fated Las Vegas road trip in the first place. "I came here to Daphne's home because I didn't really like Daphne. She was supposed to be flighty and undependable. I needed to get away from the one person I loved most."

"Charlie," Sandy said.

She nodded. "Daphne wasn't supposed to offer me a new family to join." Miranda waved in Sandy's direction. "She wasn't supposed to open a door into a new life full of people I could maybe count on. I've never in my life had people I could count on, except Charlie." Miranda ran her hand through her damp hair. "I see them—Daphne and Marlon, Greta and Timmy, *you*—and all I see is me, holding up a gun."

"There aren't any guns in this house, just so you know."

She had to resist the urge to stamp her foot like a child. "I think you're missing the point. I bought a motorcycle so no one would ask me to drive them places. I didn't want to be responsible for them getting hurt. Back home, I'd been driving more and more recklessly— sometimes. Did you know my mother always took a car service? Now I know why."

"Say what you aren't saying."

How did he know? Maybe Sandy's intuition—and the fact that he wasn't afraid of her—was why she wanted to be around him now. "I should have died. They should have let me die."

He grabbed her by the shoulders, holding so tightly his grip nearly hurt. "No. They shouldn't have."

"I have bipolar disorder. The worst kind. I'm sick, and I know it. I'm not taking my medicine, and I know enough now to know what I'm feeling. I've been hypomanic the whole time I've been here—even diving into mania sometimes. I know it. Any idiot can tell."

"Not a reason to let you die."

"I'm only alive because Charles Senior is a stubborn ass, and he would never let his daughter die. Not because he loves me, but because it would be unseemly."

"I don't know your dad. But I know my fair share of shitty dads."

"Yours."

"Mine. Greta's. Daphne's. You're in the right club."

"What about Marlon's?"

"His adoptive father is great, actually. His own dad died when he was young, but he was all right."

She chewed her lip. "I have a prescription in my bag that the psychiatrist back home wrote for me. Three bottles. A three-month supply. I'm supposed to take it every day, but I never started it. I can't decide if I want to see if I can be better. It seems like such a false hope, too far-fetched to be real."

"How were you planning to kill yourself in Las Vegas?"

Sandy talked about her committing suicide with no hesitation, no choking on the words. She appreciated that. "I was going to take all of the pills at once. It would have worked. I looked it up."

"Why there?"

"I wanted to do it someplace where I wouldn't know anyone. Where I wouldn't hurt anyone, except some strangers who would have to deal with my anonymous body." She looked out the window. "A lot of people go to Las Vegas to die."

"That motorcycle race up the Strip was pretty crazy."

"That wasn't deliberately self-injurious. That was mania."

"So what's changed now? How do I know I'm not going to find you dead in your room tonight?"

Miranda nodded. It was a fair question. "Honestly? Seeing Charlie. If he hadn't come, nothing would be different. But he's my world, always has been. I can't do that to him. When I saw him in Las Vegas, I realized I could never do that to him, not on purpose. Not while I'm," she paused, gesturing at herself, "doing it on purpose. I know the difference."

Sandy nodded. "You're not the first person I've ever met with bipolar disorder, you know."

Miranda eyed him. "I'm sure. That's the worst part. I feel remarkably mediocre and remarkably dangerous at the same time. I'm having a hard time reconciling the two."

Miranda realized then that she was pacing. She hated pacing. Her mother used to pace. She'd pace when she was thinking, when she was excited, when she was trying to figure out a problem. She'd pace when she couldn't sleep. She'd pace and pace and pace.

Miranda used to take care to never, ever pace. But lately, when the urge struck, she'd been unable to stop herself. The feeling was too strong, the feeling that, if she could just move her feet, the churning in her stomach might relent.

Sandy had turned his back to the counter to face her as she walked back and forth the length of his kitchen, releasing the emotions inside of her. Pacing was soothing, but it was also symptomatic.

Damn it. She sat back down on the stool.

"You can stay here as long as you want to," Sandy said. "But I do have rules. Two that I've thought of so far."

She rolled her eyes. "Of course you do."

"No hitchhiking. You're welcome to walk to the shops down the street—we can go together tomorrow so you can learn the way—but if you hitchhike you have to go stay with your brother. No driving, either, obviously. And you have to start taking your medicine like you're supposed to, under the care of a doctor."

"That's four rules."

"I can set as many rules as I want. It's my house."

"Can I bring guys home?"

Sandy coughed like he'd choked on something foul. "What?"

She grinned. "No?"

Sandy looked at her with an assessing gaze, then finally shook his head.

She shrugged. "I guess that's five rules then."

"I guess so. Can you live with that?"

"I can."

That night, under Sandy's supervision, Miranda took her first pill. She climbed into his bed and fell asleep by the lights of Hollywood, wondering, for the first time in years—maybe ever—what her future might look like.

Chapter Sixteen

At ten o'clock the next morning, Wednesday, Miranda woke in Sandy's blue guest room to her phone ringing. She was still exhausted after three straight days with little-to-no sleep. Last night hadn't been very restful.

She'd intended to sleep in Sandy's room. But then, at two a.m., she'd awoken, unable to sleep, anxious, worried about being in Sandy's bed. The insomnia was familiar. So was the anxiety. But she'd been so afraid of bothering Sandy, she'd crept from his room. She'd sat in the living room for a couple of hours, staring outside, mesmerized by the lights, wondering what she was going to do now that she had no anchor, no one who needed her. That wasn't true, though, she'd reminded herself. Charlie was at the W, needing her. Mostly she'd spent the hours concentrating on staying inside. Going out on the deck seemed like a bad idea, like walking on the moon without a space suit. Around four o'clock, sleepiness had crept up on her again, so she'd headed back to the room where she'd showered the day before, and slept there.

John's name flashed on the phone screen. She considered whether she should answer. Half of her wanted to hear his voice more than anything. He was wonderful. He made her want *more*. And that's why the other half of her needed to keep him at a distance.

She flipped the lid open. "Hello."

"Hey." He sounded morose.

She felt sympathetic. "Hey."

"We didn't get a chance to speak alone much the past couple of days. I was wondering if you'd like to have breakfast with me." He paused. "I have some things to say."

Those words sounded ominous. She supposed he deserved to have his say. "Where should we go?"

"Where haven't you been yet?"

"I haven't seen the ocean."

"You haven't?" He sounded surprised, like seeing the Pacific had been the first thing he'd done when his Midwestern self had moved here.

Miranda smiled, picturing the younger John gaping at the ocean. "Nope," she said.

"I'll be there in thirty minutes."

She got up and pulled on her clothes, thinking about sand and ocean water, wishing she had flip-flops to wear. She grabbed some of her cash and stuffed it in her pocket. She'd buy a pair while she was out. Surely there'd be a surf shop.

She left her bed unmade—she never made her bed—and headed out into the living area and into the kitchen. She never did have a chance to figure out the coffee maker the last time she'd been here. She'd been too busy dodging Marlon and making a mad escape.

She was standing in front of the espresso machine, trying to remember any of the Italian she'd picked up on her family's many trips to Europe, when Sandy slid open the deck door and joined her in the kitchen.

"Good morning," he said.

"Can I get a lesson for this thing? Either that or a French press?"

Sandy opened a cabinet door and pulled out a French press, then an electric teakettle.

"Oh, I love you," Miranda said. "Well, not like that, obviously."

"Obviously." He pointed to the machine in front of her. "You can grind the beans using that." He demonstrated, holding the glass container of the French press under the grinder, filling it with the proper amount of coffee, then turning off the grinder. Then he filled the kettle with water, and set about making coffee for them both.

Miranda sat on a stool to watch, noting where he'd gotten mugs, and spoons, and the rest of the supplies she'd need each morning.

"I guess we could text each other to see if we're up in the mornings."

"Or you could come into my room and say hello, considering you were there until two a.m."

She was surprised that Sandy had noticed she'd left. Maybe he was a light sleeper.

"I'm sorry I woke you."

"You didn't have to go," he said.

"I had trouble sleeping."

He studied her to see if she was lying. As though he'd be able to tell—she nearly snorted. Only a George could tell when a George was lying.

But this time, she happened to be telling the truth. Although her anxiety about Sandy—about holding his interest, about whether she was making a terrible mistake about John—might indeed have been one of the reasons she was driven from bed.

"Okay, fine," she said. "I'll just come say hi when I wake up in the morning."

He nodded.

There was a knocking at the front door. Miranda turned toward the door in surprise, but the dogs didn't bark. *Marlon*, she thought. *Crap*.

"One sec," Sandy said, making his way out of the kitchen to answer.

She stayed in the kitchen, readying herself. At least she had on pants this time.

The teapot began to whistle, so she poured the water into the French press and set the lid on top. She needed caffeine if she was going to defend herself against Marlon while she was this sleep-deprived.

But Marlon didn't appear. She heard the murmuring of conversation in the foyer, and then Marlon left. Sandy returned with a white paper bag in his hand.

He dropped the bag in front of her. "I had Marlon pick this up for you."

From the bag, she pulled a pill box, one that could hold two weeks of pills, day and night. It was enormous, plastic, brightly colored, and revolting.

"So you won't forget," Sandy said.

She nodded. She turned the pill box over in her hands. It looked like something an old person would use to keep track of a collection of medication. She didn't need this.

Did she?

"Let's fill it up together," he said.

She couldn't meet his eyes. She realized what she was feeling. Embarrassment. She'd seen the same emotion on her mother's face hundreds of times over the years. She was embarrassed that her brain was broken.

"Miranda," Sandy called, snapping her attention to him. "Don't be a chicken."

She narrowed her eyes. "Seriously?"

"Turnabout is fair play and all that. Go get your pills. I'll finish up the coffee."

She called over her shoulder, "I want a normal coffee maker. An expensive one. A MoccaMaster, dammit."

She heard him laughing.

She returned with her pill bottle. He'd set out two mugs of coffee. Together, they filled the pill box. Every pill that dropped in felt like the tolling of a bell.

"If you can make a pill box appear, you can get me a coffee maker," she said.

"Sure thing."

She was aggravated. She didn't like watching the large gray pills filling up the box. Each one looked like a bruise. She hated that he sounded so happy.

She was angry. Irritated. So she struck out, hard, to make him hurt. "John is picking me up soon. In like ten minutes. We're going to the beach for brunch or something. I don't know how long I'll be gone."

She kept dropping the pills into the pill box, but Sandy's silence was noticeable. No more sly chuckles. Good. She wanted him to hurt like she was hurting. After the box was full, she picked up a pill, tossed it in the air, and caught it in her mouth. She swallowed it with coffee.

"Want to check to make sure I took it?" she said.

Sandy looked at her sullenly. "I'm not your jailer, Miranda."

"Super." She slid off the kitchen stool, strode angrily from the kitchen, and grabbed her bag from the foyer where she'd dropped it.

She waited outside for John. Sandy's enormous house felt too small for all of the emotions she was feeling.

She was afraid of what she'd say to Sandy. Every word coming out of her mouth seemed to be carved from glass.

———

JOHN PULLED THROUGH THE GATES OF SANDY MARTIN'S HOUSE FOR THE third time in his life and nearly turned around and left. What on earth did he have to offer a girl who'd chosen this *fantasyland* over him? He had nothing but a dingy studio and a very ordinary income. From what he'd gathered from Charlie George, Miranda was far more accustomed to castles than one-room apartments.

He should leave now.

But she'd never made him feel like he was inadequate. She'd made him feel great, actually, even as she'd snarked and argued. Maybe she made everyone feel that way. Maybe she had been using him like Charlie had said, but he doubted it—for a couple of reasons. Mostly, there was the fact that she'd kept showing up when she was most vulnerable, not when she was most ready to party, as though she'd wanted him to see her like that. And then there was the big one, what he hadn't told Charlie—he and Miranda had never slept together. They'd never done more than kiss, once.

Looking at Sandy's house, at the choice she'd made, he was thinking that maybe turning her down had been his only mistake.

He pulled around the circular drive, and Miranda stepped from the shadows of the front porch. When he saw her, he remembered that he was here for a reason. He had to convince her. He had to win her back. Or just win her, period. The past few days had showed him how much she'd come to mean to him. And the thought of her staying with another man felt like his gut was being ripped open.

She hopped in the car, looking like she always looked, as though her escapade to Las Vegas had never happened, as though she hadn't sat at a bar and told him she might kill herself.

He felt his heart squeeze. "How are you feeling?"

She narrowed her eyes at him. "Is that pity in your voice? Why the hell is there pity in your voice?"

He nearly grinned. Miranda was back, and he loved it. "I just wanted to be sure you got all of the jail out of your hair."

She leaned back against the seat. "Take me to a store where I can buy flip-flops."

He did grin this time. "Anything else?"

"A caramel. Sandy is a teetotaler."

"It's ten-thirty in the morning."

"Don't be a baby."

He pulled out of Sandy's driveway and headed toward Laurel Canyon. He'd then drive down the hill to Sunset, where he would cross Sunset, continue to Santa Monica Boulevard, and turn right—west—and take Santa Monica all the way to the beach. On a weekday morning they could find parking in one of the Promenade garages easily, and the drive would be chill. She hadn't seen much of Los Angeles, so he'd show it to her.

He sighed, opening the center console with his right hand. Inside was a caramel.

She plucked it out. "You put this here for me."

He nodded, hating himself a little bit.

Then she surprised him by tucking the caramel into her jeans pocket. "You're right. It's too early."

He felt a glimmer of hope.

As they drove down Santa Monica, he pointed out places that he liked, places that she might have seen in TV shows or movies, and places that were historic. If she were going to live in L.A. for a while, she might as well see what there was to see.

"You really like Los Angeles," she said as they neared the Promenade in Santa Monica.

"I do, yeah."

"So does Daphne. She loves it here."

"She told you that?"

"No. But I can tell."

John wondered if there were a place that Miranda loved. And if there were, if she would tell him.

He parked in a garage at the south end of the Promenade, and they exited at street level. He pointed. "That's the Promenade. It's kind of a boring outdoor mall. The beach is that way." He pointed west. "If we walk south we'll get to Venice Beach, which is something you should see at least once in your life."

She nodded. "Flip-flops."

"Yeah, there'll be a store for those."

They headed west down Colorado. As they neared the ocean, Miranda tilted her head. "That's the Santa Monica pier. You didn't mention we'd be seeing that."

He hadn't. He figured a few surprises would be all right. "Do you want to go up there?"

"No. But I'm glad we came this way." They turned south on the ocean front walk, the paved sidewalk that wended its way as far as you could see north and south along the beach. She looked back over her shoulder at the roller coasters and rides on the pier, her face unsmiling. He considered whether anyone had taken her to ride roller coasters as a child, or a merry-go-round.

"Do you want to—"

"Jesus, John. I said no."

He stopped. "Do you realize that you are attacking with all weapons every time I push back about anything?"

She drew her eyebrows together. "Yes, I think I do know. I don't know how to stop. I'm sorry. I promise it isn't you." She scrubbed her hair with her fingers. "I was doing it to Sandy before I left. It's like I have a thousand butterflies in my stomach and they won't stop. They're making me so irritated."

"Is that a new feeling?"

Her eyes looked extremely tired. "No. Honestly, it's why I wanted the caramel."

He nodded, and they started walking again.

After a while, they passed a large, paved parking lot, and then another. "Why didn't we park down here?" she asked.

Of course she would notice the public lots. He confessed. "I thought you might like to see more of the area," he said. "And I wanted to have more time with you. I wanted to talk with you. About your living arrangements."

She sighed, looking around for a moment. She spied a metal bench, headed over to it, and sat. She untied her boots, pulled off her socks, and tucked them all into her bag. Then she started trekking across the expanse of sand toward the ocean.

He followed after her, kicking off his Vans and picking them up.

He met her at the water's edge. She was letting the freezing cold water lap over her toes.

"I know why you did what you did with Sandy last weekend," he said.

She laughed, but she didn't sound happy. "You couldn't possibly."

"I know you wanted to push everyone away, including me."

She watched the horizon, shaking her head slightly. She looked like she was keeping in words. Miranda wasn't one to pull punches.

He exhaled, trying a different approach. "Why didn't you come back to me?"

She was angry. "Come back to you? You kept holding me away from you." She took a deep breath, trying to calm down. "You treated me like I was some fragile, precious doll. I'm none of those things. And I don't want to be those things. I just want to be me."

"I didn't do that."

"Of course you did. She imitated his voice. *Miranda, stop getting high. Miranda, I won't sleep with you. Miranda, don't get a motorcycle.* It was a constant parade of trying to keep me pure and Midwestern or something."

John thought back over the past week. He had done those things. But not for the reasons she thought. "You're wrong, and I think you know it. But you're looking for a bullshit reason to attack me."

Miranda said nothing, just wrapped her arms around herself and stared at the horizon. The sky was a blue untouched by clouds, the haze of the city pollution behind them. They were clear of it here.

———

Miranda let her toes sink into the damp, frigid sand and wondered what it would be like if the sand kept pulling and pulling until her entire body sank under and she was gone. The pressing would feel so good. It would settle her, calm her. It would probably crush her bones and organs, but at least she'd stop feeling like she was about to crawl out of her skin.

"I did want to push everyone away," she finally said. "Including you. But I'm still going to stay with Sandy."

"You don't have to. You could stay with Daphne. She's sad you're not."

"Let's not exaggerate." Miranda scoffed. "And like I said, I don't want to stay with Daphne if Marlon is moving in. Obviously that's on the horizon."

"She told you that?"

"I realize that you are a man and are therefore not able to notice things, but Marlon is moving in, shortly. He'd probably be there already if I weren't around."

"They've only been together a week."

She paused. "Have you ever been in love, John?"

He shook his head.

"I have. And if I hadn't had to take care of my mother, I'd have moved in with him after two days."

He turned to face her, dropping his shoes in the sand, taking her hand in his. "Don't do it, Miranda. Stay with your brother instead." He looked away, shaking his head as though arguing with himself. Then he met her eyes again. "I care about you."

She inhaled deeply. She'd known this admission was coming when John had called her that morning. She'd known, and she'd come anyway. He deserved to have her listen to him. After all, she cared about him, too. But she was never going to tell him that.

He deserved someone better than her. Someone who wasn't broken.

"Staying with Sandy has nothing to do with you."

John let go of her hand and started pacing. He paced away from her, passing her on the hard-packed sand, then back again.

Watching him pace made her feet twitch with the desire to do the same. She buried her feet in the sand to keep them still.

"It has everything to do with me. I basically told you that I'm putting it all on the line for you, and you ran and slept with someone else."

"You didn't say anything of the sort." He hadn't. She remembered. She could remember every word.

"I would have if you had let me."

Miranda remembered what he'd said. *What I want to do is remove your clothes and toss you on my bed. But that want conflicts with what I want even more.*

The day before she'd slept with Sandy, John had said those words to her, and Miranda had known what John had meant. Of course she had.

"I didn't ask you to put anything on the line for me. I didn't ask for anything at all except for a friend and a fuck. But you said no to both of those things."

He stopped in front of her, blocking her view of the ocean. "I'm still your friend." He spoke so quietly she almost didn't hear him over the waves.

"Are you? Because you seem pretty well pissed off for someone who's my friend."

"Is this because I wouldn't sleep with you?"

Miranda burst into laughter. "No, John. Don't be ridiculous." She almost went a step further. *Sleeping with you wouldn't have mattered at all.* But she didn't. Not that she had a problem with lying. But he didn't deserve that kind of meanness. After all, he'd come after her to Las Vegas. He'd stood up to her brother, keeping his promise to her at the bar, and that couldn't have been easy. John really was her friend. And those were rare.

"Thanks for bringing me out here," she said. She almost added, *I know you want what's best for me.* She didn't say that either. He'd try to mount another defense. And that would just be a waste of energy.

He looked at her from beneath his brows, which were drawn together as though in pain. "There's nothing I can say to convince you not to stay with him?"

"It's not that big of a deal, John."

"It really is."

She placed the palm of her hand on his cheek. His gaze never wavered from hers.

"I have to go."

He didn't speak.

"I have to, John. I don't expect you to drive me back."

He stood, hands in his pockets. He might never forgive her for this, and she'd deserve it. And it would be for the best.

She tried the only explanation she had. "I spent so much of my life just trying to keep the people around me alive that I forgot how to live. So I'm living now."

John turned from her. "At least you want to live. That's a step up from a few days ago."

She flinched, backing away from him.

"I'm not going to wait for you," he said.

"I didn't ask you to." She turned to go.

"Wait, Miranda. I'll drive you back," he said.

"You don't have to."

"No, but I'll do it anyway." He sounded both resigned and determined.

———

ON THE TRIP BACK TO SANDY'S HOUSE, JOHN DIDN'T TRY TO MAKE HIS case again. He seemed to have accepted her decision. Miranda was relieved. She would have gotten out at a stoplight if he hadn't relented.

When they pulled in front of Sandy's porch, he killed the engine and opened his door.

"What are you doing?" Miranda asked, startled.

"I have a few things to say to Sandy."

"What? No." Miranda nearly grabbed his arm to hold him in the car.

"This is a conversation between me and him."

"But it's about me!" She ran to the front door and stopped, blocking his way. "I'm not letting you in."

"That's fine." He stood on the porch with a peaceful expression on his face.

Miranda felt panicked. She entered the house, closing the door in John's face with a glare.

The doorbell rang. The dogs started barking.

No, this couldn't be happening.

Sandy came into the foyer from the kitchen. "Hey, Miranda. Was that you at the door?"

She could lie to Sandy, say that she'd rung the bell—but John would just ring the bell again.

"John is at the door. He says he wants to talk to you." She grabbed his hand. "Please don't answer."

Sandy smiled, patting her hand as though everything would be fine.

She knew that everything would not be fine. She'd created an enormous, stinking mess and brought it home with her.

Sandy opened the door. "Hi, John."

Miranda backed into the living room until she was nearly at the bar. Wait, the bar. She grabbed a bottle of vodka and a can of soda and poured herself a drink. A big one, in a pint glass.

"Do you want to have a seat?" Sandy said to John.

"Not really."

"Suit yourself."

They faced off by Sandy's seating area, where she'd taught Sandy to play spades not too long ago. She wanted to jump off of Sandy's deck, but this time from embarrassment.

John said, "I want to know why you lied to me in Las Vegas."

Sandy's tone was mild. "I don't recall lying."

"Give it up, old man. You sit up here in the hills with your Obi-Wan Kenobi act, but it's all bullshit. You are bullshit. Being rich doesn't mean that you get to do whatever you want with no consequences."

"Actually," Miranda said, "that's exactly what it means."

They both ignored her.

Sandy crossed his arms over his chest. Wow. John was starting to get to him. "What was the lie, John?"

"You told me that Miranda slept with you as a ploy, to drive people away, more specifically, to drive me away."

"I did."

"And you said—I think I have this right—that I'm the only one who'd been making smart decisions about Miranda."

"Yes."

"And you knew, you *knew*," with those words, John punched his palm, "that I was after her heart, not just an easy lay."

Sandy's jaw muscle flexed, and he nodded.

"And yet the first chance you got, you invited her to move in with you? Are you serious? How long, exactly, did you wait after I left yesterday before you were fucking again?"

Sandy, for the first time since Miranda had met him, looked murderous.

Miranda took a big chug of her drink and then spoke. "Approximately three minutes."

Both heads whipped in her direction.

"I think it was three, right?" She looked at Sandy for confirmation. "I was naked before we reached the kitchen."

"You are making things worse," Sandy ground out.

"Really?" She gasped, laughing. "How could things be worse?"

"This isn't about you, actually," John said to her. "This is about him."

"That's a whopper," she said. "But okay. I'll sit here and keep my mouth shut."

"Why don't you go elsewhere?" John said.

"Don't bother trying to get me to leave. I'll just eavesdrop."

John shook his head, taking a deep breath. He was working really hard not to lose his shit entirely. He spoke again to Sandy. "You led me to believe that you weren't after her."

"That's not exactly lying."

"Don't split hairs."

"You've come into my house to accuse me of wrongdoing. I'll do whatever I want."

"Of course you will. You always do. You're the King of L.A. Who the hell is going to tell you no?"

Sandy's hands actually flexed into fists. Miranda had to cover her mouth to stop an inappropriate laugh from escaping.

"You're acting like Miranda didn't have a say in the matter," Sandy said. "As I recall, she made a choice of her own yesterday."

"You offered." John pointed at Sandy's chest. "You opened your home to her. You didn't have to do that. She wouldn't have asked to stay here if you hadn't offered."

That was probably true, Miranda thought. If Sandy hadn't offered, she'd be at the W with Charlie trying to figure out her next move.

Sandy glanced over his shoulder at her, realizing that John spoke the truth. She turned her back to him, taking another chug of her drink. She didn't want him to see the truth on her face and maybe— *maybe*—make her leave because of it. She didn't want to leave.

She liked it here. John was going to ruin everything.

She was nearly finished with her drink. She needed another.

Wait, she had something even better, something that had the added benefit of distracting John. She fished her hand into her jeans pocket and pulled out the pot caramel from earlier.

She started unwrapping it, loudly crinkling the cellophane. John looked her way when he heard the noise. "Jesus, Miranda."

"What? I'm supposed to just tolerate this male posturing while sober? Are you insane? Wait—no. That's me." She popped the entire caramel in her mouth. Then she set about mixing another drink, pouring the second half of the can of soda into her pint glass, adding a handful of ice, and then filling it to the top with vodka.

"Miranda, quit it," John said.

"No, you quit it." She swallowed the last of the caramel and dropped into one of the chairs with her glass, staring over his shoulder. "Just go."

John turned back to Sandy. "You lied, and you know you lied. You can keep kidding yourself if it makes you feel better. But you know, deep down, that I'm right."

Then he left.

———

Sandy watched John leave, and felt all of the anger leave his body. What remained was a bit of adrenaline, and a lot of confusion.

Miranda let out a whistle from where she sat on the chair, and his dogs, Jodie and Foster, came scrambling up to her. They were twin Hungarian Vizslas, with sleek golden-brown fur, golden eyes to match, and velvet ears. He'd trained them within an inch of their lives. Although they weren't typical guard dogs, they served that purpose for him.

Jodie and Foster hadn't barked at her when she'd entered today, though. It appeared that whatever John thought, Miranda was at home at his house. The dogs lay down at her feet.

He sat on the couch next to her. "They like you."

"I like them."

"Do you like all dogs?"

"Most of them. Even overbred rich-man's dogs like Vizslas."

He laughed at the jab. "What dog did you have as a kid?"

"Are you joking? We weren't allowed to have dogs." She scoffed. "I always wanted one, though. Dogs are something you can count on. They're reliable, and so much of my life has been so, so not."

She stood and headed to the kitchen. On the counter next to the electric teakettle was a MoccaMaster coffeemaker in a sunny yellow color. She shook her head, turning to look at him. "I guess I should be unsurprised by you and your magic tricks."

She ground coffee into the coffee filter using the espresso machine, filled the water heater, and set the machine to brew. Then she slid open the deck doors and collapsed onto one of the loungers.

He headed into his bathroom to throw water on his face. He needed a moment after that confrontation with John. He was starting to wonder if letting Miranda George into his home had been a terrible idea. But there, on the counter, he'd set her pill box. One pill already taken. One down, a lifetime to go.

No, he decided. Having her here was not a terrible idea. She needed him, even if only for this one thing. He headed back to the kitchen to find her, to talk about that terrible fight. Surely she was going to want to know what John had been referring to, the promise made in Las Vegas.

The coffeemaker had finished its brew cycle—it only seemed to take a minute, the girl knew her coffeemakers—so he poured two mugs and joined her on the deck.

Miranda was sound asleep, or rather, passed out from booze and pot and maybe lack of sleep.

He set her mug next to her, covering the top with a coaster to keep it warm. He lay in the adjacent chair, drinking his coffee, appreciating, as he always did, his view of the city below.

He thought about the confrontation with John. John was right, of course. Even if Sandy had never spoken the words aloud—that Miranda was John's, and Sandy would leave them be—John had sensed the promise, inferred it, from all of the other things Sandy had said. John had a right to be angry. He had a right to fight for the girl he could love, might already love.

The thing was, the girl didn't want him. Not like that. Not right now. He looked at her, asleep on the reclined chair, her lips parted slightly. Stoned and a little drunk. Who could blame her, having to listen to him and John talk about her like she was a horse at auction.

He should have shut that conversation down. But he hadn't been able to. He'd wanted to fight for her.

He looked out over the city and wondered what Miranda George was doing to him.

Twenty-five minutes later, she stirred. She stretched her long arms over her head, the hem of her black shirt riding up a little to reveal just a small line of pale skin above her jeans. Sandy's eyes caught there for a moment, and then he met her eyes.

She was looking at him, eyes narrowed, wearing a half-smile that predicted trouble. "How long have you been lying next to me, creeper?"

"I made you coffee, but it probably needs reheating."

She grabbed the mug from the side table so quickly she nearly spilled it. She took a deep sip. "It's perfect." Miranda was silent for a long time.

"Everything John accused me of is true."

Miranda nodded, thoughtful. "It all sounded true." She took another sip of coffee. "So, you think I should dump you for John, then? Since he's after my heart instead of a fuck?"

Sandy felt a stab in the center of his chest.

"No? Yes?" She giggled like a kid. "Help me Obi-Wan Kenobi."

"Stop it, Miranda."

She tilted her head, examining him. "I'm sorry. That really hurt you. I didn't think it would."

"How could you think that acting so cavalier with my feelings for you wouldn't hurt me?"

She raised her eyebrows in mirth. "Really? We've slept together like, twice. You're—you. I'm *nobody*. How could I possibly think that you would care what I do?" She stood, carrying her mug of coffee with her. She leaned forward against the railing, keeping her back to him. "I never asked how many other women *you're* sleeping with. It's not my place."

He'd never thought about it that way. But from the stiff line of her back, he could tell that she had, a lot. He stood and joined her at the railing. "John loves you. I think he made that clear today."

She rolled her eyes and groaned.

"And he's not just some loser wannabe with nothing to offer you. He's a decent guy. Really smart. Makes a good living."

"He lives in a room."

"He's saving his money."

Miranda smiled darkly. "It sounds like you are pushing me off on him."

"I want you to know that you have choices. That I would let you go."

Her voice lowered. "You don't have me now."

Sandy sighed. "Don't I know it."

She stared off into the far distance. "You and John—you fought over me like animals. I asked you not to let him in the house, and you didn't listen."

"He deserved to have his say."

Miranda scoffed. "No he didn't. And now he's put doubts in your head and in mine." With those last words, her voice rose.

She was right, of course. He was going to wonder if she wouldn't be better off with him—that's why he'd just offered her that choice. He was going to wonder what would have happened if he'd kept his mouth shut when she was trying to find a place to stay. There were so many what-ifs, now, because he'd let John in the door.

Miranda spoke. "I should go to Charlie's hotel. The whole point in staying here was that it was safe. Certain. You are supposed to be the steady one. What the hell, Sandy. Why'd you get in a knife fight with that dope?"

"He's not a dope."

"He's a child," she spat. "And you acted like one, too."

She was really angry. And she still wouldn't look at him. And the thought of her leaving upset him more than he cared to think about.

Her short hair was tucked behind her ears, and her feet, he noticed, were bare. She'd chucked her shoes and socks when she'd lay down for her nap.

He reached over and traced the exposed line of her jaw with his thumb.

She shut her eyes.

He did it again.

"I'm so angry I could spit," she said.

"I know."

She took his hand and led him to the deck chair she'd been sleeping on. It was still reclined nearly flat. She sat at the end, pulling him between her knees, looking up at his face. She yanked the hem of her shirt up and over her head and tossed it on the ground. She reached forward and unbuttoned his jeans, sliding a finger under the waistband of his boxers, then pushing her hands up under his shirt, wrapping both hands around his waist. She kissed his belly button, then kissed lower.

Oh, Jesus.

She was out of her jeans in seconds, reclining on the chair in only a black lace bra and panties, eyes narrowed at him like a cat. And he knew that he was exactly the liar John accused him of being.

He pulled his t-shirt off, then kicked off his jeans. He crawled up the chair until his body covered hers. He kissed her neck and she arched off the cushions like her body was on fire.

How could she possibly think he was sleeping with someone else while she was staying in his house? She was downright mesmerizing.

"Make it good, old man," she hissed. "And then I'll forgive you."

Forty-five minutes later they were in the kitchen. Miranda wore his t-shirt and nothing else. Between bites of a croissant, Miranda heaved a sigh. "I guess I should call my brother before he comes storming over here and you have to fight him, too."

Sandy nodded from where he leaned against the counter, wearing jeans and no shirt, wondering what he was going to do when she finally decided to go.

Chapter Seventeen

Thursday morning around seven o'clock, Miranda flopped onto Sandy's bed fully clothed and barefoot. He vaguely remembered her leaving in the middle of the night, again. He wondered what drove her from his bed in the night and wished he could convince her to stay with him, to wake up with him.

She picked up a mug of coffee from the nightstand. "Want it?"

Sandy scooted up so he was reclining against the headboard. "Sure."

She picked up a second mug for herself. "I need a job."

"I'm not sure 'need' is an accurate word." After all, she had free room and board and nearly twenty grand in cash. She'd be fine for a while. Plus, he imagined Charlie George would give her whatever spending money she might want.

"It is, though." She paused. "I need a job. I don't care what it is."

Sandy considered why Miranda George might need a job if it wasn't about the money. "Did you take your medicine this morning?"

"Stop changing the subject."

"You first."

"Yes. You can check the pill box."

"All that'll do is show me that you emptied the pill box."

Miranda laughed, and a real smile lit her eyes. "You are correct. But I did take it. I want to take it." Her smile turned wry. "Years ago I had this tough conversation with my mom, and she told me that her medicine worked. This was the most frustrating thing about living with her. She'd be fine for six months or a year, and then everything would collapse. And it wasn't till this particular conversation that I learned that those awful times were when she'd stopped taking her medicine. I wanted to hug her and murder her at the same time."

Sandy raised his eyebrows at Miranda to convey *I know the feeling.*

She slapped him on the arm and almost made him spill his coffee. "The point is, the medicine worked. And with you on me about taking it—the literal opposite of my dad—I'm thinking I might be all right. At least I might stop trying to jump off your deck naked."

He turned to her, eyebrows drawn. "What?"

"Oh, that happened the first night we got here from Las Vegas. Charlie saved me. It felt like the air could hold me up or something." She took a sip of coffee as though what she'd said was no big deal. "Anyways, I need a job."

"You don't need the money. And John told me you actually have some part-time work you do."

She waved her hand. "I can do that work in my spare time. I'm very efficient."

"You have twenty thousand in cash. Why do you need another job?"

She set down her coffee and stood, staring out the window, as though her words were too important to say lying down. "I don't expect you or Charlie or anyone else to understand this." She crossed her arms. Sandy couldn't believe it—Miranda George was nervous. "When you've spent years and years living only half of a life, and a whole life finally becomes yours to live, you need to make that life mean something."

Sandy nodded. That was a really good reason. "And you truly don't mind doing anything?"

"I'll do anything."

Thirty minutes later they were strolling through Laurel Canyon to the small shopping district near his house. They were going to get her a job at the café there. "You need a job close by because of your suspended license situation," he said. "And the owner of Mode owes me a favor."

As they walked, he started to feel a little dizzy. He coughed, then coughed again. Suddenly, he was hit with a feeling of nausea.

"Are you all right, man?" Miranda asked.

"I think breakfast is sitting wrong in my gut."

"Are you going to boot on the side of the road? Let me know so I can take a picture and sell it to a tabloid."

He tried to suppress the feeling of nausea and lightheadedness. He stopped walking. "Just a second. Let me get it together."

After a few minutes, the nausea and dizziness subsided.

"Sorry about that." He glanced at her. She looked far more concerned than her tone of voice had let on.

Among the storefronts in the small shopping district were a dry-cleaners, a market, and the café, Mode, where he liked to buy meals to have delivered to his house. He opened Mode's glass front door for Miranda, and she entered.

They grabbed a table, and Miranda sat. Sandy said, "I'm going to order us some drinks. I'll be right back."

At the counter, after placing the order, he asked to speak with Patricia, the owner.

Patricia was a short woman in her mid-forties with red hair cut in a *Rosemary's Baby* pixie and a rail-thin figure to match. She came bustling out of the swinging door leading to the kitchen.

When she saw Sandy, she smiled. "Hey, old man," she said.

Sandy was struck, again, by how lovely Patricia was. "Hey, young lady. I have a favor to ask."

"Shoot."

"I have a friend who needs a job. Do you need any help around here?"

"One of my bussers just quit to learn to be a stunt man. Will he bus tables?"

"She."

Patricia raised one, perfectly arched brow.

"I have no idea how well this will work out. If she's terrible, send her back to my place, no harm done. But busing tables might be something she really needs." That word again, *need*.

"All right, sure. Introduce me. I'm guessing she's waiting outside?"

"She's at the table in the corner. Black shirt."

They both glanced over at Miranda. Miranda, of course, had been watching him. And she waved with a charming smile.

"Not your usual type." Patricia said.

Not long after his wife left him, he and Patricia had had a thing. The thing had ended, and they'd become close friends. When she'd needed to upfit her kitchen equipment, he'd loaned her the money at a much lower rate than a bank would have. In exchange, he got priority as a customer. Seemed fair to him. He'd been happy to help keep her in business. Without Mode, his neighborhood would be a much less enjoyable place to live.

"She's not my type, period. I'm not sure she's anyone's type, to be honest." For some reason, it felt right to keep Patricia in the dark about his relationship with Miranda, at least for a little while. He led the way to the table, carrying a coffee for Miranda and a sparkling water for himself—hopefully it would settle his stomach.

After making the introductions, Sandy let Patricia make her offer to Miranda. Twelve an hour, more if there are tips, but because there wasn't table service, tips tended to be small. She'd be clearing tables, loading and unloading the commercial washer in the back, bringing out clean dishes to the front, and assisting the baristas. She could train to be a barista if she wanted to, so she could cover when others took breaks or things got busy.

Miranda laughed. "That's probably a good idea. That's the exact same model espresso machine Sandy has in his house, isn't it?"

It was. He'd bought one at the same time Patricia had. The dealer had given them a discount for buying two. Of course Miranda had noticed—she remembered details. But now Patricia was going to know that Miranda was living with him.

"It is, yes." Patricia said, her voice even. Too even.

"The other day when we were all at his house, I wanted to make a coffee, but I don't speak Italian." After she spoke, Miranda cut him a look as if to say, *I'm not a dummy*.

Patricia smiled. "Well, that is one of the drawbacks. We used a label maker to mark ours."

"Brilliant," Miranda said. "I'm in."

———

Miranda's hair was tied back with a rubber band she'd found on the floor of the kitchen. It had likely come off of a bundle of celery. Her shirt was damp with sweat, and she wished she had a pair of Vans like John wore all the time instead of her boots, which were both hot and uncomfortable on the red tiled floor.

John. She shook her head. She refused to think of John. Especially after that scene he'd made in Sandy's living room.

Instead she thought of her work. She loaded dishes from the table into her gray plastic bin. She set the bin on her hip, pulling the damp cloth from her apron and wiping down the table. Then she carried the dishes through the swinging door to the back.

But now it was the lunch rush, and every table was full. Prepping tables as fast as possible was a priority. Getting the dishes cleaned and back up front and ready to use was imperative. And everything was twice as hard because the *other* busser scheduled for the lunch-to-dinner shift had been a no-show. Patricia had said that Miranda would have a trial-by-fire, and she would either make it or she wouldn't. Miranda had grinned back, accepting the challenge.

Miranda pulled a square, green rack from the commercial washer and loaded it with dishes from her bin, then slid the rack inside, hitting the green button to start the cycle. The clean dishes emerged on the other side. She stacked the large plates near the food prep area, where the lunch cook and Patricia were prepping food. Then she stacked the small plates, juice glasses, cups, and saucers inside a clean bin to take up front. She carried the dishes back through the door to the front of house and behind the counter, being careful to stay out of the way of the baristas, and put them on the shelves.

Then she took her bin and headed out to the front to bus the next tables. There weren't any ready for her yet, so she stepped back through the kitchen door to wait.

Patricia joined her. "You're very efficient."

"Thank you," Miranda said.

"One would think you were actually enjoying this."

"One would be right." Miranda peered through the window, trying to see if patrons at one of the outdoor tables were preparing to leave. Something outside caught her eye, a flash of blond hair.

No. No way. She had to be wrong.

"You can't know what the future holds, though, can you," Patricia said.

"I can promise I won't go into stunt training." Miranda set her bin on the stainless steel counter, gripping its sides, and took a deep breath. Then she peered through the window again.

"What is it?" Patricia asked.

Miranda threw her shoulders back, readying herself. "Patricia, I'm so sorry for what is about to happen." Charlie had just stepped into Mode, and he was prowling around. "My brother is here. I'll do everything I can to avoid a scene. Can I take some kind of break? I know it's the middle of rush. It shouldn't take long to chase him off."

"Are you in danger, Miranda?" Patricia's voice turned deadly serious.

"Only of being annoyed to death."

"Fine. Call him back here, and try to keep it down. Use the back door if you can't."

Patricia headed over to the food prep area and started chopping scallions with an overly large knife. It seemed she didn't trust Miranda's words about not being in danger.

Miranda pushed open the kitchen door. "Charlie."

He looked over to her, raising his eyebrows in surprise. He took in her sweaty appearance and her apron, then stormed through the door.

He glared down at her.

"Hello, Charlie. What brings you here?"

"Daphne said you had a job working at this place."

Daphne had told him? The gossip moved fast.

Miranda gestured at her apron. "Correct. I needed a job. I have one now."

"You don't need a job. People like us don't need jobs."

"Never say *people like us*. It induces vomiting."

"Yes, I'm a snob. Of course I'm a snob. We are us. We're Georges."

"Can you even hear yourself? Did you see the people you passed out there?" Miranda gestured at more than a few famous faces seated around tables at Mode.

"Hollywood is garbage, Miranda."

"Say that to Sandy's face."

"He'd probably agree with me. He didn't get rich off of

Hollywood. He's a real estate mogul and owns half of L.A." Of course Charlie had had Sandy investigated. Of course he had.

"Can you keep your voice down? You're embarrassing me. And you're going to get me fired." She nodded toward the kitchen prep table.

"Let's walk out of this shithole right now."

"Charlie!" Miranda was officially embarrassed by her brother. She grabbed his hand and dragged him toward the back door. She stopped near Patricia first.

"Patricia, Charlie here is going to order a case of your most expense sparkling wine. Please deliver it to Sandy Martin's house as a gift for me." She smacked Charlie on the arm. "Give me your credit card." He pulled it out of his wallet on her command, and she passed the card over to Patricia. "We're heading out back to finish this conversation, and I'll return in five minutes."

"Sounds good," Patricia said. "You sure you only need one case?"

Miranda smiled. "You're right. Make it two."

She dragged Charlie through the back screen door and stood him next to the dumpster. Fitting.

Charlie said, "You just need to get better. Most people would take six months or a year after what you went through."

For a moment Miranda considered what Charlie had also gone through, and wondered when he would take care of himself. She filed that thought away for later. Right now she needed to get him off of her case. "Most people would go back to their jobs. Because they need money."

Charlie ran his hand through his hair in frustration. "We do not need money. Will you please stop talking about money?"

"I don't want to take anything from Charles Senior. He's the reason she's dead."

"Take it from me instead."

"It's the same thing."

Charlie was silent for a moment. He knew she was right.

He put his hands on his hips, looking to the side, frustration showing in the tightness of his shoulders. "This job is so beneath you."

"Maybe." She thought about the methodical work, the cleaning of dirty things, the teamwork, how even right now her work wasn't getting done because Charlie was wasting her time. "Or maybe it's too good for me."

"Look," Charlie said. "The only reason I'm working in the law firm now is because I want to. I love the work. I want to be like Mom."

Miranda sighed. "I think I have you beat in the be-like-Mom department."

"You know what I mean. I love what I do, and that's why I do it. Not for the money. And you can't possibly love bussing tables. What you're doing right now is mindless."

"Right now you sound a lot more like Dad than Mom. She would never let you get away with saying bullshit like that." Sorcha had believed that all work was important and deserved respect. It was their father who was the unmitigated snob.

"Isn't there anything you've ever really wanted to do?" Charlie said, getting desperate now. "Don't you have any dreams, sis?"

Miranda nearly exploded. The only thing holding her back from a meltdown was the screen door between her and the people in the kitchen. "No, Charlie, I don't. My whole life I've lived for other people. For you. For Mom. I never had time to come up with dreams for myself. I had *nothing* for myself."

"What about Matthias? You had him, didn't you?"

"Yeah, sure. I fell in love with a lawyer who worked in our parents' law firm and lived next door to our parents' law firm, a firm where I worked as a part-time paralegal." She paused. "Dating him was basically like dating you, now that I think about it. It's kind of weird." She waved her hand. "And then he moved away, and that was that."

"He still loved you even after he moved. And he didn't go that far."

"You know I don't do long distance."

"Only you would think two hours is long distance."

"It totally is. What a pain in the ass."

"You're the pain in the ass." He suppressed a smile.

She grinned, nodding in agreement.

The mood had lightened. She was Big Sis, and he was Little B, and they were going to make it through.

"So you're really going to work here," he said.

"I don't know who I am or what I should be doing, so I'm going back inside to bus tables. It's good, honest work. You should try it sometime."

"Come here," he said, pulling her into a hug. He spoke into her hair. "Everything is changing so fast."

"I know. It'll be all right. I promise."

Chapter Eighteen

One week later, on Thursday evening, Sandy dropped Miranda off in front of Rivet. She wore the same black dress and shoes that she'd worn to Greta's wedding. Tonight was a celebration, Daphne had proclaimed. They were going to celebrate Miranda's first week at her new job. Miranda wasn't sure that bussing tables for a week was something to celebrate, but Daphne had insisted.

Miranda surprised herself by feeling nervous.

She entered Rivet, and found three women waiting for her at the bar: Daphne, Greta Donovan, whose wedding she'd crashed with John, and, surprisingly, the emergency department doctor who'd patched up Daphne's shredded feet the same night of Greta's wedding. Tory Something.

Daphne had always been good at making friends.

John. She had to stop thinking about John. But it was hard. He was everywhere she turned.

Miranda took a deep breath and joined the women at the bar.

"Miranda!" Daphne exclaimed and pulled Miranda into a hug. Miranda bent down slightly to allow the shorter Daphne to reach.

Greta gave her a genuine smile, which struck Miranda as odd. Tory held out her hand, and Miranda shook it.

"I'm Tory Murphy," she said.

"I remember."

"We only hung out for a moment," Tory said. "How do you remember?"

"Miranda remembers things," Daphne said. "Consider it her superpower."

"And making friends with strangers is Daphne's," Miranda said.

Greta laughed. "I'm Example A."

Daphne frowned. "I'm not sure I like where this conversation is going."

"Why?" Miranda said. "I couldn't make friends with a Care Bear. I didn't mean my words as an insult. I'm certain Greta didn't."

"It's hard to tell with you, Miranda," Daphne said. "As precise as you claim to be, your words can always mean multiple things."

Miranda nodded. "Lawyer as charged." She paused. "Except not really. Which is why I'm bussing tables."

Dr. Tory Murphy had been easy to recognize, even out of her scrubs, with her thick black hair pulled back in a low ponytail, big brown eyes, and girlish freckles over pale, pale skin. She was probably Miranda's age, maybe older, but she looked twenty-two. She talked even faster than Miranda did. In the emergency department, she'd been smart, and funny, and very, very competent. Miranda would never have let her touch Daphne otherwise.

And now, it seemed, Tory and Daphne were friends, a friendship forged in fire and all that. But this is what Daphne did—Miranda hadn't been kidding. Daphne collected people like artifacts. Fortunately, she usually had good taste.

Miranda's phone rang then, and she pulled it out of a small black clutch. Her brother. She silenced it. She'd talked to him that morning, and everything had been fine. They'd reached an understanding: she had to call him once a day, ideally in the morning, to check in, and he promised he wouldn't worry.

They'd had lunch at Mode a few times over the past week during her lunch break, outside on the front patio. He was adjusting to life at his law firm, where he'd started working as an intern. The firm had already made him a job offer for after he graduated, which would happen in May. His law school didn't seem to care that he'd completely ditched classes for the spring semester so long as he returned for finals in early May. He'd told them his mother had died, and used his various means of Charlie persuasion to convince them to allow him to complete his classwork from afar.

He also seemed to be adjusting to the idea that his sister was living with a movie star and working as back of house help in a small café.

He still believed that she wasn't sleeping with Sandy, but what he didn't know wouldn't hurt him. Honestly, she didn't know why he cared. He'd never cared before whom she'd slept with. By now, he'd probably forgotten about the promise he'd tried to extract from her, and she was pretty sure he'd never extracted one from Sandy. That would have been preposterous.

"Do you want to get a booth or stay at the bar?" Greta asked. "We can do either."

As the owner of Rivet, Greta could probably kick the three soap-opera stars off the high-top right behind them without any fuss, but she never would. Even after five years, Greta was still a little abashed that she was associated with such a flashy locale—*Rivet*, for god's sake. Miranda admired Greta's humility, though. She could only imagine what her brother would say about Greta's unwillingness to embrace her good fortune.

She loved Charlie, but he had his flaws.

"Let's stay at the bar," Miranda said. "Standing shows off my legs."

Daphne laughed. "Between John and Sandy, you'd think you had your hands full."

"Not my hands. And never full."

Even Greta laughed then.

Tory's eyes got large. "You're dating Alexander Martin?"

"I'm cohabitating with Sandy Martin and sleeping with him once or twice a day."

"I think that counts as dating these days," Greta said.

"It counts as dating to me," Tory said. "Holy shit."

"My god," Miranda said. "He's just a dude."

"Is he hot naked?" Tory asked.

Miranda pulled her eyebrows together. "Of course. What's the point otherwise?"

The three women laughed, and Miranda, with some small pleasure, joined them.

Greta waved at the bartender, who'd been giving them their space. Miranda recognized the guy as he approached—really hot, dark hair, mid-thirties. Quentin. He'd served her and Sandy on Saturday, the night she'd first seduced him.

Greta ordered a Wild Turkey on the rocks, which caused Miranda to raise her eyebrows in surprise. Daphne ordered a Cosmopolitan martini, of course, and Tory joined her with the same.

Miranda found herself wondering if she maybe shouldn't drink.

She knew, from experience and research, that alcohol interacted with the medicine she was taking. She knew that her body was getting used to the medicine, and that the medicine had an effect on her liver.

She wondered when precisely in hell she'd grown a sense of self-preservation.

"I'll have a soda water with lime," she said.

Daphne looked at her closely. "Just like college."

"Yeah. Sort of."

Tory and Greta were talking to Miranda's right. Daphne stood on Miranda's left. Daphne kept her voice low. "So how are things with Sandy. Still good?"

Miranda rolled her eyes. "You heard what I said."

"I heard what you didn't say. Tonight, and all week."

Miranda would never get accustomed to Daphne's intuition, or her nosiness. All she'd told Daphne on the phone the few times they'd talked the past week was that Sandy was her friend-with-benefits and her pharmacist. When Daphne had tried to dig deeper into Miranda's feelings, Miranda had changed the subject. To be fair, whenever anyone tried to talk to Miranda about her feelings, she usually changed the subject.

But maybe Daphne and her intuition could help Miranda out. "I can't stay the whole night in his room. I don't know what's wrong with me. I know that I have insomnia—I always have. But when I wake up in the middle of the night, instead of trying to go back to sleep with him, I leave and go to my room."

"You have your own room?"

"I want to have my own space, and for him to have his own space."

Daphne nodded. "You're keeping your distance, then."

"At first I was afraid he would get sick of me. But now—part of me knows that, although we're friends, and he's helped me a lot, and the sex is amazing," Miranda raised her glass, toasting her reflecting the mirror behind the bar, "it's not permanent."

"It's not love."

"No." She shook her head. "I feel like I'm a broken toy that he wants to fix. At the same time, I feel like I've hypnotized him somehow, and he'll snap out of it one day and not want me anymore."

Daphne took a careful sip of her martini. "Don't you worry about hurting him?"

Miranda scoffed. "No."

"From what Charlie tells me, you've left a pretty long trail of hurt boys in your path."

"You've been talking to Charlie about my boys?"

Daphne shrugged. "We're friends."

Miranda raised a brow. "You think you're friends."

"What does that mean?" Daphne demanded.

"And Sandy is hardly a boy," Miranda said.

"You don't think Charlie is my friend?"

"Charlie is difficult to become friends with. That's all. As difficult as I am, if not more so."

"But he's so—"

"Charming?"

"Yes?"

"Snakes are beautiful, Daphne. You should know that."

Daphne nodded. "Yes. I should."

Miranda was worried, though. If Charlie had been pumping Daphne for information, what had he learned?

Around nine-thirty, after dinner and drinks, Daphne declared that they needed to hang out more that night. "And since Miranda doesn't have a car, we should hang out at Sandy's."

"I'm not sure there's logic there," Miranda said.

"There's totally logic there," Greta said. Greta was infallibly logical, and Miranda knew she was right.

"Thank god," Tory said. She'd never been to Sandy's house, of course, so the idea of hanging out there probably had her fainting with joy.

Greta and Tory followed in their cars while Miranda rode with Daphne in hers.

After getting them onto Santa Monica Boulevard heading east, Daphne turned to Miranda. "I know that this was a party to celebrate your first week of work. But I have a question."

"Of course you do. But you should let me call Sandy to ask permission first. He might not be okay with this little party."

"You're not allowed to have friends over?"

"Shut up, Daphne." Miranda dialed the phone.

Sandy answered after a few rings. "Hey, Miranda."

"You home?"

"I'm at Mode."

Miranda's curiosity sparked. Mode closed at nine. "Say hi to Patricia for me."

"I come down here sometimes for wine with Patty and her manager after closing."

"Fascinating. I'm having friends over."

He paused. "Who?"

"The girls." For a moment, she'd considered needling him. Considered taunting that she'd picked up a new guy. Anything to rile him up. But they were past that, she and Sandy. Even if she'd felt a prick of jealousy that he was out late with *Patty*.

"I'll be home in an hour or two."

"Are we all clear?" Daphne asked after Miranda hung up.

"Yeah."

They drove for a while in silence, and Miranda noticed the places on Santa Monica that John had pointed out to her—the places where he liked to have lunch, the places that still served reasonably priced beers. She thought about what Daphne had told her earlier, that maybe she had the power to hurt Sandy, too.

———

GRETA OPENED THE DOOR TO SANDY'S HOUSE AND LED EVERYONE INSIDE. Daphne followed closely behind, and she marveled that she was finally feeling comfortable here, after the struggles of the past couple of weeks. She and her friends gathered in the living room seating area near the kitchen, just past the foyer, where Miranda had been dealing spades only a couple of weeks ago, the night Daphne's world had almost gone to pieces.

Daphne didn't mind helping Miranda put her life back together. Miranda had done the same for her.

Miranda offered to make drinks at the bar. "Same cocktails as before? Or should I surprise you?"

"I like surprises," Tory said.

Miranda picked up the martini shaker and began pouring in liquids.

Daphne's phone flashed. Marlon. He was home, and he'd spotted her car. He wanted to know if he could join them. Daphne tapped her lip. She knew that Miranda had been avoiding Marlon. But it was time for her to make up with him. He certainly felt bad about his role in chasing her out of town the week before.

"Marlon wants to join us. Do you mind, Miranda?"

Miranda was pouring from the shaker into three rocks glasses. "Sure. Invite him over." But there was an edge to Miranda's voice that implied she'd bite if cornered.

Fair enough. Daphne texted Marlon.

Miranda carried the three drinks over to the table and set them in front of Tory, Greta, and Daphne.

"Why aren't you having one?" Daphne asked. Something must have happened for Miranda to have suddenly stopped drinking again.

"I don't feel like it." She headed back to the bar and poured herself a soda water.

"Only a couple of weeks ago, we were drinking greyhounds and smoking weed in my apartment because I forgot to get pain medicine from her." Daphne pointed at Tory. "And now you don't drink?" Daphne was worried. The last time Miranda had made a drastic change—lopping off her hair—she'd taken off for Las Vegas the next day.

Tory cut in. "Daphne, maybe it's a good thing. Let it be."

Miranda, still standing at the bar, scanned the bottles in front of her. She picked up a bottle of brown liquor, tipped her head back, and chugged. She set the bottle down hard. "Happy now?"

"That was Sandy's favorite scotch," Greta said, eyes wide.

Miranda stormed out onto the deck and leaned forward on the railing, tension apparent in the set of her shoulders.

Greta hissed. "Daphne, what is wrong with you?"

Daphne defended herself. "You weren't there. The days before she took off. She acted so strangely, with all of these drastic changes. Suddenly not drinking? I'm worried."

"Don't be an idiot," Greta said. "There's a material difference between buying a motorcycle and choosing not to drink."

Daphne nodded. Miranda had not seemed self-destructive tonight, not at all. Daphne rushed outside and joined Miranda on the deck.

"I'm sorry," Daphne said.

Miranda kept her eyes on the valley. "Go away. Y'all should leave."

"I was worried about you."

"I heard everything you two just said. You should learn to whisper better."

Daphne grimaced. "Then you know I want the best for you."

"I'm a science project you watch for any strange behavioral changes."

"That's not what I'm doing."

Miranda turned to face her, raising her eyebrows. The look told Daphne, *That's exactly what you're doing.*

"What will it take for you to forgive me?"

"I'll think about it."

Daphne leaned forward on the rail, looking out. Miranda leaned back against it, looking into the house.

"Why didn't you come back to live with me?" Daphne asked.

"Honestly? Because Marlon's going to ask to move in soon. I want you to be able to say yes."

"No he isn't. He loves living up here with Sandy."

"He loves you more." Miranda tapped her glass of soda with her finger. "What if he asked you to move into his apartment with him?"

"He knows I love my condo. My neighborhood."

"You'd choose your condo over Marlon?"

Daphne paused. "Of course not."

"I'm glad you said that. Hey, Marlon."

Daphne whipped around. Marlon stood in the doorway to the deck.

Miranda passed Marlon on her way into the house. He stood, listening, mouth open slightly. Miranda called over her shoulder to Daphne. "I forgive you now."

"She set me up," Daphne said to Marlon. "Why didn't you say that you were there?"

"I think I was in shock. She was staring right at me, and yet talking about me like I was invisible."

"At least I answered correctly." Daphne held out her arms, and he came to her for a hug.

"Do you want to move in together?" he said.

"Don't you think it seems a little fast?"

He lifted her off her feet, burying his face in her neck. "No."

"Your place or mine?"

"Yours. Of course yours."

Miranda sat next to Tory on the couch. Greta sat in the armchair, which left the other couch for the lovebirds. She was still mad at herself for allowing Daphne to goad her into sucking down that whiskey. What a waste of good scotch.

Marlon and Daphne took their seats. They were holding hands. She was happy for them, really. It was easier to be happy for them now than it had been before her trip to Las Vegas. Before she'd decided to have a future, too. Even if that future didn't involve the person she might sit on a couch holding hands with.

Suddenly, the front door flew open. Her brother Charlie stepped in, looking mad as a wet hen. She rolled her eyes. What had she done now?

He took in the group seated around the coffee table, and headed over with a fake smile on his face. Miranda stood, putting the same smile on her own face. To the world, they looked affable, cheerful even.

The world was wrong.

"Hey Big Sis," Charlie said to her. Then he nodded at the group. "Friends of Big Sis."

"Hi Charlie," Daphne said. "You know Greta. This is Marlon, and this is Tory."

Charlie catalogued their names, Miranda knew, but he didn't care who these people were, not in the normal way that people cared about other people. Charlie had arrived for a fight, and the others were merely witnesses to be managed.

"Miranda," he said. "I heard some interesting news from a mutual friend. I thought we could talk about it privately."

Miranda considered the wide-eyed group watching the beginnings of the glorious George sibling showdown they didn't even know they were about to witness. It wouldn't be fair to hide such a treat behind closed doors. Also, she wanted Daphne to see her brother had been using her for information, and this was the best way to do it.

"I think sunlight is the best disinfectant, don't you?"

Charlie glanced over at the seated group again, then raised a brow at her. "Venue is your call."

"Charges?"

"You're still sleeping with Sandy."

"The plea is guilty." She stepped closer to him and poked him in the chest. "Very, very guilty."

"Miranda, Jesus. I thought we agreed you'd cut that out."

"You made a suggestion that I took under advisement."

"That's not what I remember."

She cocked her head and waited.

She knew the moment the memory came back to him. "You did! You weaseled!"

She nodded. "I did."

"You're staying in this house, and you're sleeping with an old movie star. He's what—your sugar daddy?"

She cracked up laughing. "Don't forget I bus tables. If I had a sugar daddy, why would I do that?"

"Sleeping with him looks bad."

"There it is." She smiled. "Charlie George and his constant concern with keeping up appearances. You don't think I know about keeping up appearances? After all of these years lying for Mom? You don't get it—I just don't care anymore."

Charlie looked to the side, and then back at her. "I have an offer for you. From Charles Senior."

"You can take anything Charles Senior has to offer and drop it into the L.A. river."

"He's willing to give you a stipend. All you have to do is live with me in whatever apartment we find together. We'll buy you a car as soon as you get your license back and provide a car service until then. The stipend is all yours. It's twenty thousand a month."

Someone seated by the coffee table coughed.

Charlie's voice was strangely urgent. He seemed to really want her to take the offer. "You can have a job or not have a job. That's up to you. I'm taking the California bar this summer and I already have my firm job, so I'm staying here with you no matter what. Take the offer, Miranda. What does it hurt?"

Miranda shook her head. She thought of all the times her mother stopped taking her medicine because her father wouldn't help her stay on it. The day Miranda found out that there was good treatment for bipolar disorder had been—until then—the best and worst day of Miranda's life. The best, because she had hope that her mom could get better. And the worst, because she knew that her father would never help.

Then the worst day of Miranda's life had happened, and she'd sworn that she'd never take anything from her father again.

How could she? How could Charlie?

And here Charlie stood, a proxy for Charles Senior, and the betrayal was crushing her.

"A quarter million dollars a year and a sweet apartment isn't necromancy, Charlie. Mom will still be dead no matter how much money he throws at us. And it will still be his fault."

"That's not the point."

"What happens when he decides he doesn't want to pay the money anymore? What happens when the terms change? He's always changing the terms." How could Charlie not see? Miranda thought. How could Charlie take their father's side?

Charlie pressed his lips together. He knew she was right.

For a moment, Miranda felt relief. She pressed on. "I can't be dependent on him like that. It'll never work. I'd hate myself. You know I would."

Charlie paused, looking uncertain. "It's already there."

"What?" For a moment, she took in what he said. Then she ran through the kitchen, through the doorway into Sandy's suite of rooms, and into Sandy's office. Using his computer, she logged onto her bank account's website. She'd opened the bank account just that week to deposit her paychecks from Mode. There—twenty thousand dollars on top of her paltry busser's wages.

She was furious. Charlie had betrayed her. Charlie might as well be her father. The one person in the world she could count on had become the person in the world she hated most.

She wanted to cry. She bit her fist to stop the tears.

She stormed back out into the living room. Daphne, Marlon, Greta, and Tory sat, eyes wide, watching her as though she were about to do something that would require immediate evacuation.

"I hate you," she said to Charlie, voice low.

"You don't mean that."

"Right now I do."

She took a step forward. He took a step back.

"Don't you see I'm trying to make my own way for once? And you and Charles Senior just ruined that?"

"Now you can buy more clothes than the two pairs of jeans you wear every day."

"I'm working so hard at Mode every damn day. I'm working and working. I realize you don't know what it's like to work hard, Charlie, to work and work and sweat and work some more. And then to have that money from that asshole appear in my checking account, it's like he's trying to make my work meaningless. And you helped him."

"Your work isn't meaningless. You're the best damn paralegal in Los Angeles. There's no one who comes close, I'm sure of it. Come work for me."

"I don't want to work for you. You're a pompous douchebag."

Charlie's jaw dropped.

Miranda rolled her eyes and sighed. "Well you are. And you know it."

"We're throwing ad hominems now? Is it my turn?"

"I'll win." She leaned closer, putting her face in his. "I'm meaner."

Charlie grimaced.

"I'm going to blow that money on something stupid. I'll buy another motorcycle."

"You can't buy a vehicle without a driver's license."

Miranda scanned the people seated in the room. "Tory will help me."

Charlie looked at Tory over his shoulder.

Tory leaned back in her seat, a horrified look on her face. "I would never. I work in an emergency department. Motorcycles are death machines."

"You're a nurse?"

"You are such a douchebag," Miranda muttered.

"Doctor," Tory said.

Charlie raised his eyebrows, reassessing Tory.

"Get out," Miranda said to him. "You weren't invited."

"All right. Lunch tomorrow?"

"You helped Charles Senior steal my bank account information and put his dirty money in it. I don't want to see you again until I've spent it all."

"You didn't care when you took that twenty grand in cash before your field trip to Las Vegas."

Was he really unable to see the difference? "First of all, I stole that money from him. It wasn't a bribe or blood money."

"Oh, well then. Stealing makes it better."

"And I needed that money to hide from you so I could kill myself."

Shocked silence filled the room even more than it had before.

"What is it?" Miranda said. "We all know it's true." She glanced at the people on the couches. "Everyone's been gossiping. That's why he's here, isn't it, Daphne?"

Daphne nodded meekly, realizing her mistake in sharing too much information with Charlie.

"You're right, Miranda." Charlie said, shaking his head. "You are meaner."

She nodded. "That has never been in doubt. But unlike you, I never betrayed you to our parents."

"Is that what you think?" Charlie said. "That I sided with him against you?"

"Of course that's what I think!"

Charlie shook his head. "No, no, that's not it. God." Charlie's voice had dropped to nearly a whisper. "I would never do that." His brows drew together, and his eyes dropped to the floor.

Miranda stepped closer, putting her hand on his drooping shoulder. "What is it, Charlie?"

He met her eyes, and for the first time since he'd flown west, she saw the haunting there. And she remembered. Back in January, Miranda had almost died. But Charlie, he'd shot his mother dead.

"It was my idea to set you up with the funds, not his. I was the one who wanted you to come live with me." His voice dropped to a whisper. "I need you. Just, for a little while."

At the pain in his voice, Miranda threw herself at him, wrapping her arms around his neck, squeezing him to her. They hugged, releasing all of the tension that had built during their confrontation.

When they let each other go, he spoke again. "I don't want to be a burden on you. I'm fine, really. There are just times when things get a little hard."

Miranda wondered what *things* Charlie was talking about, exactly. "Lets have a day together, and we'll come up with a compromise. Tuesday? Can you take off Tuesday?"

"Yeah, I can manage that," he said.

"Do you want to stay tonight?"

He looked around the room, at the gaping faces. Miranda suppressed a smile. When he met Tory's eyes, he winked. Tory's eyes widened.

"Naw. I have a client thing tonight at this horrible nightclub on Sunset. Everyone under thirty is required to go."

"Break all the hearts."

He grinned at her. "*Res ipsa.*"

She shut the door behind him, then pressed her palm against the warm, dark wood. She took a few deep breaths to calm herself. Finally, she turned back to face her friends.

Marlon had his arm around Daphne. Daphne had her hand over her mouth, her eyes wide. Greta looked unperturbed for the most part, which was one of the reasons Miranda had always liked Greta.

Tory was grinning. "Wow," she said. "Your brother is really hot."

"That's what you took from all that?" Miranda said. "Really?"

"Well, he is," Tory said. "Anatomically speaking."

"He is, anatomically speaking," Miranda agreed. "And you don't get shocked by much, do you?"

"I'm an emergency department doctor in the city of Los Angeles. By choice." Tory raised her glass. "It either makes you or breaks you."

Her job was probably a reason why Tory was hard to shock, Miranda thought, but it wasn't the only reason.

Chapter Nineteen

Monday morning, Sandy left early for a meeting with a real estate developer in Orange County. Miranda sat in the kitchen, a cup of coffee to her left, her phone on the table in front of her.

She was a chicken.

She picked up the phone. Dialed.

"Miranda?" John answered. "I, well, didn't expect to hear from you."

"Whyever not?" she said in a sweet voice.

He sighed. "I was really angry at him, but I shouldn't have taken it out on you both like that."

"Thanks for apologizing."

"I've wanted to call you and do it sooner, but I figured you'd hang up in my ear."

"Today I'm going to use your feelings of guilt against you. I need a favor. It's my day off, and I really need more clothes."

"You want me to take you shopping?"

"It should be painful enough penance for acting like a caveman."

He laughed. "I'll see you in an hour? I have to wrap up a few things here, and then I'll pick you up."

Precisely one hour later, Miranda was in John's car heading toward the shops in Brentwood.

"Are you sure you want to go back here?" he said. "If you're on a budget now, we can head someplace less pricey."

"You haven't heard." She pulled her debit card from her pocket. "My father tried to bribe me. I'm currently flush with ill-gotten gains."

"Did his bribe work?"

"No."

She watched John's face as he expertly parallel parked in an empty spot on Montana, his fine nose and well-shaped jaw catching her attention. She'd thought he was average before, but he wasn't. He was handsome. And cool-headed. And reliable.

A week ago, standing in the sand with him, she'd believed he needed someone better than she was, someone who wasn't broken. She'd hurt him by walking away, but she'd believed it was for his own good. But over the past week, she'd begun to wonder if maybe some honesty might not be better. After all, if the roles had been reversed, and someone tried to tell her what was best for her, she would have been ripping mad.

And maybe she wasn't so broken after all.

They headed down Montana to the boutique where she'd bought her dress for Greta's wedding. They had good denim, and the slim-cut t-shirts she liked. They even had flip-flops, and she still wanted a pair. She stopped to gaze in the window. The dress on the mannequin caught her eye, a dress she'd never wear, of course. It was yellow, the same sunny yellow as the coffeemaker Sandy had bought for her, and sleeveless, with a short, A-line skirt. It was so cheerful.

"Do you like it?" John asked her.

"Not really."

They entered the store. She grabbed a few pairs of jeans in her size, and some shirts, and some sweaters to layer over the shirts, and a few rolls of Hanky Panky underpants because she was low on those, too. She tried on flip-flops. She glanced out the window at the blue sky.

"It's May," she said to John, who was sitting in the man-chair by the dressing room.

"Yeah," he said.

"I've been working so much I hadn't realized."

"It's only been May for a couple of days. You haven't missed much." He smiled.

"I'm going to try on these jeans. Just a sec."

She looked at the rack by the front of the store where the yellow dress hung in a variety of sizes. She dashed up, grabbed two, and brought them into the dressing room with her.

She pulled on the dress over her head and zipped up the side. She couldn't remember the last time she'd worn anything so colorful. She leaned close to the mirror, pressing her fingers into her cheek, making sure it was her in the reflection. Her short hair swept around her jawline, and the dress seemed to emit an energy of its own.

She stepped out into the shop.

John stood, nearly dropping his cell phone. "You. Ah."

"Do you like it?"

He nodded.

"I don't wear things like this." She felt nervous. She hated feeling nervous, usually. But for some reason, she didn't mind feeling nervous around John.

He stepped close to her and whispered. "You look like sunlight. And I want to stand in it." He nodded toward the dressing room. "Can I talk to you for a sec, in private?"

She backed into the room, and he shut the louvered door behind them.

He rested a hand on the wall as though to steady himself. "I don't know what you have going on in your life with Sandy. I don't want to know." He shook his head as if to clear it. "I just know one thing."

He put one hand on her waist and pulled her to him. He waited a moment, letting her close the last inch.

She did.

When she kissed him, she understood so many things.

————

John waited while Miranda paid for her *wardrobe supplement* as she called it, which included the delicious yellow dress. It had taken all of his energy to keep from throwing his fist in the air after that kiss in the dressing room. He had to focus on keeping his cool in this high-end shop, full of rich daughters of studio executives and prime-time dream girls. And Miranda.

His Miranda. He didn't bother to think of her otherwise. What was the point? She was his. She'd been his since the first day they'd met. He wasn't going to stop trying to win her back.

Once her two bags were filled—one held her boots on the bottom, because she insisted on wearing her new flip-flops—she led him out of the store.

"Do you want to go back to Didier's?" she asked.

Didier's, the restaurant where they'd first met, where he'd approached her asking about Daphne, but ended up hanging out with Miranda instead.

"If you'd like."

"I thought maybe we could start over."

"That seems like a good reason." Actually, that seemed like a fantastic reason.

"I want to tell you the things you still don't know."

"Even better."

They walked to Didier's, where they'd first met and become friends almost instantly, even though Miranda had pulled a trick on him at Greta's wedding, and that had hurt a bit. But he'd known he'd just been in the crossfire, and he'd known that she'd needed a friend, so he'd forgiven her.

Didier's, a French bistro in Brentwood, had black-and-white tiled floors, a long bar, wicker chairs and small wood tables.

"I've been to Paris twenty-nine times," Miranda said as they entered the restaurant.

"You know exactly how many?"

She cut him a look. "This place is trying too hard. It would never make it as a Parisian café."

"But as a bistro in Brentwood, it isn't bad."

"No, it isn't bad." She followed him as he led her to two empty seats at the bar.

Miranda flagged down the bartender and ordered two mimosas.

"Just like the first time," John said, remembering that day. She'd entranced him immediately.

"Yeah." She handed the bartender her card to start a tab.

"You don't have to pay."

"I'm not paying," she said. "Charles Senior is." She explained how, the night before, a lot of money had appeared in her checking account. She also described an absurd offer that Charlie had brought to her on behalf of her father.

"You aren't afraid that the money will disappear from your account?" He remembered how upset she'd been when her father had cut off her mother's credit card.

"That's not how banks work. You can wire money to a person if you have her account number. But you can't take it away." She frowned. "Well, not without committing bank fraud. But my father would only bother to commit bank fraud if he thought the situation were dire."

And the situation was no longer dire, her words implied. John smiled. This was the Miranda that he knew had been underneath the terrified and tortured girl he'd spent the past few weeks with. But seeing her at her worst only made him love her more.

Love, he thought. That word was accurate.

But she was still living with Sandy Martin.

After that terrible fight at Sandy's house, he'd thought he'd blown whatever chance he might have had with Miranda. But somehow, he had hope again. Something had changed in her. He just needed to know what.

"Thanks for helping me out today," she said. "And for taking a risk on me, again."

"This might strike you as odd," he said. "But I actually don't think you are much of a risk."

"Why the hell not?"

"Why'd you call me today?"

She looked away from him, at the bottles lined up behind the bar. "Six months before my mother died, I broke up with my first and only boyfriend. His name was Matthias. We'd been together since just after I graduated from college. He was the only guy I've ever loved."

Sandy, then, was not on the list. John did not let his relief show. "Why'd you break up?"

"He moved away. He had a good reason for moving—an important job—but I don't do long distance."

John suppressed a smile. Of course she didn't. "Why not?"

"It's impractical. Odds are a relationship won't survive it. And what is the point if you can't be together? Do I have to go on?" She sounded aggrieved.

John laughed. "No. But he still wanted to be with you?"

"Yeah."

"And you still loved him?"

"You don't just stop loving somebody—even I know that. But eventually, as the months went by, things faded. We stayed friends, and he stopped being so annoyed with me. And then, one day, bang."

Bang. He tried to picture the awful scene Charlie had described in the car on the way to Las Vegas. Miranda, dying on the floor. Charlie, shooting the mother they had both loved.

Their mimosas arrived in the hands of the bartender, who set them on the bar.

"I haven't spoken to Matthias since my mom died. I don't know what I would say. He still has a job at my parents' firm—at my father's firm—once his two-year clerkship is over. He might take a firm job in Raleigh or D.C. or whatever, though. But he has family ties in Winston-Salem, so he might go back to George Law." She took a sip of her mimosa. "But I'm gone. And Sorcha is gone. We were his two favorite people in the firm. We tried a lot of cases together."

"You should call him." John didn't particularly want Miranda having heart-to-hearts with her former love, but he also knew something about unfinished business. He was also pretty psyched to learn that Miranda knew what it meant to love someone.

"I should." She nodded. "You still haven't told me why you don't think I'm risky."

"You haven't told me why you called me today."

"I asked you first," she said.

"Seriously?" John chuckled.

"Fine." She sipped her drink, as though she were gathering courage. She seemed nervous.

John was surprised. Miranda George didn't seem like she got nervous often.

She gazed at him with eyes that seemed to have doubled in size. "That day on the beach, I wanted to say yes to you. I wanted to do everything you asked of me. But I was afraid that something was broken in me. And I thought that you deserved someone who wasn't broken."

At her words, John finally dared to hope. "So you tried to push me away."

She nodded.

"And today?"

"I thought maybe you wouldn't mind trying anyway. And also, maybe," she looked away, "I'm not so sure I'm broken."

It was like she was waiting for him to laugh at her. To tell her that she was an entire cart of baggage, a natural disaster, anything.

"I never thought you were a risk, not in the way you mean. Just in the normal ways. I thought you might break my damn heart. But I never thought I was risking more than that. And you're supposed to risk your heart, Miranda." He stood up from his stool and wrapped his arms around her shoulders, dropping a kiss on her head. "Those are risks we're supposed to take."

Her voice was muffled into his chest. "I should've known that moving in with Sandy would hurt you so badly."

"Yes, you should've."

"I didn't believe you cared about me that much."

"No, you didn't."

"I believe you now." She looked up at him. "I'll move my things to Charlie's place tomorrow."

John would've preferred her to say *in five minutes*, but tomorrow would do.

———

WHEN MIRANDA ENTERED THE HOUSE AT FIVE O'CLOCK MONDAY NIGHT, Sandy was in the kitchen sautéing bratwurst in a frypan. He had sauerkraut in a pot, and sourdough rolls for the sausages ready for the toaster oven.

The food smelled good, he knew, but the bout of indigestion from the other day was back, and he'd lost his appetite. He finished preparing the meal for her, though, and maybe he'd want some later. Once he felt better. Less sick to his stomach, less dizzy.

But when Miranda called his name, he turned off the heat to all burners, and took a seat at the bar.

He could tell, by the tone of her voice, that it was time.

She entered the kitchen wearing jeans, a black t-shirt, and flip-flops. It was the first time he'd seen her toes while she was wearing shoes. She carried two large shopping bags from a pricey shop he knew—a shop that everyone knew. She'd been putting her father's money to good use, then.

Good for her.

She set the bags down at one end of the long kitchen table, then sat next to him.

"The food smells delicious," she said. "I didn't realize you cook."

"This is hardly cooking. More like reheating food from the market's prepared-foods section."

"Better than I could do. Charlie and I just eat room service."

Ah, there. She and Charlie, in her mind, were already living in the hotel together. She was moving out. Miranda was always so good at hiding her tells. Perhaps she was letting them show tonight on purpose.

"How is Charlie?" he asked.

"I haven't seen him since he barged in here Thursday night. We're having Apology Brunch tomorrow."

"Is that a George Sibling ritual?"

Miranda nodded. "Can I make us drinks? You want something?"

The thought of drinking alcohol made his bout of dizziness surge. He shook his head. "Why don't you just tell me what's on your mind."

She cocked her head to the side, as though he were a scientific specimen. "It's over, and I'm moving out tomorrow."

Her words hit him in the sternum like a well-thrown punch. Even though he'd known what she was going to say, all the preparation had made no difference. Her words hurt.

He nodded.

"I owe you my life." She placed her hand on his forearm and squeezed.

"That might be an exaggeration," he said.

"It's not."

Plus, Miranda wasn't prone to exaggeration. She had a bad temper, and her words could cut, but they cut because their aim was true, not hyperbolic.

"Did I do something wrong?" he asked.

"What could you possibly have done that was wrong?" She

sounded immensely irritated. "You're great. You're basically perfect. But surely, with all of your years of experience, you can tell that you and I aren't going anywhere."

Of course he could tell, when she forced him to examine things more closely. That didn't mean he wanted their thing, whatever it was, to end. Having her vibrant presence around the house had been glorious these past weeks. Her energy permeating the house, her beautiful naked body in his bed (on his couch, on his kitchen table, on his deck), her smartass attitude—he'd miss it all.

Miranda looked away from him. "You and I each deserve someone who will love us completely. We both know what that feels like. And this isn't it."

Ah. Sandy had his answer now. "You have someone already. I suppose John finally stepped up."

"I didn't cheat on you or anything. I wanted to talk to you first. I'll move out tomorrow, unless you want me gone sooner."

"I'm not going to kick you out. Take your time. You're going to stay with Charlie?"

"Yeah. That puts a cramp in my work schedule at Mode, though."

"I can tell you a secret, then."

Miranda raised her eyebrows.

"Patricia didn't think you'd last this long. She already hired your replacement."

"She did not." Miranda sounded horrified. "I was an excellent busser."

"You were. But she knew you were temporary. She's been in the business long enough."

"Please don't hate me." Her voice dropped to a whisper.

"Never."

"Oh jeez, don't say that either. It's a curse. Words like *never* and *forever* tend to be followed by terrible things."

Sandy felt a twinge at her superstitious words.

"I don't hate you for this," Sandy said.

"That's better."

Chapter Twenty

Miranda tossed the tennis ball high, her visor blocking the sun to her left. As she tossed, she cocked her right hip back and squatted low, building power. The ball kept climbing. In the same motion, her right arm looped behind her back, behind her head, elbow cocked, her racquet loaded at her spine. Then, boom—her right hip exploded forward, her knees upward, her elbow, carrying her arm, and her wrist, and her racquet in one smooth motion like a catapult, launched her from the ground until her racquet hit the ball, crash, and sent it over the net toward Charlie. It flew right down the T on the ad side. He'd been standing too wide. Ace.

"God damn it, Miranda."

"No cussing, Charlie. They won't let us come back."

"I thought after a four-month break from tennis your serve would have gotten sloppy."

"Everything else has. You're still winning, you big baby."

"I'm only up a break."

"Which means you're probably going to win."

"You were in a *coma*."

"I've totally lost my edge."

They changed sides. It was four games to three, with Charlie still ahead. Miranda set the three balls on Charlie's racquet as they passed each other, then she grabbed a sip of water. Everything she had with her was new or borrowed—the shoes, socks, skirt, and tank she'd just bought in the pro shop while Charlie had bought shoes and clothes for himself. The racquets they were playing with were demos. They'd bought the can of balls and their water bottles. They were guests at the club where they were playing, recommended by Charlie's colleague at his law firm. The place had thirty courts, plus two golf courses and a pool. Charlie had told her most of the firm's attorneys were members.

A pool and a place to beat Charlie at tennis—Miranda had to admit it was nice. She would never join, of course. Charlie would. That was fine—she only wanted to go with Charlie anyway.

She probably couldn't beat him at tennis today, she knew. She had indeed lost her edge after months without playing. But she'd beat him next time.

After their match—he won in a tiebreaker—they showered and dressed for brunch by the pool. Miranda had packed her yellow dress and flip flops.

Charlie was waiting for her by his new car, a black M5 that looked a lot like the car he'd rented and returned. Charlie always had a type —whether it came to cars or girls.

He raised his eyebrows when he saw the dress. "That's cheerful."

"Bite me."

He held up his hands. "I like it."

"I don't care."

You look like sunlight, John had said to her at the store, like she'd been something he'd needed to live. Sunlight, as vital as water and food. She didn't care if Charlie wanted to make fun of her yellow dress. She'd seen it in that shop window, and she'd known.

"Fine," Charlie said. "It'll take some getting used to, if you're suddenly going to dress like a rainbow. But on balance it's probably a good thing."

"Charlie, either you're going to see me for who I am—even as that person keeps changing before your eyes—or you're not. I'm not the person you went to high school with, or college with. I'm not the person who was always waiting at home for you on school breaks. I'm none of those things."

He rubbed his face with his hand as he looked at her, and she imagined what he saw: her cropped hair, shorter than she'd ever had in her life, her bright clothes, when she'd always favored black or dark jewel tones. Her flip-flops, when she'd always worn expensive flats even to the pool. Before, everything on the outside was designed to keep the inside together, even as her insides were falling apart.

He nodded, opening her door for her. "Let's eat."

———

THE POOLSIDE RESTAURANT REMINDED CHARLIE A LOT OF THE ONE BACK home. He glanced at his sister, who sat next to him at the square table. If the familiarity made him comfortable, it probably hurt her. He was starting to get a feel for things now, for why she might cut off her hair or start wearing yellow.

She'd spent her whole life shielding him so he could have good memories. But while he'd been making those good memories, she'd been suffering.

It was time for her to let that suffering go.

He'd been trying to get the old Miranda back to make himself feel better. But she'd never left. She was still there, cussing and kick-serving. She just wasn't willing to play stupid rich-kid games to keep him happy anymore. She was going to bus tables if she felt like it. She was going to find herself, or something. And he was going to let her.

"I'm moving out of Sandy's today," she said, sipping her soda water with lime. She'd turned down a bloody mary, and he restrained himself from asking why.

His eyebrows shot up. After all of his throwing down last Thursday night, today she decided to leave? "Can I ask why without you poisoning my food?"

"I ended things with him—amicably—and I'm going to start seeing John."

John Wesley. He'd grown on Charlie. Charlie would have him checked out, of course, but he seemed like a good guy. He definitely seemed devoted to Miranda, which was a good start. "How did Sandy take the news?"

"Like a grownup. As I expect you to do."

He laughed. "John's cool. He didn't let me push him around."

"So he passed your macho test." She rolled her eyes. "Super-duper."

But Charlie remembered when John had kept his promise to Miranda at the bar in Las Vegas. Lying to Charlie for her couldn't have been easy. He knew he could be a pain in the ass when he was angry.

"You going to take a car service to bus tables then? That might look a little funny."

"You are such a dick."

"Here comes Miranda, our table busser, in her limo."

"I'm quitting that job today."

Charlie hid his relief.

"And I'm moving in with you. I hope you have a two-bedroom suite."

"Of course I do. I was expecting you."

"I need a bikini for the hot tub."

"It's a pretty sweet hot tub."

"I also need that paralegal job you mentioned."

"Consider it done." Charlie couldn't hide his smile now.

Her voice got small. "I still hate our family."

Charlie picked up her hand in both of his, squeezing it. "Miranda." She looked away from him, at the glistening blue water of the pool. "Big Sis." She looked at him, her eyes red at the edges. "I'm your family."

Tears gathered in her eyes. "Okay." She nodded. "You're right."

"We outnumber him now. We've won, okay? He can't hurt any of us anymore. Do you understand? Any of us."

He left the most important words unspoken: *including Mom.*

"Okay."

He kept hold of her hand while they waited for their food.

"Have you thought more about your future? The dreams thing?"

She nodded. "Prepare to be shocked."

He smiled. "Okay."

"You were right. I am the best paralegal you've ever seen. I was telling John about how Matthias, Sorcha, and I used to try cases together, and I realized how amazing we were."

"You miss it."

She nodded. "I'm going to go to law school. Follow in my little brother's footsteps."

"Seriously?"

"Yep."

"You hate lawyers."

"I hated *those* lawyers."

Charlie felt a big caveat coming, one he wasn't going to like.

"I'm going to get a job as a public defender, if they'll have me.

"You're not. No. No way."

She smiled, close-lipped and pleased with herself. "If Charles Senior wants to give me three hundred thousand a year, then I'll take it. And then I'll do something he would find absolutely distasteful. I'll throw the might of this big legal brain behind defending the rights of the defenseless."

"You'll have to hang out in jail. A lot. And not the nice ones."

"Yes."

"You'll change your mind before you graduate."

"Remember Matthias's mom?"

Charlie remembered. Matthias, Miranda's ex-boyfriend and first love, had gone into law because his mother had been sent away for a decade by an over-zealous prosecutor and an understaffed public defender's office.

Shit. Miranda was not going to change her mind.

"Yellow dress, Charlie," she said. "Get used to it."

CHARLIE PULLED UP IN FRONT OF SANDY'S HOUSE AND PARKED NEXT TO Sandy's car. Miranda took a deep breath. She didn't think leaving would feel so final. Of course she'd be back to visit, wouldn't she? Leaving Sandy's didn't mean leaving them all behind, did it? Sure, Marlon mostly thought she was awful, but Daphne liked her—and Greta too—she hadn't imagined that, had she?

She didn't want to lose them. Suddenly, she cared very much about the offer of a new family that Daphne had made before she'd left for Las Vegas.

Charlie stood next to her. When she looked at him, he said, "I'll help carry your stuff. And I want to thank him."

Miranda agreed, and she led the way inside. "Sandy," she called out. When he didn't answer, she dashed upstairs to see if he was in his sound-proof viewing room. He wasn't.

"Miranda!" Charlie called from downstairs, with an edge of panic to his voice that had her flying down the stairs, chased by adrenaline.

Charlie was squatting on the deck. Sandy was lying on his back, eyes open, clutching his cell phone in one hand.

"No," Miranda said, running out, sliding to her knees. "No."

"He's awake and breathing, but not well. Call 9-1-1."

Miranda laid a palm on the deck for stability, fighting off a sense of vertigo. The George siblings, and once again someone was dying on the floor. There was that kid in college, there was Sorcha, when she'd overdosed by accident. And finally there was January, when everything had shattered.

Maybe Charlie was right. Maybe she and Charlie *were* different. They wrecked everyone around them except themselves.

That couldn't be right. It couldn't be.

"Take his pulse," she told Charlie, waiting for an answer from 9-1-1. "Charlie," she was practically screaming. "Does he have a pulse?"

"Barely."

When the emergency person answered, she gave Sandy's address and demanded an ambulance. "I think he's had a heart attack."

"Does he have an Automatic External Defibrillator?" the operator asked.

Good question. She leaned toward Sandy. "Can you hear me, babe? Do you have an AED?"

Sandy managed to choke out one word. "Closet."

He had one thousand closets, but she ran to the one in his bedroom. There, on the floor, was a portable AED. "Found it," she told the person on the phone. "Will this harm him?"

"No. It doesn't do anything if it senses a heartbeat. Only if his heart stops—fibrillates. Just follow the directions."

Only if his heart stops.

She and Charlie operated the AED as though they'd done it a thousand times before, ripping open Sandy's button-down on the deck, attaching the sticky pads, hoping to save his life under the unrelenting Los Angeles sky.

As soon as Charlie's hands were free, Miranda told him to call Daphne. "And tell Daphne to call everyone. I don't know where he's going, or what's happening. But they all need to know."

Charlie nodded and made the call.

Miranda wasn't supposed to touch Sandy, in case the AED had to fire, but she didn't want to let him lie there without any human touch. Letting him lie there, alone, was killing her.

The guilt was killing her.

Yesterday she'd come home to find him cooking her dinner. And she'd thrown all of his generosity back in his face so that she'd could fool around with John. Yesterday seemed like a million years ago. She couldn't leave Sandy now. If he survived this, he'd need someone to take care of him. He'd need her. Recovery might take weeks, even months. He had saved her life. She couldn't abandon him now.

She could never be that selfish.

She and John—they just weren't meant to be.

Charlie came back from the other end of the deck where he'd been speaking in rushed tones with Daphne. Ambulance sirens wailed in the distance. "I'll go open the front door."

"The dogs. Lock them in the bedroom, okay?"

He nodded, then ran off.

"I'm not going to leave you, Sandy. I'll be here for you. I'm not going anywhere."

Sandy's face was turning ashen, the pinkness leaving his skin.

"Come on, Sandy." She started to cry.

The paramedics entered, and she sat back against a deck post and sobbed.

———

At eight-thirty that night, they all gathered at Sandy's house: Greta, Marlon, Daphne, Patricia from Mode, who'd acquired food for everyone, even Tory, who'd been so helpful at the hospital, translating what the doctors were telling them, and Charlie, Miranda, and John.

Miranda didn't know who'd called John, telling him to meet them at the hospital, but whenever he'd tried to sit near her, she'd moved and sat next to Daphne or Greta or Charlie.

She couldn't bear the twin aches in her heart. The hole that leaving John was going to cause, and the hole that her guilt over Sandy had already torn.

The group of friends occupied one end of Sandy's kitchen table, where they'd gathered after leaving the hospital. The Coronary Care Unit kicked out all visitors at 8 o'clock.

They hadn't been allowed into the Unit anyway, with the exception of Marlon, Greta, and Tory. Tory had privileges at the hospital, so she was allowed to talk to the doctors, thank god, and she kept them all posted on what was happening with Sandy's health. Marlon and Greta, it turned out, were listed as Sandy's medical Powers of Attorney. No one had been more shocked than they were by the discovery.

In the waiting room, Tory explained that Sandy had had a heart attack.

"But, he's so fit," Daphne argued, refusing to believe it. "How is it possible?"

"The left anterior descending artery is particularly susceptible to cholesterol buildup, cutting off blood flow to the main artery. I've seen healthy men in their late thirties drop dead from heart attacks caused by this particular artery." Tory paused. "We call it the *widowmaker*."

"Well that's grim," Marlon said, hugging Daphne to him.

"But in this case," Tory said, "Charlie and Miranda got there in time. The AED defibrillated his heart while the paramedics were still in the driveway. Getting that sinus rhythm back kept his heart pumping relatively normally for the trip to the hospital and into surgery."

"And the surgery is minor?" Greta asked, the stiffness of her shoulders and shaking in her voice revealing how afraid she was.

"As far as heart surgery can be minor. He'll have a cardiac catheterization to open up the obstructed artery via angioplasty and then placement of a stent to prevent collapse in the future. He must have had a genetic predisposition toward this kind of heart condition. Like Daphne said, he's very fit. His checkups would have caught anything out of the ordinary. But bad genes—you can't control those. He'll have to take heart medicine every day now."

Miranda thought about the medicine box he'd gotten for her. She would get Sandy a matching one. They could keep them side-by-side in his bathroom.

She wouldn't leave him.

She couldn't.

"Anyways," Tory continued, "he'll stay here in the CCU for a few days, and then he'll be released home. But he'll be pooped, and he won't be able to do much. He'll need to go to rehab. And he should have someone stay with him, probably for a few weeks."

In the car on the way to Sandy's, Charlie drove silently while Miranda sobbed. He didn't make any snarky comments, and he didn't try to make her feel better. He was exactly what she needed him to be.

Finally, before they pulled into the driveway, Miranda said, "I can't move out now. I have to stay and take care of him."

Charlie was quiet for a moment, taking in her words. "What about Marlon and Greta? The others? Isn't that their job?"

"He took care of me, Charlie. I owe him."

Charlie parked down by the garage. "Let's see what the others have to say."

Miranda knew a delay tactic when she heard one. "I'm not going to change my mind."

So now everyone sat at the table, while Patricia handed out sandwiches that someone from Mode had brought by.

Miranda stood to make a pot of coffee in her coffeemaker. She poured six large mugs, then set another pot to brew. She opened the fridge and pulled out the cream, turning her mug of coffee light brown.

Daphne appeared at her side. "I can help carry those."

"Okay."

"How are you? It must have been such a shock finding him."

"I wasn't alone. Charlie was with me."

Daphne chewed her thumbnail, giving her a skeptical look. "Sandy owes you his life. You're basically a hero."

"No, I'm not."

Daphne raised her eyebrows at the hardness in Miranda's voice.

"I feel like I did this to him. I broke up with him, and then he had a heart attack."

"You broke up with him?"

"Last night during dinner. I'd come home today to pack my things and move out."

"You blame yourself for his heart attack?"

Miranda frowned. That didn't sound right. "Not exactly."

"Someone recently told me not to take all the credit for bad things that happen to other people. I think it was you."

"That's not what I'm doing. I don't blame myself for his heart attack. I just feel like I owe him for everything he's done for me." But she did feel guilty. There was no escaping the guilt.

Daphne nodded.

"So I feel like I need to stay here and take care of him while he recovers, the way he took care of me."

Daphne glanced over her shoulder to where John sat at the table. Miranda followed her line of sight. John was watching her intently. But there was a sadness to his gaze as well, as though he knew what she was going to tell him tonight. As though he knew that he'd already lost her.

"You and John," Daphne said.

"We figured things out yesterday. That was why I was moving out. And also, I'd decided to apply to law school. I was going to go work with my brother as a paralegal during my application year. I'd made a plan, finally."

"But you're setting all of that aside for Sandy?"

"I have to."

Daphne nodded, a thoughtful look on her face. Then she carried three of the mugs back to the table.

Miranda picked up her own mug along with two more and followed

Daphne spoke first. "I think we should make a schedule for Sandy's care. Tory can be our medical consultant. The rest of us can take one day of the week. How does that sound?"

Miranda whipped her head in Daphne's direction. "That sounds like a no. Did you not hear me?"

"I heard you. I'm proposing a better solution."

"What was your solution?" Greta asked, sounding curious.

"I was going to stay here and take care of Sandy."

Marlon snorted. "Because you do such a good job taking care of yourself?"

Miranda rolled her eyes. "You're like a canker sore that won't heal."

"Marlon," Daphne said, annoyed. "Will you give her a break?"

"Why should I?" Marlon spoke to Daphne. "Why does she feel like it's her job to take care of Sandy? She hardly knows him."

"She's willing to sacrifice weeks, maybe months, of her life." Daphne said. "Show some empathy."

"She saved his *life*," Greta said to him.

"It's okay, y'all," Miranda said. "He can be mad at me. I'm sure I did something to deserve it at some point." She stood, looking down at Marlon. "You're still a canker sore."

Marlon stood too, looking angry now.

Miranda spoke to Greta and Daphne. "I feel that I owe Sandy, for everything he did for me. I also feel guilty. It's no secret that I broke things off with him yesterday. The timing is awful."

"Are you saying that you actually, physically broke Sandy's heart?" Marlon laughed. "You sure do think highly of yourself."

At his words, Miranda's patience snapped. She launched herself at Marlon. Everything—Sandy's ashen face, his still body on the deck, the look of loss on John's face right then, her dreams, set aside once more—she couldn't take Marlon's taunting on top of everything else.

Before she could land a punch, Charlie caught her around the waist and hauled her back.

Marlon shook his head. "For rich kids, you two sure act like punks."

Miranda hissed, Charlie's arms around her the only thing holding her still. She was at the end of her control. "Not him, you imbecile," she said. "Just me."

"Watch it, Marlon," Charlie said.

"Or what? You'll sue me?"

"Can't you see she's hurting?" Charlie said scornfully. "How many times are you going to make the same mistake?"

With that, Charlie wrapped his arm around Miranda's shoulder and led her back toward her bedroom.

Chapter Twenty-One

As soon as they were away from the kitchen and out of earshot, Miranda started crying. Once they entered her bedroom, Charlie closed the door, put his hands on her shoulders, and turned her to face him. "Do you want me to beat him up for you? He looks tough, but I think I could take him."

She burst into sobs. "Why is he so mean to me?"

Charlie chewed his lower lip. "Honest assessment? He's jealous of Sandy's relationship with you. And he doesn't like unpredictable things—I'm not sure why just yet, but I'd imagine there's some sort of horrible loss in his childhood that makes instability the bane of his existence. And let's be honest, you knock people off-balance."

She sniffed. "I agree with your assessment. But I'm tired of his shit."

"Do you want it to stop, or do you want to just go away?"

"I don't want to go away."

He exhaled. "That's a relief."

Miranda's heart clenched at the pain hidden under Charlie's words. She should never have abandoned him after their mother's death. And she should never have run away to Las Vegas. It would take a while for him to have faith in her again.

She rubbed her face with her hands. They were shaking. "I thought Sandy was going to die."

"I did, too." He held her shoulders, leaning forward until his forehead touched hers, and she remembered why she was so very glad she had a brother.

There was a knock at the door. Charlie raised his eyebrows. She nodded that it was okay to answer.

Charlie cracked the door open a couple of inches. "Seriously, dude?" Charlie said, annoyance in his voice.

"I screwed up." Marlon spoke. "I need to apologize."

"It's not her job to relieve your guilty conscience."

"It's okay, Charlie," she said. "You can let him in." She sat on the edge of the bed, suddenly exhausted.

Marlon stepped into the bedroom, and she realized how haggard he appeared. He must have been the most worried of them all. His lashing out was rooted in fear, nothing more. She knew that, rationally.

It still hurt, though.

He sat in the armchair in the corner, the one where she usually tossed her clothes before hanging them up, resting his elbows on his knees. Charlie remained standing, arms crossed like a bouncer.

Marlon spoke. "My father died of a heart attack when I was twelve. Then, a little while later, my mom died in a car wreck, and I had to go live with my aunt and uncle. Sandy basically adopted me when I was a teenager."

Charlie had been right, then. Something awful in Marlon's past had indeed been triggered by everything happening with Sandy lately. And then, today, the heart attack had pressed on that trigger point harder than anything else. His surrogate father had nearly died in the same way his real father had. It was amazing Marlon wasn't in pieces, poor guy.

"It's no excuse for how I've been treating you. You didn't do anything wrong. You're a little reckless for my tastes, but as Daphne will tell you, I drive five miles under the speed limit, so just about everything falls into that category."

"Even Daphne falls into that category," Miranda said.

"I know." And the love in his eyes when he said those words cracked Miranda's heart open. He ran his hand through his hair. "The point is, I'm sorry. I've been taking all my stress and worry out on you." He narrowed his eyes. "You let me do it, though. At least you did. Today was the first time you fought back."

"I don't want to fight with you. I want you and Daphne to be happy."

Marlon nodded. "You blame yourself for what happened to Sandy, even though you shouldn't. Jesus, you saved his life—both of you. I owe you so much. You think you have to do all the work taking care of him, but you don't. We can all do it together." He stood. "Come on. Daphne's making a chart or something. We're supposed to sign up."

She stood. "I forgive you. I'd already forgiven you." She pointed at Charlie. "He hasn't."

Marlon turned to her brother. "If someone talked to my sister the way I talked to Miranda, I wouldn't have had the self-control you have right now."

"We Georges play a long game."

"Plotting my death?"

"In a way that will ensure no one knows it was me."

"I completely believe you could do such a thing."

Miranda rolled her eyes. "No, he couldn't."

Charlie grinned, breaking the tense mood. "Probably not. Our father could, though. Cold-blooded bastard."

Marlon held out his hand to Miranda. She shook it.

———

LATER THAT NIGHT, SHE WALKED JOHN TO HIS CAR. IT WAS AROUND TEN o'clock, after the food, after the happy phone call from the hospital that told them that Sandy was doing fine, was awake, and would be released by the end of the week, and after the schedule sign-ups that gave Miranda one twenty-four-hour duty shift per week at Sandy's house.

While they walked, John was oddly silent, especially compared to the day before, when he'd been so free with his words. *You look like sunlight*, he'd said. *You're supposed to risk your heart*, he'd sworn.

When they reached his car, he leaned back against the driver's-side door, his face inscrutable. Maybe he should be her new spades partner, she thought. She couldn't get a read on him at all.

"You were going to leave me again tonight," he said.

She exhaled. He'd known, then. She considered lying to him, denying the accusation, but he deserved the truth. "I was, yes."

"Do you love him?"

Did she love Sandy? Is that what he thought? "I love him as a friend. No more than that."

"But you would have left me anyway because of a sense of duty?"

She paused, and then she nodded. "I didn't want to. I felt like I had to."

He nodded, fishing his keys from his pocket. "Ever since I met you, I've been in second place. Yesterday was the one day when I was first for you—and that day was amazing, Miranda. You made me want to change my life. To, I don't know, live for you." He shook his head.

"You made me feel the same," she said quietly. "You still do."

"Not enough, apparently."

"John, no. Please give me another chance."

"Every time a crisis hits, you're going to turn away from me. You'll turn toward your brother, or Sandy, or Daphne, or someone else. I've been here all along, waiting for you. Fighting for you. But that's not enough. I don't know what is."

"You are enough," she whispered, knowing that her words weren't going to make him stay. He was right, after all. The crisis had hit, and she'd shoved him, and everything else that she wanted most, aside.

He reached out and touched the tips of her hair. "I wish that were true." Then he climbed in his car and drove away.

Chapter Twenty-Two

On Saturdays, John didn't usually work. But after the events of the past Monday and Tuesday, he needed to keep his brain occupied and his fingers away from his phone. He was terrified he'd make a call and end up right where he'd been before—at the end of a string held by Miranda George.

So he was in his studio apartment immersed in code, and he didn't even know what time it was. He had pizza left over from the day before that he'd been slowly consuming. He hadn't cleaned in days. If this was love, he didn't want anything to do with it, not for a long while.

The knock at his apartment door shattered his concentration. Had he ordered another pizza? He couldn't remember. Was he expecting Turbo? He checked his text messages. No—that was tomorrow. He stood, and crumbs fell from his lap to the floor.

He opened the door.

Charlie George stood on his porch in all of his starched-khaki glory.

"Mind if I come in?" Charlie said, walking right past John and into his apartment.

John closed the door. "Why the hell would I mind?"

The sofa was covered in pizza boxes and dirty clothes. John was eager to see Prince Charlie handle how the other half lived.

Charlie took his bearings, examining the unmade bed, the clothes

232

all over the floor, the dishes piled in the sink, and the only seating in the apartment covered in greasy food and someone else's laundry. "Looks like my college dorm room." He reached down, folded up the pizza boxes on the couch like they were tissue paper and stuffed them in the trash can. Then he used the dirty clothes to wipe down the couch, tossing them on the floor when he was done. Then, to John's utter astonishment, he opened John's fridge and grabbed himself a beer—no, two beers—popped the lid on one with an opener on his own keychain, and plopped down on the couch he'd just cleaned. He chugged the beer until it was half gone, and set the other between his feet—for later, apparently.

"Dude." John said. "I think I'm impressed."

"Colleges don't have maids, you know. I might not enjoy other peoples' shit, but I can deal with it."

John grabbed a beer for himself and sat on one of the barstools. "Why are you here?"

Charlie gave him a skeptical look.

"Yes, okay. You're here about Miranda. What'd she tell you?"

"She told me nothing. But I know that you two aren't seeing each other, and I know she's sad about it. Therefore, I know you made my sister sad. I came to hear your side of the story before I decide whether to wreck your career."

John laughed. "You can't threaten every person who hurts Miranda."

Charlie looked deadly serious. "I can, though."

"How did you find my address?"

Charlie snorted.

"She was going to break up with me because of Sandy's heart attack."

"She told you that?" Charlie asked.

"She said she didn't want to, but she felt she had some sense of duty."

Charlie nodded. "I can see that. Very Miranda of her." He pinned John with dark brown eyes that were so similar to Miranda's own it was eerie. "You're an idiot douchebag for letting that chase you away."

"Does this winning personality help you a lot in life?"

"I'm not trying to win you over. I'm trying to decide whether to use that baseball bat you have tucked under your bed to beat some sense into your head."

John frowned. Attention to detail also ran in the family, it seemed. "I want her so much. I do. But she doesn't feel the same about me."

"Evidence?"

"Can't you see it? She keeps pushing me aside. Putting me second."

"No, you dummy. She's pushing *herself* aside. Putting *herself* second." Charlie finished his first beer, set the bottle on the floor, and popped the second. "I'm going to give you a second chance with her because you were helpful when we needed to save her in Las Vegas." Charlie took another big chug of beer. "You were helpful, by the way, because she likes you, just like you told me she does. I didn't believe you. I thought you were just another hopeless case, crushing on my sister. But I was wrong."

John could only hear the one phrase over and over. *Pushing herself aside. Putting herself second.* Charlie was saying that her decision hadn't been about him at all.

"Miranda wanted to be with you. She chose you. When she did that, she chose her own happiness. She has never, in her entire life, chosen her own happiness. And when Sandy got sick, she felt guilty for it. Probably because she spent her whole life caring for our sick mom—it doesn't take a genius hacker to make that connection. So she put her own dreams aside, again, to take care of another person who needed her. Luckily, her friends figured out what she was doing and stopped that shit." Charlie drank hard, finishing the second beer.

Apparently another shared George trait was the ability to drink like a fish with little consequence.

"Charlie, I may be a genius hacker, but she was sleeping with another guy until one week ago.

Charlie nodded in agreement. "Jealous?"

"Of course I was jealous." John stood, angry now. "Who wouldn't be? Even you would be jealous."

"I don't get jealous."

John laughed. "You're screwed now."

"How's that?"

"You just cursed yourself. I just hope I'm around to see it."

"You sound like Miranda. She has this bullshit superstitious thing too."

John scrubbed his stubble with his hand. "When she told me she was staying with Sandy after we got back from Las Vegas, it hurt. When she almost did it again on Tuesday, I realized I couldn't handle that hurt twice. The point is, I'm not being unreasonable here."

Charlie nodded. "No, you're not. She picked him for a reason, one we won't understand, at least for a while. Maybe she'll tell you if you ask her. But don't blow this chance with her over a misunderstanding."

Charlie was right. Of course he was.

"Where is she?" John asked.

"She's at Sandy's now, finishing up her shift. I'm supposed to pick her up in an hour and a half, at five. Why don't you do that instead. She'll give you another chance."

John nodded. "I'll pick her up."

"Don't be late. Marlon's taking over after her, and I still don't trust him in the same room with her for more than five minutes."

With that, Charlie George set the two empty beer bottles on John's kitchen counter and saw himself out of the apartment.

John exhaled. It could have gone worse, he supposed. Charlie could've actually beaten him with the baseball bat, like he threatened to do. Instead, John felt as though Charlie had flung words at him like grenades and left him alone to clean up the wreckage.

Yet somehow people found the guy charming.

John stood, gathering the laundry from around his apartment. Then he scrubbed the dishes in his sink and put them away. He stripped his bed, tossing the sheets in the hamper, and put clean sheets on the bed. He swept the wood floors. Finally, he showered, shaved, and dressed.

Charlie seemed to think she would forgive him for walking away. John wasn't so sure. But he would do his level best. He was a genius hacker after all.

———

MIRANDA SET SANDY'S PILLBOX—THE TWIN TO HER OWN—ON HIS

bedside table. She held out two pills, one for pain, one for his heart, and a glass of water.

Sandy plucked the pills from her palm and took the glass. "Can I take these with scotch instead?"

"No, you cannot."

"When did you become such a bummer, Miranda?"

"Shut up, geezer."

Sandy laughed, then swallowed his medicine.

He sat propped up in bed on three down-filled pillows, blankets draped at his waist. He wore one of his tight gray undershirts. He did not look like a geezer. Miranda admired his arms as she set the glass down on the bedside table next to the medicine box.

She took a seat in the chair next to the bed, an Eames lounger upon which she'd napped all night. Others had slept in one of the guest rooms, but Miranda couldn't bear staying away. Then Sandy had said she could sleep in the bed next to him, but she couldn't bear to do that either. Even though John had left her, she'd promised John things were over with Sandy. She would keep her promise to him.

She knew she looked sleepy and mussed after dozing—not enough—in a chair all night. But she knew she and Sandy were past caring about appearances. In the short time since she'd ended things, in the twenty-four hours she'd spent with him today, they'd reached a rhythm, one of friendship. Even family.

She felt such relief that she wouldn't be losing him, too.

She'd been living with Charlie, who'd stayed remarkably quiet about John's sudden disappearance from her life. He usually took it upon himself to drag her to a bar to find "new prey." That's what he'd done the summer she'd broken up with Matthias. He'd called all of his buddies to meet them out, and she'd knocked them down, one by one, over the course of a few months.

"They're damaged for life," he'd said after one particularly brutal dumping.

"That's hardly flattering."

"No one will ever live up to you."

"Which part? You can't possibly be talking about my abs seeing as how I don't have any."

"Your intensity, sister dear. You're a high, and now that they've had it, they'll remember it forever."

"They don't actually say this cheesy shit to you, do they?"

"They don't have to."

Miranda sat next to Sandy and wondered whether the relief she felt with him was that she hadn't been a drug. She couldn't possibly have been. Not to a man whose entire life had been lived on full blast.

"Can I ask you a question, Sandy?

"Of course."

"Fair warning. It's personal and also is uncharacteristically self-conscious for me."

"Now you must ask."

"Why'd you get entangled with me?" She held up her hand. "I am not fishing for compliments. I know, as an objective fact, that you could have had any one of thousands of beautiful women here in your castle in the sky. So there must have been something strange or weird about me. I want to know what it is."

"You think you already know."

"No—I think your reason is different than what other people have wanted from me."

"Even your John?"

She pressed her lips together. She didn't want to talk about John.

"Fine. I'll answer. There were three things that became very apparent that night at Rivet, three things that caught my eye." He held up one finger. "You are utterly fearless."

She snorted. He had that backwards. She was afraid of everything.

"You are stressfully intelligent."

She nodded. That was true. A combination of genetics and survival skills developed in the George household.

"And you are," he was actually pointing at her now, "if not beautiful by Hollywood standards, sexy. I'll never forget that silky not-a-shirt thing you wore. On a motorcycle. Christ."

She laughed. Wearing that shirt had been a strong move on her part. She'd intended to stir up trouble, and she had.

"Why do you ask?" he said.

"Charlie's got these friends. They're all a bunch of dumbasses."

"Why would your brother be friends with dumbasses? He's not stupid."

"I think they make him feel normal. I never tried to fit in, but he did."

Sandy nodded.

"I was always some sort of prize to these guys. I was their buddy's big sister. I knew it, but I didn't care. When I hooked up with one of them, I never saw him more than once or twice. I'd delete his phone number, you know? And then later, my brother would come home with these ridiculous stories of heart-crushing loss." She narrowed her eyes. "For the record, none of them actually have hearts."

"Noted."

"But then he told me something, shortly before our mom died, and I've never been able to forget it. He said that I make them high, like a drug. That that's the kick I give. So when I drop them, they're like, junkies I guess. I think Charlie meant it as a compliment. But thinking about it now, I feel awful. Like the only thing I have to offer a person is a wild ride."

She felt tears prick her eyes. Here was why she'd stayed with Sandy, why she hadn't stood up stronger for her and John. She hadn't believed any of them would want her forever.

Matthias had wanted her, hadn't he? They'd been together for years. But he'd basically been a George. He was an exception. She wouldn't find two exceptions in her lifetime.

"John isn't addicted to you. Anyone who plays a game as slow as his can't be after a high."

"That's what I thought. But now he's gone."

"What do you mean, *He's gone?*"

She hadn't yet told him about that final night with John. So she did.

"You dumped me for this guy who's supposed to treat you properly, and this is what he does? If I weren't geezed up in bed, I'd kill him."

Miranda laughed. "I didn't dump you. We broke up."

Sandy's face turned solemn. "You dumped me. I didn't choose to end things."

"Wow, you're serious." Miranda was taken aback for a moment. She thought of Daphne's warning, that she might hurt Sandy, and how she'd scoffed at Daphne's words.

"I am serious," he said. "I'd take you back right now."

"If you weren't geezed up in bed, that is."

Sandy smiled at her words. "You weren't a high, but you were dazzling. That's not a bad thing."

No, she supposed it wasn't.

"Thanks, Sandy." She stood, and kissed him on the forehead. "Marlon will be here any minute."

"I wonder what he'll gripe about today."

"Hopefully not me. I left the house to his exact specifications."

"I'll see you in a week?"

"Friday at five. Maybe sooner if I decide to come bug you."

He held her eyes for a moment longer than a friend would, and then he nodded. She nodded back, and left his bedroom.

She packed up her things, waiting for Marlon to arrive. As she set her bags by the front door, Marlon let himself in.

He didn't smile when he saw her, but he didn't make the pinched face he used to make, either. "How is he?"

"Good. He's awake, waiting for you. He just took his medicine. I wrote everything on the chart."

"Thank you. For, you know, everything."

"Sure." She waited awkwardly for him to tell her to take off. Thankfully, there was a knock at the door to break the silence.

"That would be Charlie, my ride," she said, as Marlon reached to open the door again.

"What are you doing here?" Marlon fairly snapped to the person outside.

"I'm here to pick up Miranda." That was John's voice, Miranda realized. How did John know she was here?

She glanced through the open doorway. John met her eyes over Marlon's shoulder.

"I don't believe she's expecting you." Marlon sounded very grumpy.

She stared at Marlon's profile. Was he acting protective of her? What on earth was going on?

"She isn't, no. Charlie asked me to give her a ride. That is, if she doesn't mind."

"I'll ask her." Marlon shut the door in John's face.

Miranda laughed, covering her mouth with her hand.

"Well?" Marlon asked.

"What are you doing?"

"Daphne told me he dumped you the day you saved Sandy."

"How does Daphne know that?"

"Charlie told her."

"Y'all are a bunch of gossipy old ladies!"

"Fair." He pointed at the door. "Do you want me to tell him to leave?"

She thought about it. Maybe Sandy was right about John, that he wasn't like Charlie's friends. And if Charlie had sent him—maybe she and John had a chance after all.

"I've got this." She opened the door. Marlon, she noticed, remained a few steps behind her, arms crossed protectively. What a difference a week made.

"Hey," John said when he saw her.

"Charlie sent you?"

"That's the short version."

She nodded in understanding. With the Georges there was usually a long version.

"I'm sorry, Miranda. I made a horrible mistake."

"You did, yes."

From behind her, Marlon snorted with laughter.

She looked over her shoulder at him. "Will you shut up? You're ruining our moment."

"Are we having a moment?" John asked, eyebrows raised, looking hopeful.

"I'm considering it."

"I thought you were choosing him over me again. But I see that you weren't doing that at all."

"I believe the proper wording is something about how Charlie made you see that."

"Charlie helped, yeah. But I would have figured it out eventually. I might have been too late, though. Everyone needs a little help seeing things clearly sometimes." John nodded at Marlon. "Like he did."

Miranda looked over her shoulder at Marlon again, whose eyes had narrowed in annoyance. John was right, of course. A few weeks ago, it had taken their collective will to get Marlon to see how wrong he'd been about Daphne. Marlon was the most stubborn of all of them.

"Fine. I'll go check on Sandy," Marlon said. "See you later, Miranda."

"Bye, Marlon." She turned back to John. "Sure, you can drive me home."

She reached for her overnight bag and her satchel with her laptop, but John got to them first. He carried them to his car while she shut Sandy's door. When she turned, he was leaning against his car, waiting for her.

"You know," she said. "This is very *Say Anything.*"

"I don't have a boom box."

"*Sixteen Candles*, then."

"I don't have a Porsche."

"Problem solved. Let's go buy one."

"You don't have a license."

"I was going to buy one for you, not me."

John smiled. "I like my car. It's reliable."

She sidled toward him until they stood knee-to-knee. "I'm sorry, too. I won't put you second again."

He wrapped his hands around her waist and pulled her close. "You don't have to worry about that, Miranda. I know what I did wrong. You felt like you had to choose between me and your family. But you don't. You can have both." He nodded at the house. "If that Neanderthal can figure that much out, so can I."

She threw her arms around his shoulders, laughing into the crook of his neck. "I won't tell Marlon you called him that."

"God I missed you this week."

"Of course you did." She smiled at him. "Apparently I'm dazzling."

He picked her up off the ground, and she laughed again. She hadn't thought she would ever feel this happy again.

He carried her to the passenger side of the car. "In. Buckle up."

"Where are you taking me?"

"My place."

"It's about goddamn time." She gave him a close-lipped grin.

He wrapped his hands around her smooth jaw, her neck, and kissed her until she was breathless. "It is," he said.

What's Next for the George Siblings?

You can read more about Miranda and Charlie in *Take Your Charming Somewhere Else*, which tells the story of Charlie and a homicide case that kicks up some really unhappy memories. Good thing Dr. Tory Murphy is around to help him sort things out.

The Hollywood Lights Series is now complete with the publication of *Take Your Charming Somewhere Else*, which won the IPPY Gold Medal for Romance!

Be sure to catch the rest of the Hollywood Lights Series, which is now complete, starting with *Entanglement*.

To learn about my books and writing life, subcribe to my Substack at pryalnews.com.

Acknowledgments

This is the fifth book in the Hollywood Lights Series, and part of me can't believe it's real. This was a hard book to write, and it took a long time—the longest of any novel I've ever written.

Fallout Girl wouldn't be here without Lauren Faulkenberry, for lots and lots of reasons, many of which she and I will keep secret for now. But Lauren is also my dear friend and editor. She always provides excellent editing and helpful comments on the story. She lets me call her when I'm panicking, and then I stop panicking. I quite literally couldn't do this without her.

Thank you to Alexa Chew, my first early reader, for her comments and for reminding me never to be boring. Thank you to my second-round early readers: my sister, Chris Adigun, MD; my world-class copyeditor, Janet Linger, who also happens to be my cousin; and novelist and fellow Tall Poppy Writer Kelly Harms. And thanks to novelist and friend Emily Colin who has been a great supporter.

Thank you to local businesses who support me: Annie Johnston and La Vita Dolce Café in Chapel Hill for providing me coffee and a cozy place to write, and also the café manager Erin Farmer Pacheco for helping with the book's title. Thank you to Jamie Fiocco and Flyleaf Books for supporting local authors and hosting readings and launch parties over the years, including the one for this book.

Thank you to my author friends for support, including Sonja Yoerg, Sandra Block, Susan Bishop Crispell, and Amy Sue Nathan, who have been extra helpful with this particular book. I appreciate all you've done for me.

And thank you to my family, always.

An Interview with the Author

Why did you choose to write about mental illness?

Miranda has Bipolar I Disorder—as do I. Like many authors, I try to keep fiction and life separate, but I also try to write about what I'm familiar with. It took me until the fifth book of this series—and my fourth full-length novel—to finally write a heroine who has BD.

Sometimes writing close to home is the hardest and scariest thing to do. I really wanted to get it right. I felt like I had a duty not only to show what it was like for the main character to struggle with this disability, but also for her to make out all right in the end. I didn't want her to "overcome" her disability (I can't stand "overcoming disability" narratives), but rather to just *be a disabled person*, living her life, in fiction. Stories like that are way more radical than you might think.

What kinds of writerly strategies did you have in mind when you were writing this book?

I thought about point of view (POV) a lot while I was writing *Fallout Girl*. Point of view is a writing strategy that lets your readers into your characters' heads—POV is how your characters see the world, and therefore how your readers see your characters.

In fact, POV was so important to this book that I wrote a short essay about POV and *Fallout Girl* before the book was published. The essay is about POV and using fiction to witness mental illness.

Here's an excerpt from the essay:

When I was writing this book, it was very important to me to have the reader be in Miranda's POV when she is in crisis or witnessing her mental illness.

In other books I've read, when the main POV character who has a mental illness hits a crisis point, the POV suddenly shifts to those around the character. The shift signals that the disabled character is unable to express herself any more, and the only credible witnesses to the disabled character's experiences are those who are not disabled. That signal might not have been the intention of the author, but that's the signal nonetheless.

Furthermore, that signal reflects what happens in the real world. People with mental illnesses—people like me—aren't seen as credible witnesses to their own lives and experiences. I didn't want my fiction to reinforce stereotypes like that.

Therefore, I wanted Miranda to have her say. I wanted her to be her own witness.

You seem to know a lot about motorcycles. Why?

Back in my twenties, when my BD was under-treated, and I was making not-so-awesome decisions, I bought a Suzuki sport bike and rode it way too fast. I know what it feels like to go one-hundred-and-twenty on a motorcycle. Doing that sort of thing is not normal—I know that now—but back then, I couldn't sense the danger, only the thrill. That's symptomatic.

Part of me has always thought it was important to be able to operate vehicles properly in case of emergencies—manual transmission cars, two-wheeled vehicles—but what I was doing on those motorcycles had nothing to do with safety in emergencies. It had a lot more to do with what Miranda described when she rode her bike in *Fallout Girl*.

More recently, I wrote about riding motorcycles in an essay for the gorgeous *Motherwell Magazine*, called "With New Life Brings Fear of

Death." I talked about how having kids can make you fear death in a way you never did before—and how I couldn't possibly ride a motorcycle now. (That essay is collected in my book, *Life of the Mind Interrupted*.) Also, back when I bought my bike, I could never have afforded the gorgeous motorcycle that Miranda bought. I bought a low-rent imitation. It still went way too fast, though. And my dad was really mad at me when he found out. I'm sure he still remembers, even though it's been fifteen years. (Hi, Dad.)

> Although Miranda has bipolar disorder, most of the time she's not actively talking or thinking about it.

That's right! Most of the time, disabled people don't talk or think about our disabilities. We just hang out, being disabled people. Our disabilities are indelible, and they make us who we are, but they are not *all* that we are. We have to think about all the things non-disabled people think about, like bedsheets, melted cheese, and yoga pants. I think this is one reason why it's so hard for non-disabled people to write disabled characters. I would imagine that, when writing a disabled character as a non-disabled person, striking the balance between the character's constant awareness of her disability and her just living life isn't easy. After all, I never stop knowing I have BD. But if you were to ask me how many minutes during an average day I spend thinking about having bipolar disorder, consciously, it's not that many.

But then again, if you ask me how much difficulty and pain bipolar disorder has caused me—then you would get a very different answer.

There's the average day, when things are going well. Then there's the off day, or off week, when things are dark. BD has no cure. But I'm so much better now than I was in my 20s, because the treatments are great these days, and dark weeks are usually days, and sometimes only hours. And the dark times are so much shorter than they used to be.

But I want to say this: I have good health insurance and enough money to pay for my care. I have excellent doctors and excellent medication. I have the support of my husband. I have everything a person needs to live a good life with bipolar disorder. If you take away any one of these things—insurance, money, support—a person would have a nearly impossible time living with this deadly disability. We have a social duty to care for one another.

What helped you get over your fear of writing about a character who has bipolar disorder?

I want everyone who reads this book to realize that many, if not most, people with mental illnesses are like Miranda is by the end of *Fallout Girl*. They're like me. We are okay—not scary freaks or weirdos, like we're depicted in some popular media. We are your neighbors. We're moms; we're on your tennis team; we do book signings at your local bookstore. We're just people—accountants, lawyers, doctors, and baristas. We got dealt a different hand, but, for the most part, if we have enough health insurance, financial stability, and emotional support—then we're all right. Chances are you are friends with someone like Miranda. Take care with your words and prejudices. She might need you some day. And you might need her.

About the Author

Katie Rose Pryal, J.D., Ph.D., tells stories about the outsiders, the misfits, and the beautifully complicated. She is a Bipolar-AuDHD author of many books of fiction, nonfiction, and memoir.

Her books include *Your Kid Belongs Here: An Insider's Guide to Parenting Neurodiverse Children* (Johns Hopkins, 2025), *Life of the Mind Interrupted: Essays on Mental Health and Disability in Higher Education* (Blue Osprey, 2017), the IPPY-Gold-winning *Even If You're Broken: Bodies, Boundaries, and Mental Health* (Blue Osprey, 2019), and the IPPY-Bronze-Winning *A Light in the Tower: A New Reckoning with Mental Health in Higher Education* (Kansas, 2024).

Her Hollywood Lights romance series includes *Entanglement* and the IPPY-Gold-winning *Take Your Charming Somewhere Else*. Like all of Katie Pryal's writing, the series centers neurodiversity, in addition to angsty romance, star-crossed lovers, sexy woodworkers, movie stars, and happily-ever-afters.

She lives in Chapel Hill, North Carolina, with her spouse, children, and many, many animals. Subscribe to her monthly letter at pryalnews.com.

www.ingramcontent.com/pod-product-compliance
Lightning Source LLC
Chambersburg PA
CBHW031441200726
48289CB00007BB/2061